THE GAUNTLET

***Other Five Star Titles
by Max Brand:***

Sixteen in Nome
Outlaws All: A Western Trio
The Lightning Warrior
The Wolf Strain: A Western Trio
The Stone That Shines
Men Beyond the Law: A Western Trio
Beyond the Outposts
The Fugitive's Mission: A Western Trio
In the Hills of Monterey
The Lost Valley: A Western Trio
Chinook

THE GAUNTLET

A Western Trio

MAX BRAND™

Five Star
Unity, Maine

Five Star Western
Published in conjunction with Golden West Literary Agency.

November 1998

First Edition

Five Star Standard Print Western Series.

The text of this edition is unabridged.

Set in 11 pt. Plantin by Al Chase.

Printed in the United States on permanent paper.

Library of Congress Cataloging in Publication Data

Brand, Max, 1892–1944.
    The gauntlet : a western trio / by Max Brand. — 1st ed.
      p.   cm.
    "A Five Star western"—T.p. verso.
    Contents: The blackness of MacTee — The king of rats — The gauntlet.
    ISBN 0-7862-1164-4 (hc : alk. paper)
    1. Western stories.   I. Title.
PS3511.A87G38 1998
813'.52—dc21
                                            98-29041

Table of Contents

The Blackness of MacTee   7

The King of Rats: A Reata Story   85

The Gauntlet 181

The Blackness of MacTee

In 1933, Rogers Terrill, editor of Popular Publications' *Dime Western*, had reached an agreement with Frederick Faust's agent, Carl Brandt of Brandt & Brandt, to buy three short novels by Max Brand to be published in the magazine. Originally, these novels were to be interconnected insofar as they were to feature the same principal character, and Faust wrote them while on a trip with his family in Egypt. Perry Woodstock did appear in the first of them, "The Strange Ride of Perry Woodstock," included in THE FUGITIVE'S MISSION: A WESTERN TRIO (Five Star Westerns, 1997). In the second, "The Stage to Yellow Creek," included in THE LOST VALLEY: A WESTERN TRIO (Five Star Westerns, 1998), Perry Woodstock is the narrator of the story. In this, the third so-called Perry Woodstock short novel, he is nowhere in evidence. It first appeared under the title "Black Thunder" by Max Brand in *Dime Western* (7/33). For its appearance here, the author's original title as well as his full text have been restored.

I

"A VISITOR FROM DUNPHYVILLE"

The stone was quartzite and the drill was dull — yet Harrigan sank the hole rapidly, swinging the twelve-pound hammer in a sort of fury. The hillside was a burning furnace of noonday heat — yet Harrigan would not abate his labor.

The sweat blackened the back of his flannel shirt in an irregular pattern that was water-marked with salt at the edges. That back rose and fell a little with every stroke. The shoulders worked. Two mighty elastic ropes of muscle sprang up from the waist and spread powerful fingers across the shoulder blades. But in spite of the strength of this man, one could not help expecting him to weaken and seek rest. Yet he did not rest. He continued steadily at his labor. An inexhaustible fuel, in fact, was being fed into the furnace of this man's strength, and the fuel was anger.

It was not merely the heat of the sun or of his labor that kept the face of Dan Harrigan red. It was not the effort of his labor that made his blue eyes gleam. It was a steady passion of anger that set his jaws and lighted his eyes from a fire of the soul. Rage was to him like a sustaining food.

A mule brayed in the valley, and Harrigan leaped to his feet. He looked down toward the water hole in high hopes. But those hopes vanished. It was not MacTee, returning at last from town. Their mule was a piebald brute, and this was the usual dust-covered beast of burden, with a man on its back. The rider, plainly not MacTee, had just left the water hole, and was

9

heading his mount up the half-mile grade toward the mine.

Harrigan pondered this. For twenty-four hours MacTee had been due back from town with supplies. Yet he had not come. What, then, had happened? Had he fallen into a brawl in the town? Had the dark passions of his Scotch nature boiled up until a Forty-Five caliber bullet quieted them forever? Had that great soul, that stark and terrible spirit, vanished from the earth?

Harrigan was stunned by the mere suspicion that such a thing might be. He looked up at the sky, that was pale with the flood of sunlight, and told himself that if MacTee had died, those heavens would be overcast by thunderheads. There would have been a sign of some sort even in the middle of the night. Lightning and sounds of doom would have accompanied the passing of MacTee.

And yet what could this be but a messenger to tell him of MacTee? What else would bring a man into the white heat of this desert? Not even buzzards wheeled in the air above the waste. Only the partnership of a MacTee and a Harrigan could have produced enough vital energy to drive men out here prospecting for gold. For two months they had broken ground, hoping that a thin vein of ore would widen. It had been bitterly hard, but Harrigan and MacTee were used to bitter hardships. They were, in fact, used to one another.

The mule came nodding up the slope. The rider had bent his head. His hands were folded on the pommel of the saddle. He would be terribly thirsty. Harrigan turned with a sigh and contemplated the jug wrapped in sacking that was placed in a shadowy nook where the wind would strike it.

The man came nearer. The bristles on his unshaven face glinted in the sun. He was as big as MacTee, Harrigan decided. He carried a rifle in a long saddle holster. There was a gun belt wrapped about his hips. A big canteen bumped against the

10

front of the saddle. That was good. At least, he carried his own water with him.

Now he pulled up the mule close by the mine and dismounted. He looked young in years but old in the West. He stood still for a moment, staring at Harrigan, and the waves of heat rose with a dull shimmering from his sombrero. He was as lean as a desert wolf, all skin and bones and sheer power.

"Howdy," he said. "This is about the middle of hell, ain't it?"

"Yeah," said Harrigan. "This is the corner of Main Street and First Avenue, in the center of hell. You couldn't be wrong."

"All right," said the stranger. "Then you're Harrigan."

"Yes. I'm Harrigan."

"If you're Harrigan, where's MacTee?"

"He's not here."

"You lie," said the man of the guns.

Suddenly Harrigan straightened. He seemed to grow younger. A tender light came into his eyes.

"Brother," he asked in the softest of voices, "did you call me a liar?"

"I asked for MacTee, and you say that he ain't here?" protested the other. "If he ain't here, where is he?"

"He's in Dunphyville, yonder."

"You lie again," said the stranger. "There ain't hardly enough left of Dunphyville to cover a prairie dog. If a jackrabbit tried to hide behind what's left of Dunphyville, his ears would stick up behind the heap."

"That's twice in a row that I've been a liar," counted Harrigan, rubbing his hands together and looking rather wistfully into the face of the newcomer. "What's your name?"

"Rollo Quay," said the big man.

"Rollo," said Harrigan, "it's a funny name. It ain't the only

11

funny thing about you neither. But before I make you any funnier, I want to find out what happened to Dunphyville."

"It was wrecked," said Quay.

"I don't know how God, man, or the devil could want to waste time to wreck that dump," said Harrigan.

"It wasn't God, man, or devil that wrecked the place. It was MacTee," said Quay.

Harrigan nodded. "MacTee got restless, did he? Well, if he got careless and stubbed his toe on a place like Dunphyville, I guess there's not much left of the town."

"There ain't gonna be much left of MacTee, when I find him," said Quay. "Not when I meet him, there ain't gonna be! I'm gonna take payment out of his black hide for everything he did to my saloon back there in Dunphyville!"

"Brother," said Harrigan, "I hear you talk, and I'd certainly like to save you till you had a chance to meet him. But I don't think that I can wait that long. What was the last seen of MacTee in Dunphyville?"

"The last seen of him," said Quay, "was a cloud of dust with a streak of lightnin' through it. Nobody knows exactly where it landed. And nobody knows exactly where it disappeared to. But before I talk about Black MacTee any more, I'm gonna do something to make Red Harrigan a little bit redder. You Irish son of a hoop snake and a bob-tailed lynx, I'm gonna take you apart, first, and find out where that skunk of a MacTee is later on."

He stepped straight forward, feinted in workman-like manner with his left, and drove an excellent right for the head.

Harrigan ducked his head half an inch and shed that punch as a rock sheds water.

"Here's the same sock with a hook in it," said Harrigan, and knocked Mr. Quay under the feet of the mule.

Rollo Quay sat up half a minute later and laid one hand on

the side of his jaw. Then he saw that Harrigan was sitting on the back of the mule. The revolvers that Quay reached for were gone.

"I'll leave the little mule in Dunphyville, safe and sound," said Harrigan.

"Damn the mule," said Quay. "What I want to know is . . . where did you hide that blackjack when your sleeves was turned up to the elbow."

"That was no blackjack. That was the hook in the end of that punch," said Harrigan. "I'm going to look for MacTee. If he happens to drop in here while I'm gone, talk soft and low to him, brother. I'm only a sort of chore boy around here. But Black MacTee is a *man*."

II

"WHERE THE LIGHTNING STRUCK"

There were only a dozen buildings in Dunphyville, but they all seemed in place to the eye of Harrigan, as he drew near the town. In spite of the storm of which Quay had spoken, nothing appeared wrong, until Harrigan entered the single street. Then he noted sundry details of interest. Most of the windows were broken. The chairs on the front verandah of the hotel were missing one leg or two, and several of them had been converted into stools. All the "e's" in the sign **General Merchandise Store** had disappeared and were represented by ragged eyeholes of light. And the whole side of the blacksmith shop was scorched and the ground blackened beside it, as though the dead grass had been kindled in an effort to burn the town.

Harrigan stopped the mule in front of the saloon. The two swinging doors were gone. The two front windows were smashed out. Broken glass glittered in the dust of the street. One of the frail wooden pillars that held up the roof over the verandah was broken in the middle and sagged to the side. The darkness inside had about it an empty air of desolation.

"Yes," murmured Harrigan, "it looks like Black MacTee."

He dismounted from the mule, made comfortable the revolver which was under his coat, and entered the saloon through the open doorway. It was, indeed, an empty spot. Of the long mirror that had reflected so many sun-burned faces, there remained against the wall only a few shreds of brightness

14

and gilding. Of the long array of bottles whose necks and brilliant labels had shone on the shelf behind the bar, all were gone except half a dozen lonely last survivors. The brass rail was bent and broken from its brackets. Bullets had ripped the polished surface of the bar itself. And behind the bar leaned the one-time stalwart figure of a fat man in a dirty apron. He wore a plaster over one cheek, a leather patch over one eye, a red-stained bandage around his head, and his left arm was supported in a sling.

"Hello," said Harrigan. "What happened?"

The barman looked toward Harrigan with one dull eye.

"Hullo," he said, in a hollow voice. "There was a kind of an explosion. After that, I don't seem to remember nothin' very clear."

"Let's have a drink," said Harrigan, putting one elbow on the splintered edge of the bar.

"There ain't nothing to drink except brandy at a dollar a throw," said the barman. "All the rest. . . ." He made a vague gesture with one hand. He turned to follow his own gesture and survey the destruction.

"We'll have the brandy, then," said Harrigan.

The barman found one of the few bottles that remained and set it with a glass before Harrigan.

"You're drinking, too," said Harrigan.

The barman filled a glass for himself sadly.

"Now," said Harrigan, "what happened the other day when Black MacTee was here?"

"It all started right over there in the corner," said the barman. "MacTee was loaded up to start for his mine. His mule was hitched outside the door. He was settin' there in the corner, readin' a stack of the old newspapers that we keep around. There was a dozen of the boys in here, most of them from the Curley Ranch." He paused, re-filled his brandy glass by sense of touch while his eyes still contemplated the memory.

"All I recollect after that," said the barman, "ain't very much. I remember that MacTee come over here to the bar and set 'em up all around for the boys. They all drank, and he set 'em up again. And then he lifted up his whiskey glass and he hollered out . . . 'To Kate, boys. . . .' "

"My God!" said Harrigan. "What was it he said? . . . 'To Kate?' What put him on that track? What newspaper was he reading? Tell me, man . . . what newspaper was he reading?" The flame of his hair was the flame of his eyes. He devoured the very soul of the man before him.

"Wait a minute. Don't hurry me, or I'm gonna have a relapse," said the bartender. "He ups the glass and says . . . 'To Kate.' And everybody hollers out and downs the drink, except me. And when he sees that my glass is still full, he says what's the matter with me, and I say no disrespect to the Kate that he knows, but that once I got tangled up with a freckle-faced snake by that name, and ever since, when I heard the name of Kate, I got shootin' pains and colic. Well, I no sooner says that, than he reaches across the bar and slams me, and I drop off into a deep sleep. When I wake up, this here is what I see."

"Kate," said Harrigan. "He's spotted her! He's gone! For the love of the dear God, tell me, man, where's the newspaper that he was reading when he let out that Indian yell?"

"Where's the beer gone, and the soda, and the bar whiskey and . . . ?"

"Shut up!" said Harrigan. And the barman was silent, for he found in the eye of Harrigan something that was hard to meet. The blank fury of the great MacTee was not as terrible as the blue lightning that was now in the eyes of Harrigan.

"How far to the railroad?" demanded Harrigan.

"Seven miles," gasped the barman.

16

"Tell Quay, when he comes back, that his mule will be over at the railroad. So long."

And Harrigan fled through the doorway and leaped into the saddle on the mule's back.

III

"ON THE TRAIL
OF BLACK MACTEE"

The town of Caldwell Junction contained not a great many more buildings than Dunphyville, outside of the railroad station and the sheds. In such a small town it was not surprising, therefore, that the first thing Harrigan saw was the pinto mule with the black and white tail, standing outside of the grocery store. The grocer himself was loading a wicker basket filled with supplies into a cart to which the mule was hitched.

"Where'd you get the mule?" asked Harrigan.

The grocer was pink and white. All grocers have that complexion. His pink turned to red, and his white turned to pink, when he faced Harrigan.

"There was a man here the other day . . . ," he said.

"Big . . . black hair . . . drunk . . . happy?" asked Harrigan.

"Yes," said the grocer. "What has he done? Are you after him? Who is he?"

"He's a double-crossing Scotch black-souled hound," said Harrigan. "Did you buy this mule from him?"

"Yes," said the grocer, shrinking from the red and blue flame of Harrigan.

Harrigan groaned — in his mind's eye was the haunting picture of a lovely girl whose given name was Kate.

"The big man with the black eyes, he pulled out of this town on a train, I don't doubt. What train was it?"

"It was headed south. It was a freight," said the grocer, rather frightened.

18

"What train is this one?" asked Harrigan suddenly, as a whistle shrieked up the track.

"That's the Overland, bound south," said the grocer.

"Then it doesn't stop here?"

"No. It just takes the grade slow, and. . . ."

But Harrigan, without waiting to hear more, turned and sprinted down the street. He saw the engine's head come nobly into view, swaying with speed. He saw that speed quenched somewhat by the upgrade passing the junction. But still the train was thundering along, dust and cinders whipping under its wheels as it shot by the station.

Harrigan, turning with it as the tender went by, sprinted with all his might. He reached his full speed as the observation car went past, and he leaped high and far for the iron balustrade that fenced in the rear platform. He caught with both hands. The grip of one was broken. For an instant his body streamed out behind the flying train. Then he drew himself lightly up and scrambled aboard.

The conductor came on the run, half a minute later. He took Harrigan by the collar. "Bums like you *oughta* die," said the conductor. "I've a mind to throw you off now. If we weren't behind time, I'd stop the train on the trestle and heave you off into the gulch. But when we hit the next stop, you'll be on your way to jail, young fellow!"

Harrigan replied: "You're mistaking me, my friend. My brother-in-law, Mister Peter Van Houston Dyce, is on board this train. I had to ride fifty miles to get here to tell him that his father has just been roughed by a bear on my ranch."

"Get out of this observation car and stand on the front platform, you lying bum!" shouted the conductor.

So Harrigan stood for eighty miles on the front platform and smiled as he heard the roar of the wheels and their rapid syncopation over the tracks.

* * * * *

It was nearing dusk when they reached the next stop. Harrigan slid off on the blind side of the train and walked ahead as far as the first signal light. When the train passed that point, gathering speed, it gathered Harrigan, also, into its blind baggage.

The vigilance of the conductor, who was led by a spirit of eerie inquiry, found Harrigan on the blind baggage, fifty miles farther south. He tried to brain Harrigan with a signal lantern, but the red-headed man escaped. He rode another seventy miles on the tops of the coaches, or between them, but at the last he was driven from this refuge.

The whole train crew, by this time, had sharpened its eyes, hardened its fists, and roused its soul for this contest with a daring tramp. But it was not until the gray of the dawn that Harrigan, after haunting that express all through the night, at last, left the Overland. He would not have left it even then, except that he began to feel that perhaps he had overstepped his proper distance south. Therefore, in fear that Black MacTee might have ceased traveling in this direction, he dropped off at the railroad yards of a big cattle-shipping town to look about and make inquiry.

Three railroad detectives closed suddenly upon him like three little kingbirds on one big hawk. He did not run. He did not fight. He let two of them hold him by the arms while the third rammed the muzzle of a revolver into the pit of his stomach.

"You're Harrigan," said the third man.

"With that gun in front of you, you can call me worse things than that," said Harrigan.

"It's a big rap that you've got to stand for," said the detective.

"What's the charge against me?" asked Harrigan, "and who made it?"

"You murdered Joe Chantry, up yonder," said the man who carried the gun. "And the gent that told us about you is the man that you're chasing south. He's the next man that you want to bump off. He didn't look like the sort of a bird who'd run away, neither."

Harrigan blinked.

"As big as me, or bigger?" he asked. "Black hair and black eyes and a dark skin?"

"Yes," said the man with the gun. "Come along, Harrigan. He warned us that you're likely to make trouble. But the first trouble you start with us is gonna break your back and split your wishbone. Understand?"

"I understand," said Harrigan, "that he'd have me hanged to get me off his trail, and be damned to him! It's Black MacTee . . . and gone blacker than ever! Oh, yes, I understand. I never heard of a man called Joe Chantry . . . but I understand!"

He was marching forward with a man on either arm, and the man with the gun behind him. Now he stumbled, or seemed to stumble, and kicked out behind him with the fine precision of an army mule. The gun carrier shot a hole in the morning sky and went down with a pair of battered shins. Harrigan threw the other two detectives on top of him, collected three guns, and ran toward the rumbling sound of a long freight that was pulling out on the southern route.

It was a train of empties. He hooked his ride, found a boxcar, and slipped through the open door. He sat on the floor while the dust danced on the trembling boards and the landscape swept by him. Mountains near and far, then a series of black tunnels with open country beyond, a smiling land of rolling hills with groves of trees shading it, and the flash of water running in every valley.

They passed the scattered houses of another large cow town. As the train slowed, Harrigan left the three revolvers in the box-

21

car and swung down to the ground. He had to sprint hard, because the train was still traveling fast. And while he was still helpless with the speed of his running, trying to keep from pitching forward on his face, leaning back his head and shoulders, he saw a long, lean man with a deep-visored cap pulled well over his eyes come out from behind one of the piles of ties that were corded at the end of the railroad yard.

This man raised a hand with the bright flash of a gun in it. Harrigan had been running as fast as he could, before this. He tried now to increase his speed. The end of the freight train went by with a departing thunder. He heard the voice of the man with the gun shouting for him to stop. A gun barked. But the next instant Harrigan dived around the corner of one of the big stacks of ties. There he waited. He looked down at his shoulder and saw the glint of bare skin. The bullet had nipped away a bit of the strong flannel shirt.

Footfalls rushed up, crunching on the cinders. A shadow sloped over the ground around the corner of the ties. So Harrigan sprang and laid the barrel of his gun along the head of the pursuer. Immediately he sat the limp body on the ground and waited for life to return to the eyes. He picked up the fallen revolver. Inside the coat of the man he found the shield of a railroad detective. Up the sleeve of the coat, he found a handy blackjack. His victim groaned. Harrigan took the man by his long chin and shook his head violently.

"Brother," said Harrigan, looking down into the bright, dangerous eyes, "you're another that MacTee has made a fool of. He's told you to look out for Harrigan. He's told you that Harrigan is wanted for the killing of a fellow named Chantry. Well, boy, I never heard of a gent named Chantry and that's a fact! But I've heard of Black MacTee. Where is he? Which way did he go? Further south?"

The bright little eyes looked at Harrigan without expression. They were simply bright.

"All right," said Harrigan. "I hate to do it, but I'm fighting against time."

He took the hand of the detective, pulled his arm rigid, and then tapped him with the blackjack across the ridge of the tight shoulder muscles. The detective closed his eyes and turned gray-green. Harrigan took the other arm, jerked it tight, brought down the blackjack on a similar spot.

"All right," said the detective. "That's enough." His eyes opened again. "Why not?" he said. "I don't know what the game is that you two thugs are playing, but I know that I *want* you to meet. He left the railroad line, right here. I dunno where he faded to."

Harrigan went to a barber shop for a shave. The barber was so fat that even the effort of standing made him pant a little.

"I read something in the paper, a while ago," Harrigan remarked, deciding to try a shot in the dark. "The news came from here. It was about a girl with an Irish name. Her name is Kate Malone. . . ."

"She ain't from here," said the barber. "You mean the schoolteacher that saved her pupils when the school caught on fire?"

"That's the one," said Harrigan.

"She ain't from here," said the barber. "She's teaching a cross-roads school eight miles out on the Cullen Road."

Harrigan left the shop and went to a clothing store. He bought a necktie and a cheap coat, then found the Cullen Road. A buckboard drew up from behind, stopped, took him in without a word. The driver was a grim-faced rancher who kept looking straight before him and never spoke.

"I'm trying to locate my sister, Kate Malone," said Harrigan.

23

The rancher turned his head a little, but looked at the distance, instead of Harrigan.

"I reckon she's found a whole crop of brothers, since the school burned down," he said.

He spoke no more for an hour. The green hills drifted slowly behind them, while the two mustangs dog-trotted sullenly along, heads down, enduring the miles. At last, the old rancher pulled up the team and pointed to a cluster of trees around a red roof.

"That's the Tyndale house," he said. "That's where Kate Malone is living while the school's rebuilding. I hope she remembers your face, young man."

IV

"BLACK MACTEE"

There was a pleasant wind that tumbled a few white clouds across the sky. The hills were the finest Harrigan ever had seen. Never had there been such cattle as those that dotted the wide range. The very air was different, for Kate Malone also was breathing it.

He went up the side lane, opened the gate, and passed on to the house. A Negro in a cook's apron was carrying stove wood from the woodshed toward the kitchen door. Down the slope behind the house Harrigan saw, through the tree trunks, the gleam of running water.

"I'm looking for Angus MacTee," said Harrigan.

"Yes, sir," said the cook. "I guess he ain't here, sir."

"No?" said Harrigan. "Is Miss Kate Malone here, then?"

"No, sir, I guess she ain't here, neither." The cook rolled his eyes. "She was called away, sir," he said, "by a message from town, and. . . ."

Harrigan grinned, suddenly. "How much did MacTee pay you for telling me that lie?" he asked. "Ten dollars?"

"No, sir. Five dollars," said the cook. "I mean. . . ." He stopped short, his thick lips parted, his eyes perfectly rounded as he saw that he had been so easily trapped.

"Is MacTee here now?" asked Harrigan.

"He . . . he . . . ," stammered the cook. "I guess so."

"Is he down by the creek? Is he with her?" asked Harrigan, pointing.

25

The cook was silent, agape. So Harrigan marched straight down the hill, through the heat of the sun and the cool touch of the shadows, until he came close to the edge of the water. Then he heard voices, and slipped from tree to tree until he could see Kate Malone herself, sitting on a rock at the side of the stream. The current curved toward the other bank at this point, and in the still eddy lay the image of the girl with a patch of sun in her hair. Black Angus MacTee stood beside her.

Since she was turned away from him somewhat, MacTee did not need to guard his facial expression. Under the great dark ridges of his brows, his eyes burned with a black fire.

When Harrigan saw the man, it seemed to him that he was dwarfed by the dimensions of MacTee and by the pride and furious, headlong desire in the face of the man.

"What I want to know is not much, Kate," said Angus MacTee. "It's only to find out if you mind me being here close to you. It's only to find out if you care the least mite for me, Kate."

She looked up, not at MacTee, but at the long, bright slope of the hill beyond the creek.

"I've owed my life to you, Angus," said the girl. "How could I help caring for you? Except for you and Dan Harrigan. . . ."

"Poor Harrigan," said MacTee. "*There* was a man."

The girl got up from her place and looked straight into the face of MacTee. And Harrigan would have given worlds to have been standing nearer to study her expression.

"Is Dan Harrigan dead?" she asked. Her voice was level. Who could tell what emotion was behind it?

"If he were dead, would it be breaking your heart, Kate?" asked MacTee.

"He's not dead, Angus," said the girl. "I know the two of you. I know that better friends never lived in the world than you are. If Danny were dead, you couldn't speak of him with a still eye, Angus."

26

"I was his friend," agreed Angus MacTee with a ponderous sigh. "But now I'm thinking that it might be better for Dan, if he were under the ground."

He turned away, slightly, from the girl. And Harrigan closed his hands to fists.

"What's happened to him?" asked Kate Malone.

"Whiskey got him," answered MacTee. "Whiskey got poor Dan. It was so that I didn't care to let him go to town alone. He'd spend the money I gave him for groceries on nothing but whiskey. I'd have to go in afterward, and I'd find him with his money spent, singing in a saloon for more drinks, or holding out his hand on a street corner. . . ."

Harrigan leaned his forehead against the trunk of a tree and fought back the growl that was rising in his throat.

"Poor Danny!" cried the girl. "I know how it is with great big impulsive natures like his. Oh, poor Danny."

Life returned to Harrigan, as he listened.

"If that was only the worst," sighed MacTee. "But it's not the worst. Whiskey takes hold of a man, Kate, and rots the heart in him. Whiskey turns the soul in a man. Poor Harrigan! I'm afraid he's done for now. The law's after him, Kate."

"For what?" she cried.

"Don't talk of it, Kate," muttered MacTee. "Don't have words about it. I wouldn't breathe it even to you. Murder's not a thing to be talked about, is it?"

"Murder!" she gasped. "I've got to go to him, Angus. He needs me, and I've got to go to him."

"Eh?" grunted MacTee, staggered by this result of his talk.

"I've always sworn that if either of you were in trouble, I'd go around the world to help you. And he needs me now."

"You'd do him good, if he were like his old self," said MacTee, shaking his head. "But there's little left of the old Dan Harrigan. Ah, when I think of the eye of him, and the fire in his

27

hair, and the fire in his heart, Kate, it's a pitiful thing to think of the man he is now, with his hair turning gray, and his eye dim, and his face all bloated. He looks old, Kate, and weak. The soul's gone out of him. He wouldn't want to lay eyes on you, Kate. It would remind him of the days when he was a man, and when he loved Kate Malone . . . if he really loved you, Kate. But I've always thought it was just that he saw I wanted you, and so he wanted you, too. Except for him, tell me the truth of it, Kate . . . you and I would have been married long ago. You never would have run away from me, except for Dan Harrigan."

"I won't talk of it, Angus," said the girl. "If Danny were here, I might try. But not when he's away."

"It's Harrigan that you loved, then?" exclaimed MacTee, with a terrible scowl. "When you ran away and left word behind you, you said in the letter that you really loved one of us, but you wouldn't choose him for fear the other of us would be murdering the lucky one."

"You know well how it was," answered Kate Malone. "I owed my life to you both. You were greater friends than I've ever seen in the world. But if I married one of you, the other one would be unhappy. And men like you and Dan, Angus, are sure to use your hands, when you're unhappy. That was why I ran away. But if Danny is ill, I've got to find him. You must take me to him, Angus!"

"He won't need to take you, Kate," said the great Harrigan, and stepped out from his shelter.

She put out her hands toward him. He saw the terror of inquiry turn to joy in her eyes. She ran to him, and he leaned over her and kissed her.

"Angus, Angus!" said the girl. "How could you have played such a joke on me, with Danny standing there all the time?"

MacTee was black, indeed. His great hands hooked them-

28

selves into predacious claws. His body trembled with passion. But he strove to cover this emotion with a harsh, grinding laugh. "I wanted to surprise you, Kate," said MacTee. "And then have old Danny jump out like a jack-in-the-box. Good old Danny!" Cheerfully he smote the shoulder of Harrigan, a blow that would have felled an ordinary man.

"Damn your black heart, you sneaking traitor," murmured Harrigan, adding aloud: "Well, well . . . old Angus. He carried it pretty far, though. 'Bloated face' . . . eh? There's the bright young wit for you. There's the boy to make the crowd laugh. Kate, let me look at you. Let me soak you up with my eyes. God bless me, it's a happy day, even if there's a Black MacTee in it."

Her blue eyes were shining into the blue eyes of Harrigan. But the joy bubbling up in her grew suddenly dim, when she heard Harrigan end on the remark about MacTee.

"I wouldn't want to spoil any party," said MacTee coldly. "I'll step along, Kate. You and Dan seem to have a lot to say to each other."

"Stop it, Angus!" she exclaimed. "Stop it, Dan. You're glaring at one another like two wolves. Can't we be three friends together? Can't we . . . ?" She stopped, with a groan of despair.

"Sure," said Harrigan. "We're all friends together." But still his eyes were fastened on those of MacTee, blue fire on black fire.

And the girl, glancing from one to the other, turned pale. The happiness was gone from her as suddenly as it had come. But she made herself say cheerfully: "We'll take a walk together, and talk over everything since we were last together. I'll just run up to the house for ten minutes to change these shoes, and then we'll take a stroll over the hills. Wait here!"

She hurried up among the trees toward the house, turning once to wave and smile toward them, before disappearing.

29

V

"BROTHERS OF BATTLE"

When they were alone, each of them took a long stride that left them closely confronting one another.

"Only one of us is going to be here when she comes back," said Black MacTee.

"Aye," answered Harrigan. "Only one of us. You murdering thug, I'm going to take everything out of you. You ran off with the mule. You left me to starve at the mine. You chucked away our money. You planted the railroad dicks along the trail to salt me down with lead, if they had a chance. But all that's nothing. You had to lie to Kate Malone about me. You had to tell her that I'm a worthless drunk. Damn you, I'm going to take all of that out on you."

"I told her the truth about what you're going to be, Harrigan," said MacTee. "Because when I get through with you, today, you're going to be afraid to lift your head and look anyone in the face. I'm going to grind you so damn' small, Harrigan, that the wind can blow you away."

"Perhaps," said Harrigan, "but not just now."

"You're turning yellow already, are you?" demanded MacTee. "You're trying to back down, are you? You're a rat!"

"MacTee," said Harrigan, "all the soul of me is itching in my hands. But we can't fight it out now. She'll be back before we could finish. Only, I promise you that you'll have your chance before the day's ended. We're going to take a walk, now, with Kate. We're going to be polite to each other. And tomorrow, one of us will either be dead or gone away. Is that right?"

MacTee, after fixing a glance of terrible disdain on Harrigan for a moment, turned on his heel and strode off to a small distance. He began to walk up and down, wrapped in his dark thoughts.

Harrigan leaned against a tree and smoked a cigarette and watched Angus MacTee. Dimly there passed through his mind the many pictures of the days when he had walked at the side of Angus MacTee into the face of dangers that they had met together. They had wrought such deeds for one another that the whole wide West had spoken of them. They had been such friends as men conceive, but never find.

Of these things, however, Harrigan saw only the faint pictures. For now they wanted one woman. In the old days they had done battle for her. Matched in strength, in craft, in desperate courage, Red Dan Harrigan and Black MacTee had struggled to win her, until in the end she had fled from them both for fear that they would kill one another. She had told them that they would never see her again. She had told them, in her last letter, that she truly loved one of them. But her choice she would not name. When she was gone, they were to each other more than brothers. But now that she was with them again, they mutually poisoned the air for one another.

All this was in the mind of Harrigan, as he stared at MacTee. When they had been together at the mine, the vigilance of MacTee in acts of courtesy and in kindness had never ended. He had been always first to find the water jar empty and to assume the labor of filling it. He had been the first to forage for wood. He had labored willingly extra hours sharpening the drills. The money in his pocket had been Harrigan's money; the blood in his body had been Harrigan's blood; the breath of his nostrils he would have given up for his

31

friend. But not Kate Malone!

When she entered their world, MacTee became a dark and crafty savage. A wild Indian was capable of no more atrocities. His fruitful malevolence had scattered a hundred dangers along the trail that Harrigan had just followed. It would scatter more, in the future. So there arose in Harrigan a red flame of detestation and hatred. If Kate Malone were removed, he knew that he and MacTee were welded as one flesh and one blood and one bone. That was the very reason she had fled from them before. . . .

Suddenly Harrigan said: "MacTee, it's more than ten minutes we've been waiting."

"Ah?" muttered MacTee.

"It's nearer to fifteen," said Harrigan.

"What would you mean by that, and glaring at me?" asked MacTee.

"I'd mean," said Harrigan, "that you let the brute beast come out in your face a minute ago, and she could see it plain enough. She's gone again . . . I'll bet my soul on it. She's gone again!"

MacTee gave him one stern glance. "Maybe you're right. But it's the red hell that shone out of you, that she saw!"

They were already dashing through the woods toward the house.

"I might have guessed . . . ," groaned Harrigan.

He strained with all his might to gain the lead. It seemed to him that in this contest the supremacy between them would be established. But when they issued from the trees before the house, MacTee was a stride in the lead.

Instantly they saw the answer to their fears. On a distant hill a rider wavered for an instant on the horizon, then disappeared from their view. It was a woman. It must be Kate Malone.

"Damn you!" said Harrigan, and smote the dark granite of the jaw of MacTee.

Stone is hard, but iron is harder, and the fist of Harrigan was iron. MacTee was hurled to the ground, and Harrigan ran toward a big, brown gelding that was tethered in front of the ranch house.

"Hey, boss, you ain't runnin' off with that hoss, are you?" shouted the cook.

Harrigan answered merely: "I'll send back the price in hard cash!" He untethered the rope with flying fingers. He had his foot in the stirrup, when a thunderbolt struck him to the ground.

It was Angus MacTee. And it was Angus MacTee who leaped into the saddle. Harrigan rose and laid his mighty clutch on the reins, reaching for the gun hand of MacTee at the same time, and locking his hold on the wrist.

Then a calm voice said behind them: "You two hoss thieves, get away from that mustang!"

They looked toward the house and saw on the verandah a little man with a long rifle leveled firmly at his shoulder. There is no arguing with a rifle held by such hands. One may gamble against a revolver, but not against a rifleman who kills his deer at six hundred yards. So MacTee dismounted and stood at the side of Harrigan.

"I oughta hold you and jail you, maybe," said the rancher. "But all I'll do is to get you off my place. Move, the pair of you!" He raised his voice to an angry yell, as he lost control of his temper. "Get!" he cried.

MacTee and Harrigan got. They strode rapidly across the rolling ground until they found the trail of the horse that had carried the girl away from them. They came to the hilltop over which she had dropped from view. There they paused.

They glared at one another with gloomy detestation. On the

33

jaw of MacTee there was a red lump. On the side of Harrigan's face was its mate.

"Harrigan," said MacTee. "I'm going to break you open like a crab and eat the heart out of you, before long."

"MacTee," said Harrigan, "there's nothing here but the sky and the grass to look at us. I'm better than you with a gun. I'll put it aside. I'll have you with my bare hands. There'll be more taste to the killing of you, that way."

"Harrigan," said MacTee, "it's a true thing that I'd love to be at you. But we've got a job on our hands that may use up the brains of both of us. Look yonder!" He pointed toward the wide landscape, the green hills, and the ragged storm of mountains that rose toward the horizon.

"There's our job. Kate's no fool. She's as tough as whipcord, and she'll run like a fox till she thinks that she's dropped us off her trail. She's dropped us before. She'll drop us again, unless we put our heads together and all the strength that's in us. Let's be partners again till we've found her. And afterward . . . God help you, Harrigan."

Red Dan Harrigan grinned. He held out his hand. "I'll be a brother to you, MacTee," he said, "till we've found her. And after that, MacTee, I'll work you into a red mud with my hands."

Their hands closed, joining with a mighty pressure.

VI

"YELLOW GULCH"

They traveled through the rest of that day as only Harrigan and MacTee could travel. If there was more speed in MacTee's long legs over the level, there was more agility in Harrigan when they came to rough country. In the evening, they came to a little ranch house on the southern side of a hill. In a big field near the house and barn, horses were grazing.

MacTee said: "We've got to have horses, if we want to find Kate Malone."

"We've got to find horses," agreed Harrigan. "But you know this part of the world, MacTee. They'd rather hang a horse thief than a murderer, Angus."

"There was never a rope spun that could hang me," said Angus MacTee. "If there's no heart in you, Harrigan, turn back now, and I'll go on alone."

"How could a Scotchman have the heart of a Harrigan?" asked the other. "I'll go wherever you'll go, MacTee, and do whatever you'll do, and then one step beyond."

"Go into that barn, then, and find saddles and bridles," said MacTee calmly, "and ropes. When you've got 'em, I'll catch the horses. I'm not as good a thief as you are. There's not much cat in me. But I can handle a rope."

It might seem an unfair division of the labor for Harrigan to risk the danger of men, and MacTee to take only the task of catching up horses. But Red Harrigan was not one to split straws. He circled the hill on which the ranch buildings stood,

35

came over the shoulder of it, and passed out of the twilight into the thick, muddy black of the interior of the barn. Suddenly out of the darkness he heard the overbearing powerful neigh of a stallion. A horse began to plunge and batter inside a box stall. Harrigan groaned, for the people in the ranch house were sure to hear this uproar and respond to it. He was not surprised when, far away, he heard a screen door slam with a tin-pan jingling.

He had found saddles and saddle blankets and bridles. And now he hurried back with them toward the rear door. He was not yet at it, when the other door opened. Harrigan, leaping eagerly into the outer night, found that he was lighted by the brightening moonlight. A man shouted loudly: "Stop, thief!"

Harrigan kicked the door shut behind him and ran into the field, the corner where MacTee was already holding a pair of mustangs. He reached MacTee, who held the horses steady while Harrigan began the saddling in frantic haste.

The near door of the barn opened. Harrigan groaned. But he could hear the man who stood in the entrance swearing angrily, apparently unable to see anything suspicious. The rancher had fired twice, but the bullets came nowhere near the two thieves. Then he cried out loudly, as other men came running from the house.

But Harrigan and MacTee were already spurring away. The instant they were seen, bullets came whirring. But what can a revolver do at long range, when it is fired by moonlight? They rode straight on up a narrow valley, the floor of which grew steeper and steeper.

MacTee began to laugh. "Dan, d'ye hear me? Isn't it like the old days? Were there ever any better days than the old ones?"

And Dan Harrigan laughed, too. He forgot Kate Malone. He forgot the very object of his quest. It seemed to him that there was nothing in the world that was half so important as the great Black MacTee, the companion who never failed a man in time of danger. Behind them came the noise of hoofs. But the two merely laughed again, in the highest indifference. Mere mortals could not be matched against a Red Harrigan and a Black MacTee.

For two hours, off and on, they heard the distant noise of the pursuit. Twice rifles were fired after them. Then they were left alone to travel deeper into the night.

"Suppose that she left this trail?" asked Harrigan.

"She'd keep to the valley," answered MacTee. "I know the way her mind works. She'd keep to this valley. She'd want to get those mountains for a fence between her and Harrigan and MacTee."

A wind struck them, iced by the high mountain snows. But they held steadily on, crossed the divide, and came down through tall forests. At last, staring through a gap in the woods, they made out the wide-spread, gleaming lights of a town.

"That's where she is," said MacTee, with great assurance. "There's no use killing the horses. We'll go down in the morning and find her there."

"She'll start on before morning," said Harrigan.

"She can't keep running all the way around the world," answered MacTee. "No, she'll stay there for a while and hope that we'll never find her. We'd better camp here."

So they camped. They built a bed of evergreen boughs and were soon asleep. And when they wakened, the sky was luminous with the dawn. They resaddled the horses, pulled up their belts a notch, and jogged the mustangs down toward the town.

It was sprawled like a spider, with a small body and with long arms that stretched up many narrow gulches roundabout. Twenty trails converged on that small city.

"It's a jumping-off place," said Harrigan gloomily. "She might have gone in any direction."

"We'll find her," said MacTee. "There's something in me that knows how to find her as sure as a magnet knows how to find north."

The trail down was slow work. It was very rough and entailed constant windings that absorbed much time. The sun was high and hot when at last they dropped into the hollow where the town lay. MacTee wanted to go straight to the hotel.

"Suppose a pair of stolen horses have been trailed as far as this town?" suggested Harrigan uneasily.

"We have to take chances," answered MacTee. "And in the hotel, we'll find people who'll know every stray dog that's entered the town in the last ten years."

They reached the hotel that was a square white box shouldered tightly in between adjoining buildings, with the usual verandah strung across the face of it. In a livery stable across the street they put up the horses, then entered the hotel. They washed and shaved and went into the dining room.

It was after eight o'clock and, therefore, very late for breakfast in a Western town. The chairs were standing on tables. A big fellow with a tattooed arm of a sailor was scrubbing the floor with a pail of suds and a stable broom.

"Too late, brother!" he growled over his shoulder at the pair.

MacTee took two chairs from a small table and put them in place.

"Ham and eggs, coffee, hot cakes, and anything else that's handy," he said.

The waiter walked up to him with a scowl. "Are you tryin' to start something?" he demanded.

MacTee put the end of a forefinger against the breast of the ex-sailor. It was like touching him with a rod of steel. "What I start, I finish," said MacTee. "Unless you want to be close to the end, move some chuck out of the kitchen and

38

into this room. Understand?"

The waiter understood. He moved his glance in a small arc from the third button of MacTee's shirt to his gleaming eyes.

"All right," said the waiter, and nodded.

MacTee and Harrigan sat down.

"Danny," said MacTee, "I wish that we'd never laid eyes on Kate Malone."

"I wish it, too," said Harrigan. "Except when I think of her."

"She's nothing," said MacTee, "but a snip of a girl with a brown face and blue eyes. There's a thousand prettier than she is. What is she to come between friends like you and me?"

Harrigan frowned and shook his head. "I'd like to agree with you, Angus," he stated. "But I'm just after seeing her. Besides, you'd never hold to the idea that you have right now. Not if you thought that *I* had Kate Malone."

"No," agreed MacTee suddenly. He jarred the heavy table with one fist. "You and I have fought for her and starved for her and bled for her too many times. I couldn't give her up to you, Danny. But I could wish that another man would come and take her. Not like you. Not my kind of a man. But some damned long-haired violin player that I couldn't touch for the fear of mashing him like a rotten apple. If a sneaking fool like that should come along and walk off with Kate Malone, Harrigan, I'd be a happy man, after a while. After the poison boiled down in me, I'd be a happy man."

The waiter came in, but not with a stack of dishes piled on his arm. Instead, he came with an armed man walking on each side of him, and behind this leading trio there moved others, a whole dozen or more of stalwarts.

Harrigan gave them one side glance. "They've come for us, Angus," he said.

"There's hardly a round dozen of 'em," answered MacTee

calmly. "And if they knew us, Danny . . . if they knew us as we know ourselves . . . wouldn't the fools bring the whole town together before they tried to come at the bare hands of Harrigan and MacTee?"

He who walked on the right hand of the waiter was built like a lumberjack and dressed like a lumberjack in a plain Mackinaw. On the lapel of the coat was a steel badge, brighter than silver. He was such a big man that he did not touch a weapon in making this arrest. He merely stepped to the table and rapped his brown knuckles on the top of it.

"Stand up, you bohunks," he said. "Hoss thieves get free board and room in this here town of Yellow Gulch."

VII

"THE MEN OF YELLOW GULCH"

Harrigan looked at the deputy sheriff and at the fellows ranging beside him, and realized that they were men.

"All right," he said to MacTee, "I guess we'll have to stick up our hands, partner."

"All right," said MacTee, and, rising to his feet, he brought up his fist like the head of an iron mace. It bashed the deputy sheriff under the jaw and sent him staggering across the floor. Harrigan selected the ex-sailor who had betrayed them. It was neither an uppercut nor a swing nor a straight punch that he used, but his favorite hook. The hook of Harrigan was like the snapping of a whiplash with an anvil hitched to the end of the lash. His blow struck the jaw of the waiter, and that unfortunate man fell on his hands and knees.

Then Harrigan and MacTee raised a frightful yell and charged home among the men of Yellow Gulch. Whoever they struck fell or staggered far away. That single charge should have ended the fight at once, for guns could not be used in the tangled heart of this mêlée.

But Harrigan saw a strange thing. The men of Yellow Gulch might be felled, but they would not stay down. The deputy sheriff, the first to drop, was already on his feet and coming straight into the thick of the fight. The ex-sailor was up, also, and charging. And all the other men of Yellow Gulch came in with cheerful shouts. Their eyes shone, and it was plain that they considered this a delightful game. Their bodies were of India rubber; their jaws were of whalebone; and their souls were the purest flame of battle.

Just as Harrigan finished these observations, two ponderous fists landed on his jaw from opposite sides. He dropped on his face. When he wakened, a pair of monstrous legs bestrode him. It was MacTee, bellowing like a mad bull, striking right and left.

As Harrigan gathered his feet and hands under the weight of his body, the men of Yellow Gulch fell back a little, and the deputy sheriff stood before MacTee with a gun in either hand.

The deputy sheriff was no longer what he had been. The left side of his face was a great red puff. His right eye was closed. His coat was half ripped from his body.

"Stick up those hands, or I'll blow you to hell!" shouted the deputy sheriff.

But Harrigan dived along the floor, struck the legs from beneath the man of the law, and, as the revolvers drilled eyeholes for the sunlight through the wall, Harrigan arose again into the fight.

"Harrigan!" thundered MacTee, a drunken joy in his voice as he saw that his friend was again in the fight. "Harrigan!" he roared, as though it were a battle cry. He caught up a chair and swung it. "Harrigan!" he bellowed. "Harrigan!" With each shout, he struck down a man. Half the little crowd of Yellow Gulch warriors were on the floor, and through the rest Harrigan and MacTee charged to the side entrance to the dining room.

They heard an uproar of pursuit behind them. As Harrigan slammed and locked the door behind them, a bullet clipped through and split one panel. But the door held, nevertheless, while the two fugitives sprinted with lengthened legs down a narrow alley, and straight out of the little town of Yellow Gulch into the woods.

42

The green of the trees covered them. And presently they were sitting at the side of a little brook that wandered through the forest. They smoked cigarettes, considered the brightness of the patches of the sun and the brown of shadows upon pine needles, and listened to the quiet conversation of the flowing water.

Finally MacTee announced: "We were licked and chucked out. We were chucked out with no breakfast, even. What's the matter with us, Harrigan? We used to rate as men. Now what are we?"

Harrigan shook his head. He was peeling off his clothes, and, when he had finished that task, he stepped into the water of the brook and scrubbed from himself the signs of battle. At last he redressed and lay on the bank in the shadow.

"This Yellow Gulch," he observed at the last, "is the sort of a town that we ought to know a whole lot more about, MacTee. It's full of folks that I could be glad to see, and so could you."

"I could," agreed MacTee. "It's a town worth having and a town worth knowing. Did you see that yellow-headed fellow with the straight left?"

"I did," said Harrigan, caressing his face. "And there was the short man with the big shoulders and the overarm swing. You remember him? I just managed to hit him in the pit of the belly, and, as he dropped, I was able to uppercut him, and, when he straightened from that, I clouted him on the jaw."

"With a hook?" asked MacTee.

"With a hook," said Harrigan.

"Danny," said MacTee dreamily, "there's times when I love you more than a brother. What did he look like when you last saw him? I sort of missed him in the last few minutes."

"He looked like an astronomer," said Harrigan, after a mo-

43

ment of thought. "He was lying on his back, and he seemed to be studying the stars."

MacTee laughed broodingly.

Harrigan said: "Are we beaten, MacTee, or what do you say?"

"The mountains are up and against us," said MacTee.

"They are," agreed Harrigan. "But if we lose her now, we'll never find her."

"Now," said MacTee, "that they know the quality of us, they'll be shooting on sight. And these people, they wouldn't know how to miss."

"They would not," agreed Harrigan.

"So what do *you* suggest?" asked MacTee.

"I suggest," said Harrigan, "that we draw straws to see who goes into Yellow Gulch after dark and tries his best to get on the track of her."

MacTee shuddered. "Draw to see who goes back into Yellow Gulch?" he echoed.

"That's the idea," said Harrigan.

MacTee groaned. "All right," he agreed. "Pick out some straws, and we'll see."

Harrigan picked two blades of grass. The short one he laid under his thumb projecting less than the long one. Then he changed his mind and laid them with their ends exactly even.

"The long man goes to Yellow Gulch," said Harrigan.

"Good," said MacTee, and straightway picked the shorter of the pair.

Harrigan stared, opening his palm to reveal the long one. "Well," he said, "that's the way I'd rather have it."

"You're a brave man, Danny," said MacTee. "And when we're this far from Kate, I don't mind saying that you're as brave as any man in the world. But you wouldn't be telling me that you'd rather be going into Yellow Gulch than sitting out

44

here in the woods, waiting for news?"

"I would, though," argued Harrigan. "If I sat here, and you went in, I'd go mad. For I'd see you finding Kate Malone for yourself. And I'd see you talking to her, persuading and lying, until you got her for yourself."

"She's not there at all, most likely," said MacTee.

"Maybe not," said Harrigan. "But I'll go fishing in Yellow Gulch for her as soon as it's dark . . . and I'll be a happy man to start on my way."

VIII

"HARRIGAN GOES TO TOWN"

MacTee went to the edge of the woods with Harrigan, where he looked with his friend at the glitter of the town lights.

"You're a brave man, Harrigan," he observed, "considering the sort of men they have in Yellow Gulch. Good bye, and God bless you. If a thing happens wrong to you, I'll find the man that did it, and plant him alive."

So Harrigan went like a thief into the town. If MacTee dreaded the place and the strong-handed men of it, so did Harrigan. But in his heart there was the wild and eerie passion that led him toward the girl. So he went on until, upon the dark of an alley, a kitchen door opened, a dull shaft of yellow lamplight fell upon Harrigan, and a woman's voice shouted: "It's Harrigan! It's Harrigan!"

Harrigan ran. It was as though the woman had called to furious hornets, all in readiness inside of a nest. Out they poured, the men of Yellow Gulch, to follow him. Doors slammed. The heavy feet of men hit the ground.

He fled across the main street, a gorge of revealing light that brought a shower of bullets after him. One of them kissed the tip of his right ear. He bounded like a deer into a silent byway. A tall board fence rose beside it. He leaped, caught the top rim, swung himself over, and started for the fence on the opposite side. Then the imp of the perverse made him decide to trust to his luck — so he dropped into a nest of high grass and lay still. At the same time, a pursuer swung over the top of the fence like a pole-vaulter, and another and another followed him.

What manner of men were these in Yellow Gulch, when all of them seemed able to match the best that Harrigan could do? His heart grew small in him with wonder, and he shook his head as he lay in the tall grass, murmuring: "I must be pretty far West!" A dozen, he counted, crossed the yard, vaulted the fence on the other side, and rushed away. Other footfalls stormed through the street. Then gunshots broke out, far away. The noise diminished, the shouting turned corners and was obscured.

After that, a quiet footfall drew near to Harrigan. Then the voice of a girl said: "I've got a sawed-off shotgun loaded with buckshot. I've got you covered, and I can't miss. Get up out of that, Harrigan!"

Harrigan got up at once. With a sawed-off shotgun, no matter in what hands, argument is futile. He saw that the girl was small. He saw that the gun in her hands was real. So he lifted his arms above his head. This was something for the world to read in newspapers and laugh at — how Harrigan was captured by a girl, by a child!

"March up there through that screen door into the kitchen," said the girl. "And if you try to jump one side or the other, I'll blow you out of your socks!"

If they had men in Yellow Gulch, they had women, also. Harrigan walked a chalk line to the back verandah, up the steps, and through the screen door of the kitchen. He faced the stove, his arms still lifted over his head. The screen door creaked gently behind him.

"All right," said the girl. "You can turn around."

He turned. She was not more than sixteen. She had freckles across her nose. She was rather small. But her eyes were of the divine Irish blue.

"So you're Harrigan," she said.

"I'm a piece of him," said Harrigan.

"It's you that licked Jim Bingham, is it?"

"Who's Jim Bingham?"

"You licked him, and you don't even know his name? He's my brother."

"I know him, then," said Harrigan. "He's short and wide, and he knows how to box. He's got black hair and a pair of eyes in his head."

"I'm mighty glad you noticed him," said the girl.

"Molly," groaned a voice at a distance of two or three rooms.

"Aye, Jim. Wait a minute." She added: "He's lying in there with a couple of busted ribs. But you don't look so big. Not to me, you don't."

"I'm not so big," said Harrigan gently.

"But you licked Jim," she said grimly, bitterly.

"I had the weight and the reach on him," said Harrigan.

"You had ten or twelve huskies socking at you, too," she answered, shaking her head. "I thought the Binghams were the best, but I guess they're not. The Harrigans must be close to the top."

"I got in a lucky punch," said Harrigan.

"Harrigan," said the girl, "why do you and MacTee steal horses and chase around after a girl that doesn't want you?"

"Who says that?"

"There's talk around."

"The talk's wrong," said Harrigan. "She wants one of us. We want to find which one."

"Ah?" said the girl.

"Yes. She wants one of us."

"She's mighty pretty," said the girl. "I saw her. She's beautiful. She's good, too, and she's kind, and gentle, and wise, and brave, and everything."

"Yes. She's everything," agreed Harrigan. "I've known her for a long time. I've known her since she was a ringer for you."

"Since she was a what? Are you trying to flatter me, Harrigan?"

"The truth is not flattering," answered Harrigan. "I remember her when she was a ringer for you. And I've been following her ever since."

"Never mind who she's a ringer for," said Molly Bingham, flushing. "But go on and tell me what makes you think she wants one of you?"

"She said so, one day."

"It was a long time ago, then," suggested the girl.

"Yes, it was a long time ago," agreed Harrigan, sighing.

"Suppose she took MacTee," said the girl. "What would you do?"

"I'd murder the black Scotch heart of him," said Harrigan.

The girl started. "I think you mean it," she answered. "And yet, you and MacTee fight for each other like two brothers."

"He's the best man in the world," agreed Harrigan, "except where Kate Malone's concerned."

At this, the girl chuckled, softly.

"Molly!" called her brother, in angry impatience.

"Be still, Jimmy. I'm coming in a moment," answered the girl.

"How did you know me?" asked Harrigan.

"I saw the red of your hair. And who else but a Harrigan or a MacTee would be leaping the fences around Yellow Gulch at this time of the night?"

"True. I hadn't thought about that."

"I'm going to call for help."

"If you do," answered Harrigan, "they'll never take me alive."

"Well, then, I'll give you a chance. I'll send you to where

49

Kate Malone is staying. But I'll have a promise out of you, first."

"I'll promise you the clouds out of the sky."

"Harrigan," said the girl, "she loves either you or MacTee, and neither of you can guess which one it is. And she doesn't dare to give herself to one of you for fear that the other will make mincemeat of the lucky man. But now I'm going to take your word of honor that you'll go to her, Harrigan, and swear on the Bible to her that if she loves MacTee you'll do him no harm, but you'll go far away. Will you promise me that?"

Harrigan looked up at the ceiling, then down into the face of the girl.

"Well . . . ," he said.

"Or else I'll raise a yell that'll bring all of the town to this spot. It's a mean town, too, Harrigan. There's a dozen of its best men that are wearing bumps and breaks because of you and MacTee, and all their friends, and themselves, are achin' to have another go at you."

"It's true," said Harrigan. "It's a tough town. The toughest that I ever found in my days."

"Will you promise me?"

"If she says that it's MacTee, will I go 'way off and never do him a harm?" repeated Harrigan.

"Aye. Will you promise that?"

"Yes," groaned the hesitant Harrigan.

"Good," said the girl. "Give your hand on it." She held out hers.

Harrigan looked at the hand and sighed.

"Be a man, Harrigan."

Gingerly he took her hand. He closed his eyes, and sighed. "Here's my promise, and God help me. Where'll I find her?"

"I know where she is," said Molly Bingham. "Go out to the front corner of the garden. Wait there. I'll soon be coming."

Harrigan went out through the darkness of a trance and stood in the garden. Presently the front door opened and closed. The girl stood beside him.

"Come with me," she said.

Harrigan followed her down a lane, and across an alley, and up a barren, empty street until they came to a little house retired among trees.

"She's in there," said the girl. "Wouldn't you feel shame, Dan Harrigan, to be hounding a girl like her, and making the world talk? Wouldn't you feel shame?" But she was laughing softly, as she walked up the path before him to the house. When they came to the trees, she said: "Wait here."

He waited. She went on. She climbed the steps through a soft shaft of lamplight. She knocked at the front door, then opened it, and went inside.

Harrigan heard nothing. The coldness of ice water welled up in him, covered his heart, rose as high as his throat. He felt dizzy and weak.

At last the front door of the house opened. Two women came out. One of them sat down at the top of the steps, and he knew that this was Molly Bingham. The other came with hesitant steps down the path. At last she reached a full halt, turned, and beckoned. Molly Bingham instantly ran and joined her. They came on together. A dullness of lamplight passed over them, and Harrigan saw the face of Kate Malone. His dizziness increased. He wanted to run away, leaving all questions unasked and unanswered. Then they were close. Kate Malone halted. The younger girl stamped on the gravel of the path.

"Come on to her, you great hulk," she snapped.

Harrigan strode, looming through the darkness. When he came to Kate Malone, he dropped to one knee and felt that it was the weakness of his legs that compelled him.

51

She made a gesture toward him. He caught her hand. It was cold and trembling.

"Poor Danny!" she soothed. "Did the brutes hurt you badly?"

At that, a wild hope filled him. "Fists couldn't be hurting me, Kate!" he exclaimed. "Nothing but a word from you could hurt me. That's what I've come to learn from you. Tell me, Kate, that you love MacTee, and I'll take myself from your way. I'll never bother Angus. You'll be free with him, and God give you both happiness. But tell me the truth of it. Do you love Angus MacTee?"

He listened, breathlessly. The pause was long. The moments of it stung him like poisoned daggers.

Then she answered in a broken voice: "Aye, Danny . . . I love him!"

IX

"BAITING A TRAP"

The hope sickened and died in Harrigan as a green twig withers and droops in flame. After a while he got up to his feet. He kept on rising, when he was erect. He kept on drawing himself straighter and straighter, drawing in deep breaths, telling himself silently that he would not die, that men did not die of wounds that words could make.

Someone was weeping. That was like Kate Malone. She could not endure giving pain, and she was an old friend and a dear one. Yes, Kate would weep over him. This made tears sting his own eyes, until suddenly he saw that it was the other girl who was crying heartily, stifling her sobs. But Kate stood with her hands clasped in front of her, and her face lifted toward the stars. She reminded him of a picture he had seen somewhere, he could not remember where.

He said: "Well, Kate, I'm taking myself away. If I were man enough, I'd go out into the woods and tell Angus that he's the lucky one. But I couldn't trust myself that far. If I looked at the face of Black Angus, and thought of him calling you his wife . . . I'd likely go mad. But I've sworn an oath and given my hand on it . . . and now I'll take your word and leave you."

He held out his hand. The cold hand of Kate was laid in his.

"You blithering idiot!" gasped Molly Bingham. "I never knew a red-headed man to be such a fool. Kiss her good bye . . . and then see."

There was a melancholy stirring in the soul of Harrigan.

53

"We've been through great things, Kate," he said. "Will you kiss me good bye?" He put his left arm around her, gently. She had not stirred, but still looked past him at the upper night. She was like a stone.

"Oh, Dan Harrigan, you half-wit," said Molly Bingham. "You swore that you'd leave her, if she loved MacTee. But make her swear your own oath that she loves him. Make her swear that it's true she loves MacTee."

"Almighty thunder," groaned Harrigan.

His left arm was no longer gentle. It crushed Kate Malone to him.

"Swear it, by God, Kate, and I'll leave you. Swear that you love MacTee. For if you don't mean it with all your heart . . . if it's only a trick to get me and all the murdering trouble out of the way. . . . Swear that you love him, Kate. The saying of it won't do with me."

But Kate Malone began to sob. And that baffled Harrigan. It made him more bewildered than ever.

"She's only a poor liar, after all," said Molly Bingham. "Kiss her, Dan Harrigan, and see what's left of her pretending. Kiss her . . . the silly baby."

But Molly Bingham was herself crying, and talking through her tears. And Harrigan knew that in all the days of his life he never would understand women truly.

He leaned to touch his lips to the face of Kate Malone. Her head dropped weakly against the hollow of his shoulder.

"Kate!" he cried out in an ecstasy of revelation. "You're mine. You belong to me! It isn't MacTee that you care for."

"It's you, Danny," said the girl. "It's always been you. But I've never dared to show what I feel, for fear of Angus MacTee. What can we do now? He'll kill you, Dan, if he finds out the truth."

"God means it to come to a showdown between us," said

Harrigan. "I've got to see MacTee, and face him, and have it out."

"No!" cried the girl. "You'd never come back to me alive!"

"I've got to tell him that I've found you," said Harrigan. "I came for both of us to find your trail, Kate. We're partners, Angus and I. We'll keep on being partners . . . till he goes for my throat. There's no other honest way out of it."

"Would you be honest with the devil, Dan Harrigan?" asked Molly hotly. "Well, no matter what MacTee would do to a man, he'll never touch a girl. Let me know where to find him, and I'll take him the word that you've found Kate, and that you and she are away together. I don't have to tell what the direction is."

"I can't let you go out and face him," said Harrigan.

"It's the one way to live up to your partnership with him," said Molly briskly. "If you talk to him, you know it'll be the death of both of you. Tell me where to find him."

"Tell her," said Kate Malone.

So Harrigan hesitantly, uncertainly, gave the word to Molly of how she could pass through the woods and come to the creek, and so to the camp of Black MacTee.

"I'll be on my way," said Molly. "Kate, do up your things. Get out of Yellow Gulch with Harrigan. Take the Dormer Pass and head straight for the railroad. You'll be out of the reach of MacTee before long. Go fast! You have your own horse, Kate. And in the shed behind my house there's a big bay gelding that belongs to nobody but me. You can take that horse, Dan Harrigan. Good bye, Kate. Good bye, Harrigan."

"Wait!" exclaimed Kate Malone. "Stop her, Danny!"

Harrigan barred the way of Molly. At the touch of his hand, she was still, laughing and trembling with excitement.

"What am I to say to you, Molly, darling?" said Kate. "And what's Dan to say to you? We'll owe you everything."

"I could teach Dan what to say to me," said Molly. "If I were a year or two older, I'd fight you for him, Kate. Dan, if you lose her somewhere in the mountains, come back and you can find me."

She slipped away and was instantly lost in the darkness. She had given them the means of escaping, and now she was determined to assure their safety still further, so that no harm whatever could overtake them. . . .

Running as fast as any boy, she got to the house of the deputy sheriff. He sat on his front porch with a wet towel around his head and various swellings discoloring his face.

"Hullo, Dave," said the girl. "I've got news for you that'll make you open both eyes."

"It'll be a month before I get both eyes wide open," said the deputy sheriff. He had the shamelessness of a man whose courage has been proven over and over. He sat up and took the towel from his face. "It's not mumps that I caught, but the Harrigan," he explained with a grin. "What's the good news, Molly?"

"The Harrigan's gone," said the girl.

"The devil he has. Where?"

"Through the Dormer Pass with Kate Malone, and, if you lift a hand to follow 'em, Dave, you're not a right man."

"Listen to her," said Dave's wife, chuckling. "I suppose she loves the red man."

"I do," said Molly. "Who wouldn't love a man that can beat Dave, here? And my own brother laid up with some broken ribs from the same fist. Of course, I love Red Harrigan. But there's a thing for you to do, still. You can catch Black MacTee."

"Aye," said the deputy sheriff. "He has a fist like an iron club. I'd like to put hands on MacTee, and irons on him, too."

"You'd better have the irons on him before you try your hands," said Molly. "Get some of your best men, Dave. There

56

are plenty in Yellow Gulch that'd be glad to be in at the killing of MacTee or of Harrigan. You know that."

"I know that," agreed Dave, "and I'll do it." He stood up from his chair. "You'll be running the whole county before long, Molly. You're running Yellow Gulch already."

"As soon as I outgrow freckles," said Molly, "I'm going to run for governor. You won't take after Harrigan, Dave?"

"No," said the deputy sheriff. "Not if you tell me to keep my hands off him. I wouldn't dare." He chuckled again. "But this MacTee. Where is he, Molly?"

"You cut across town till you come through the woods to the creek. Go up the creek till you find a sandbar with the creek spilling over the two ends of it. Black MacTee will be somewhere there. And go carefully, Dave. He's a tiger."

"I'll have five men with me," said the deputy sheriff cheerfully. "I'd rather walk into the cave of a mother grizzly than into a place where that black Scotchman is hiding."

X

"PURSUIT"

Black MacTee, sitting on a rock at the side of the water, trailed his left hand in the icy current. His heart was aching with desire for a smoke, but he dared not smoke for fear that even the easily dissipated smoke of a cigarette might reach inquisitive nostrils and bring danger. So, as he sat there, he occupied his mind and quelled his nerves by submitting his flesh to the biting chill of the stream. He was so engaged, when he heard a faint rustling sound. It was a very small sound. It might have been the rustling of leaves when branches sway slightly. It might have been the step of a wild beast inside the woods.

But the nerves of MacTee were drawn taut, and, therefore, he lifted his head to listen. What he heard next was hardly a sound at all. It was rather a vibration, a nothingness of tremor that ran through the ground. But it sent MacTee into cover with the speed of a slinking cat. He crouched in the shadow, looking out savagely, tensely, around him. After a time, he heard another mere whisper. It was close beside him, and now he could make out the silhouette of a man moving from behind the trunk of a tree, coming toward the sandbar.

MacTee reached out his arm, massive and rigid as the walking beam of a great engine. With the sharp, deadly knuckles of his second joints, he struck the stalking silhouette behind the ear. The sound was very muffled. It was not as loud as the noise a chopper makes when it is struck into soft meat. And yet the hunting figure relaxed, at once. MacTee, taking a single long stride forward, caught the slumping body before it could crash to the ground. With that burden in his arms, he straightened and stalked away soundlessly.

On his left, he made out another dim form, slipping in the opposite direction, and he felt that he had been betrayed, and by Harrigan. The thought stopped his heart with cold sickness. There was no rage in him, at the moment. There was only that unutterable smallness of soul and despair as he thought that Red Dan Harrigan might have betrayed a partner. He locked that misery behind his teeth and went on, stepping softly. When the burden he carried began to moan faintly and to stir in his arms, he was at a considerable distance from his starting point. So he put the man on his feet and shook him. Searching through his clothes, MacTee found a revolver and took it away from his captive.

"Who are you?" asked MacTee.

The other muttered: "Lord God, my head's smashed in."

"It'll feel better after a while," said MacTee. "What d'ye mean by sneaking through the night like a mountain lion hunting mutton? Who are you?"

"I'm deputy sheriff, and. . . ."

"Somebody told you that you'd find me here?"

"Yes," admitted the man of the law, his wits still reeling from the blow that he had received.

"He told you, then," muttered MacTee. He drew in a long, long breath, to keep away the sense of strangulation. "Even Harrigan," MacTee said miserably. "Anybody else . . . but not Harrigan, a traitor! Traitors don't wear red hair." He added: "Where's Harrigan?"

"I don't know," said the deputy sheriff. "It's MacTee that has me? What happened?"

"What's happened doesn't matter, compared with what's *going* to happen pretty soon," said MacTee, "unless you tell me what's become of Harrigan. Have you caught him?"

"No."

"He's not in jail?"

"No, he's not in jail."

"Then where is he? D'you think I'll hesitate to squash your windpipe for you, unless you talk out to me, man?"

A shudder passed through the deputy sheriff. It was a tremor imparted to his body by the quivering of the angry hand of MacTee, as it grasped the shoulder of the prisoner.

Far ahead of them a voice called, anxiously: "Dave! Hey, Dave!"

"My God, I've made a fool of myself," groaned Dave.

"It's better to be a living fool than a dead one," said MacTee. "Tell me where Harrigan is, or. . . ."

"He's in the Dormer Pass, I suppose, by this time."

"Ha? You know where he is? In the Dormer Pass?"

"Yes. They've gotten up into it, by this time."

"They? Who's with him?"

"Kate Malone," said the deputy sheriff.

"God in heaven," groaned MacTee. "The coward, the cur, the traitor! He stole her . . . and he's running with her!"

"She's gone willingly with him, MacTee," said the deputy sheriff. "She has. . . ."

"You lie!" said MacTee, and struck him heavily in the face, so that the head of the deputy bobbed back on his shoulders.

"Where's the Dormer Pass?" asked MacTee.

"There," said the frightened deputy, for he felt that he was in the hands of a madman. "There, to the right of that sugar loaf, in that cut, yonder. That's the Dormer. You can see the cloud rolling down through it."

MacTee looked, and he saw a white serpent of mist, brightened by the moon, crawling down the face of a mountain.

"The Judas," groaned MacTee. "The damned, sneaking,

Irish blarney, hypocrite and traitor! He stole Kate and he sent the law after Angus MacTee to keep me from. . . ."

"No," said the deputy sheriff. "He didn't send. . . ."

"Be still, damn you!" snarled MacTee.

He dashed his fist into the battered face of Dave again with such force that the deputy slumped senseless to the ground. MacTee let him drop. Well ahead of him, through the trees, he could hear the shouting of several voices that blended and blurred together, and yet he could make out among them the calling of the name — "Dave!"

But there was something better close at hand. He could see the glint of the metal work on bridles, the vague outlines of saddles, and one glistening spot of moonlight on the rump of a horse. Half a dozen of them were tethered in one group among the trees just before him.

"Dave! Dave!" yelled the searchers.

"Here," groaned the feeble voice of the deputy.

MacTee stepped to the tethered mustangs, chose the biggest for himself, mounted it, untied the others of the group, and led them off at a quiet walk that turned into a jangling trot, and thence into a flying gallop that swept him straight toward the Dormer Pass.

XI

"FLIGHT"

The horses of Harrigan and Kate Malone were already entering the thick mist. At once they were lost as though in smoke. Above them the strength of the moon pierced here and there through the gathering storm clouds. It peered as though through a window, and sent down a broad shaft of milky white enabling the two riders to see one another, vaguely. The way had grown extremely steep. The horses began to slip and slide. Even mountain horses, which are nearly as sure-footed as goats, could hardly negotiate those smooth rocks after the wet of the clouds had greased them.

They rode very close together for a time. Then Harrigan dismounted. His great bulk made it difficult for his horse to climb. The girl, however, could still make better progress by remaining in the saddle. It began to be difficult work. In half a dozen places, the horses could barely climb the sharp grades. They grunted. Their striking, sliding hoofs knocked long sparks out of the stones. And yet, through this difficult time, they did not speak to one another. Not until Kate said, as they paused a moment, panting: "Do you think that we were right to take this pass?"

"Molly seems to be right about everything. She told us to take this one," answered Harrigan.

"Aye, but suppose that MacTee is able to make her talk to him, and gets the name of the pass out of her, and the fact that we've gone through this way?"

62

"You don't know MacTee," said Harrigan. "He's man enough to smash a regiment, but he couldn't even whisper against a woman." He added, out of the largeness of his heart: "There's only one thing I regret, and that is that I didn't go find him myself before I left Yellow Gulch."

As he spoke, looking toward the girl, a radiance of moonlight flowed over her through the mist and made her like a form of glowing marble.

"All right, Danny. We don't care, so long as we're here together and safe for the minute. Only. . . ."

"Only what?" urged Harrigan.

"It's too happy," she answered. "It can't last. There's a pricking in my blood that tells me. There's something that follows me like a ghost."

They had come to a narrow point of the ravine, as she spoke, and here the wind, gathered as into a funnel, blew the mist rushing against their faces, then dispersed it as the wind gathers the dust of the desert and sweeps it off against the horizon. They looked back to find that the pass was clear of mist, for the moment, behind them. And that was how they happened to see, far away, laboring up the slope of a very distant incline, the form of a horseman who looked larger than human, the horse driven frantic by constant spurring.

"MacTee!" said Harrigan.

He felt, in an instant, as though he were a small child followed by a demoniacal power. The very thought of MacTee became overpowering.

"Angus MacTee!" cried the girl. For even at that distance she, also, could recognize the bearing and size of the Black MacTee.

They looked at one another silently. There was no longer a mist between them. They could see each other's face clearly, and as plainly as he could see the fear in the face of the girl, so she could see the fear in the face of Harrigan.

They fled up the pass, the hoofs of the horses striking out an iron clangoring.

Then the wind ceased. The clouds closed over them more darkly than ever. The moonlight ceased. They began to fumble forward through a wet, cold darkness.

Wind came again, but it did not clear away the clouds. It merely heaped on more and more mountainous vapors. Gusts of rain struck them wetly in the darkness. The hail came in great, pelting volleys of stones that dazed and hurt the horses. They whacked on the broad shoulders, they stung and cut the face of Harrigan, until he almost wondered that the girl could keep in her saddle. But she made no complaint.

He dismounted again, went to her during a brief halt, and took her hands. They were as ice. He made her bend down from the saddle, and he kissed her face. It was icy, also. All her body was quivering. He knew that it was not the storm but the fear that was killing her, and he wanted to say words that would start the currents of her blood again. But he was not able to speak.

He went on, leading the two horses, with an ache of emptiness in his heart. He knew that he was afraid, and he feared lest she might despise him for the terror that he felt.

The storm increased. The wind came charging. Under the weight of it and the sting of the hail and rain that charged it, the horses frequently halted and balked.

The moon shone through again briefly. Harrigan saw the mouth of a ravine that opened to the right, and into this he suddenly turned. Now the high walls shut off the main torrent of the storm. The clouds flowed higher over them, and only occasional rattlings of hail beat against them. Then the hail ceased, and it rained in torrents. The lightning sprang with it, making the mountain faces above them fluctuate wildly. It was by the lightning that he saw how the girl had bowed herself, clinging to the saddle with both hands, her head down, as one who submissively endures, without hope. He felt as though he had beaten her. He felt as though she were a child.

The next moment, they turned a narrow bend in the ravine, and the valley widened before them. The heavier roaring that he had thought to be the mere thundering of the wind he knew, now, to be the dashing of water. And on the edge of the cañon wall, he saw a small shack and shed, built together, of logs. He made for that. It was a steep and treacherous slope that they had to cover to get to the cabin. It was so steep and covered with loose, rolling stones, that it seemed incredible that anyone should have built in such a spot. Something must have altered the place in the meantime. The slope must have increased with weathering, and the treacherous coating of loose stones, like so many ball-bearings, must have rolled down from the upper part of the mountain.

They came to the cabin doorway, in which there was no door. A flare of lightning showed them that there was nothing but a bleak emptiness within the place. They entered, and the regular pulsing of the lightning showed them the vacant hearth, three broken chairs, and a loft of small poles overhead, with a ladder leading up to the attic trap door.

Harrigan climbed the ladder, tore down some of the poles, and came to the floor again. He broke up the poles and one of the chairs. Of the smallest fragments of the wood, he made a heap of tinder that had splintered off from the larger pieces. This he was able to light with his fourth match. The yellow finger of flame took hold, mastered bit after bit of the refuse, burned up strong and clear. He built up the fire, cording the larger pieces around the flame.

Now the pale flare of the lightning was not the only illumination. There was, besides, the steadier, smokier light from the fire. This showed to Harrigan the drooping figure of the girl. She stood close to the wall, one hand resting against it.

He went to her and touched her shoulder. She looked up to him. Her head fell back. She looked like one about to die.

"He could see the firelight," said Kate.

Harrigan studied her a moment. She was dripping wet, so that her clothes clung to her, and she looked amazingly helpless. It was not that he loved her less, but, for the moment, it seemed an amazing thing that two forces as great as Harrigan and MacTee should be engaged in mortal combat because of such a negligible thing. Yet there was no question that she was worth more than the rest of the universe to both of them. They knew her of old. But she was crushed and weak now. She was not the independent, strong, and almost imperious creature she had been. Strength had gone from her with hope, and Harrigan knew why. It was because she felt that terrible events lay just around the corner from them. Harrigan felt the same thing. It was a sense of inevitable and inescapable disaster.

"He would see the house, if he happens to turn down this ravine after us," said Harrigan. "But there's no reason why he should come this way. He'll go on through the pass, against the storm. That's the way of MacTee. He faces things. He fights them straight through. That's the greatness of him. Nothing turns him back. But if he happens to come through the ravine toward us, the lightning would show the cabin to him. The firelight won't matter."

"We'd better go on, then," said the girl, in a rapid, broken voice. "I don't want to stay here. It's like a cavern. I'd rather die in the open, than in a house. . . ."

He put his hand against her face. It was burning hot. Despair ran through him in a sickening current. Yet he made his voice calm to answer: "We'll have to stay here. As a matter of fact, there's no way of getting through without the danger of your catching pneumonia. I don't dare take you through this sort of weather."

"I won't melt," she said. She laughed a little, and repeated: "I won't melt."

It was like the voice of a child, trying to be brave. It was like the piping voice of a child. The heart of Harrigan was wrung by the sound of it.

"I'm taking the horses into the shed, the poor devils," he said to her. "You stay in here and take your clothes off. Take them off and wring them dry. Look at you. You're soggy. You're wet to the skin. Wring your clothes as dry as you can and drag them on again. I'll stay with the horses in the shed till I've fixed myself the same way."

She looked at him vaguely, as though she had not understood.

"Do you have to go away, Danny? I don't want you to go away. Stay here with me."

He was incredulous. He never had seen her so childish. Had the fever affected her mind? No, the dilation of her eyes gave the answer. It was not the heat of fever, but the intense cold of fear that had numbed her brain. Her lips were pale. Her eyes were as great as the eyes of an owl. He would hardly have recognized her face.

"Do what I tell you, Kate," he said sternly. He talked like a father to a child. "Do what I tell you. Take off your clothes and wring them out. I'll be in the shed. Look, you tap on this partition, and I'll be back in here before even a lightning flash would be able to jump in and steal you away from me."

"All right. It's all right." She was actually smiling, a crooked, wistful smile.

Harrigan mastered his heart and went outside. The rain blasted against his face. The roar of it was less than the sound inside the cabin, but every water drop cut at his skin.

The two horses were huddled against the wall of the house, shrinking from the sweep of the storm and wincing from the strong glare of the lightning. Overhead, the thunder broke in an endless booming, like the water of a great cataract falling on a world of tin. Harrigan pulled at the reins. For a moment the horses closed their eyes and stretched out their necks without stirring. Then they followed him to the shed.

No water entered it, and no wind. A musty smell of emptiness was there, and some of the warmth of the day that had not yet ebbed away. Harrigan stripped off his clothes. He was glad to give his strength to something. He almost tore the tough fabrics to pieces by the power with which he twisted them. Then he dragged them on again. He took a bandanna, rolled it, and used that to rub down the horses until they were fairly dry. Their body heat set them steaming. By the lightning flashes he could see the steam rising. The rank smell of their damp pelts filled the little shed.

Suddenly the rain stopped beating. He looked out and discovered that the southern half of the sky was thronged with the great black forms of the storm, with lightning leaping beneath it. But in the northern portion of the sky there were enormous white waves of clouds, with the moon riding through them. It struck a solid bank, was lost in it, then burst through, flinging a luminous spray before it. Harrigan drew in his breath. The weight of the thunder, also, was withdrawn from his brain, as it were.

He hurried around to the front of the cabin. As he strode, the stones rolled suddenly under his weight. He was thrown flat and skidded down the sharp incline until, at the very verge of the cañon, he found a fingerhold, and stayed his fall. From where he lay, he could look down a hundred yards of cliff that was almost sheer to where a river worked and whirled and leaped white in the bottom of the gorge. He remained prone for an instant, waiting for his heart to stop racing. Then he got up, cautiously, and crawled to the cabin before he ventured to rise and go weak-kneed to the doorway.

Beside it, he called: "Kate!"

"Yes!" she answered.

"Are you through? May I come in?"

"Yes, come in."

He paused to look down the ravine. A wisp of mist was standing in it like a monstrous ghost. Otherwise, it was empty, the moonlight glistening over the wet rocks. Then he stepped inside and found the girl seated in a broken chair beside the fire. Her clothes were fitted to her skin as sleekly as the pelt of a wet animal. She had not followed his instructions. And she looked up at him with the same dumb, suffering eyes of fear.

XII

"FEAR"

He crouched beside her. Bent in that fashion, he felt far more keenly the hugeness of his bulk compared with her.

"What is it, Kate?" he asked.

She shook her head.

"It's MacTee," he insisted. "You're afraid of MacTee. You think that he's sure to come."

She closed her eyes.

"Well," said Harrigan, "you can't sit here in wet clothes. You'll have to do something about it. You'll have to wring them out, Kate. I told you that. Listen to me . . . if you won't do anything . . . if you just give up like a child . . . I'll have to undress you and wring out the clothes myself."

She opened her eyes and stared at him, as one who cannot understand.

He thought he would startle her into alertness. So he put out his hand and unfastened the top button of her khaki shirt. No change came in her uncomprehending eyes.

"Kate!" he exclaimed. "For God's sake, what's the matter?"

She closed her eyes again. The firelight touched her face gently. The smoke, hardly drawn up the chimney at all from the hearth, curled behind her, and she was as the stuff of which dreams are made.

"It's MacTee," she answered. "Ever since the old days, I've been afraid, Danny. I've always known that a time would come

70

when you and he would meet for the final time. I've always known, and now. . . ."

"Now what?" asked Harrigan, staring in his turn — for the whole affair had grown ghostly.

She was silent. He touched her face. It was flushed and still burning hot. Her hands were hot, too, and dry. When she looked at him, there was a film over her eyes. A terrible feeling grew up in him that her brain was giving way under the strain.

"It's going to be all right," said Harrigan. "There's been enough to keep us apart. This is the last bad time . . . this night, the storm, and all of that. Afterward, we're going to have plain sailing."

"Not on this earth," whispered her lips.

A ghostly coldness stole through his blood. He wanted to ask her if she had the power of second sight.

She said, more loudly: "I know it's the end, Danny. I want to make the most of it. I want to be gay. I want to make you happy for the last time. But I can't. There's a shroud over me. I'm afraid. I'm buried alive in fear."

"It's because you've been thinking of MacTee too long," said Harrigan. "You've made a ghost out of him. That's all. Besides, you're too excited. And it's night. The minute the sun comes up you'll forget all of this. Everything will be all right."

She lifted her head to answer, but instead of speaking, she stared with terrible eyes of fear past him, toward the door.

Then the heavy, booming voice of MacTee said: "Everything will be all right for her, Harrigan. But you or I will be dead!"

Harrigan rose to his feet slowly, like an old man whose joints are frozen by age. He turned. And there in the doorway, filling it from top to bottom, stood MacTee. His clothes were glued to his body by the wet. The brim of his sombrero sagged heavily around his face. And the face itself was as Harrigan had seen it

71

before, in times of settled passion, like gray iron. The storm had not affected him, any more than it could affect a steel beam.

"Come out!" said MacTee.

A revolver was held in his right hand, waist high. Harrigan studied it. He was far faster with a gun, far straighter in the shooting of it. Perhaps there was a ghost of a chance that he would be able to get out a weapon and end the thing with a bullet.

MacTee said: "Don't try it, Harrigan. Don't try it!"

And Harrigan knew that it would be folly to try. He looked back at the frozen face of the girl.

"Maybe this is the end, Kate," he said. "Maybe you've been seeing the future a lot more clearly than I can make it out."

He leaned and kissed her good bye. Her face had been burning before. Now it was cold. She made no response. Harrigan was not in her eyes at all, but only the great body and the terrible face of MacTee.

Harrigan turned to the door and strode toward it. MacTee backed away from the entrance. Harrigan had stepped outside when the girl screamed suddenly, a frightful sound, as though a bullet had torn through her flesh. Harrigan glanced back. He saw that she had not risen from the chair. She simply sat as before, but with her head thrown back like a dying thing. He stepped on into the night. The storm had retreated farther away.

It was so far away now, that the voices in it could hardly be heard, and over the rest of the sky fled the shining white waves of clouds with the moon sweeping grandly through them.

MacTee still backed up, step by step. Harrigan followed him to a little distance from the hut. Then MacTee stopped and glanced around him swiftly — very swiftly, for fear lest the least absence of care might enable the magic of Harrigan to produce a gun. Then he said: "Hoist your hands, Harrigan!"

His voice had the clang of iron in it. Harrigan threw his hands well above his head. He knew that he was in touching distance, in breathing distance, of death.

"Turn your back to me!" commanded MacTee.

Harrigan turned his back. That was the hardest thing to do, to turn one's back on a nightmare terror. But he turned his back, little by little.

MacTee stepped up to him and laid the weighty muzzle of the revolver in the small of Harrigan's back.

"If you make a move . . . if you even breathe," said MacTee, "I'll blow your spine in two!"

"I won't move," said Harrigan.

The hand of MacTee searched him. It found two revolvers and threw them away. It found a knife and threw it away. The pressure of the gun was removed. MacTee drew back.

"Turn around again," he ordered.

Harrigan turned.

MacTee weighed the Colt in his hand.

"I ought to kill you like a dog," he said. "You went to Yellow Gulch to search for both of us. You found Kate. You told her enough lies to get her for yourself. Then you got hold of the deputy sheriff and told him where to find me. You're a traitor. You're a treacherous dog, and I ought to shoot you like a dog. But killing with a bullet wouldn't do me much good. I'm going to use my hands on you, Harrigan. I'm going to kill you with my hands." He tossed the revolver away and spread out his great hands. "It's been coming to you for a long time," he continued. "And now you're going to get it!"

"I didn't send the deputy sheriff," said Harrigan honestly. "I'm not such a sneak. I sent a girl to let you know. . . ."

"My God," shouted MacTee, "are you going to try to lie out of it like a dirty dog? Are you going to turn yellow when the pinch comes?" And as he spoke, he rushed in at Harrigan.

73

Harrigan struck with all his might. His fist glanced as on rock, but he was able to side-step the rush. He turned and met it again. After the first blow, his heart was working again.

"I'm going to tear you to bits," said MacTee, wiping the blood from his face.

"MacTee," said Harrigan, "there never was a time when a Scotchman could beat an Irishman. It's the end of you, damn you! Come in and take it."

MacTee laughed. It was a terrible thing to watch, and a terrible thing to hear, that laughter of MacTee. And he came in again, with a leap.

There was no stopping him. Harrigan knew it. He hammered in a long, over-arm punch that landed solidly in the face. Then he doubled over quickly and got a low hold, straightened, and heaved the weight of MacTee over his shoulder.

MacTee's hand gripped at him. With one gesture it tore coat and shirt from his back. Harrigan saw the white flash of the moon on his body. He looked down and glimpsed the corrugated strength of his muscles and laughed in turn. The battle-madness had entered him.

He ran in as MacTee arose and shouted: "Now, MacTee! Now, Angus! We'll see who's the better man!" So he plunged straight into the embrace of MacTee.

He had reason to regret it an instant later. For the arms of MacTee were iron — hot iron — that shrank into place around Harrigan and crushed him. The power of a machine squeezed the breath from Harrigan. In a sudden panic, he beat at the head and body of MacTee. He saw that it was as idle as splashing drops of water off a rock. His wind was almost gone. He tried for another grip by shooting his right arm under the armpit of MacTee and bending his forearm over the shoulder. By chance he fixed his grasp on the point of MacTee's jaw. The flesh was no more than a thin masking for the bone. It was against the bone that the grip of Harrigan was biting. His own breath was gone. He jerked with all his might. The face of MacTee was convulsed to the mask of a beast, a dead beast, glaring with eyes of glass from the wall of a hunting lodge. The great neck muscles of MacTee bulged out to meet the strain. His whole body shook as Harrigan jerked with all his might, again and again, striving to bend back the erect head.

There was a sudden giving. MacTee's head had gone back an inch, another inch. He groaned in an agony. They turned slowly. Bit by bit, the head of MacTee was going back. His body began to bend at the waist. His knees sagged. He became smaller than Harrigan. He tottered. He was about to fall, but that was not enough for Harrigan, who suddenly shifted his clutch lower. The great spread of his fingers, like talons, fastened across the throat of MacTee. That was the end. He held the life of the man. A bubbling, gasping sound came from MacTee's lips. He staggered this way and that. It was a miracle that his stalwart legs still could hold him up, when he was dying on his feet.

Dying — all that was MacTee now pinching out in darkness; all the lion of courage and savage cruelty and great-hearted friendship, also diminishing like a light that will fail and can never be kindled again.

"Angus," groaned Harrigan. "I can't be murdering you, man. Say that you've had enough . . . I can't be murdering you."

But he knew, as he said this, that it was a vain appeal, for Black MacTee had never surrendered before, and he would never surrender now. How could that nature admit defeat? Suddenly Harrigan loosened his grasp.

"I can't do it, MacTee," he groaned, drawing back.

He had been in so close that there was no chance for those hammering bludgeons, the fists of MacTee, to strike a vital

75

spot. But drawing away, he came into perfect range. At the last instant, he saw the danger coming like a shadow, from the corner of his eye. He tried to raise his left arm to block the punch. But his hasty guard was beaten down. A ponderous mass struck full and fair on the side of his chin, near the point. The shock was telegraphed into his brain like a thunderclap, while the darkness of thunder clouds spread over his eyes. The moonlight seemed to disappear. Before him all was the thick of night.

In that murk of darkness, he saw a vague silhouette drifting. He put up his hands and stretched them out. But terrible blows struck him and knocked across his brain showers of fiery sparks. They gave him only light by which to see his own coming destruction. He was beaten, and he knew that he was beaten.

A wave of sick weakness came over him. He fell on hands and knees. The darkness, at the same time, cleared instantly from his mind, letting in the fullness of the moonlight, so that he could see the valley, the pale boat of the moon, the clouds that fled down the wind. He saw MacTee in the act of catching up a great, jagged stone, and heaving it into the air. A sudden lightness of body and a strength of limb enabled Harrigan to rise. Once upon his feet, he could only stand there, tottering, his helpless arms hanging at his sides. He saw the stone heaved back, until the strain of the effort was shown in the whole body of MacTee, prepared to deal the final stroke. But MacTee did not strike. The stone dropped out of his hands and thumped its weight heavily against the ground.

"Damn you, Harrigan," said MacTee, "I can't do it. You're a traitor, Harrigan. But I can't finish you off the way you deserve to be finished!"

Harrigan pointed toward the cabin. "It's the girl that counts, MacTee. She's half out of her mind with fear of you. We've got to show ourselves to her . . . alive."

He stumbled forward. His knees were so uncertain that he was in danger of falling. MacTee gripped him by the arm and sustained him. They moved forward crookedly toward the cabin.

"Why did you do it, Harrigan?" asked MacTee. "Why did you knife me in the back? Why did you tell 'em where to hunt me down?"

"I didn't," said Harrigan. "I'll swear on the Book, MacTee, that I left a girl behind to take the news to you that I was gone, and Kate with me. Maybe she was afraid to go and thought she'd do better by sending men and guns. I don't know. But I wouldn't stab you in the back, MacTee . . . as you've tried to stab me many a time."

"You lie," said MacTee.

He released Harrigan's arm. And Red Harrigan, giving his head a shake, turned like a bull on MacTee.

"All down the railroad line, you left the railroad dicks ready to put lead in me. Answer me that, MacTee!"

"Are you going to bring up the past?" asked MacTee gloomily. "Are you going to . . . ?"

A faintly murmuring voice broke in upon them from the cabin.

"Hush," said MacTee. "Do you hear?"

They hurried into the cabin, and there they found that the girl was slumped against the wall of the shack, her head fallen on one shoulder, her eyes closed, her face crimsoned with more than the heat of the firelight.

MacTee put his hand on her forehead. "She's burning with the fever, Danny!" gasped MacTee. "Ah, Harrigan, what have I done?"

Harrigan brushed him aside. It was not hard to do. There seemed to be no strength remaining in MacTee, for the moment. Harrigan pressed his face against her breast and heard the rapid hammering of her heart.

"It's the shock that's made her sick, Angus," he explained. "And happiness will make her well again. I'm sure of that. Make her know that we're friends."

"Friends?" said MacTee. "I'd rather be friends to a snake than to a Harrigan."

"You fool," said Harrigan. "Do you think that *I* want your friendship? I wouldn't have the whole man of you, not a dozen a nickel. Make her know that you're not hounding the trail of her and me, now!"

MacTee stared sourly at the red-headed man. Then he leaned and called: "Kate! Kate Malone! Oh, Kate, do you hear me?"

She opened her eyes and looked uneasily toward him. Fear began to gather in her face.

"Hush, Kate," said MacTee. "Here's Dan Harrigan beside me. Do you see that? And we're friends, Kate. We'll be friends all the days of our life. There's nothing to be afraid of."

She looked blankly at him. "Is it true, Danny?" she asked.

"It's true," said Harrigan.

"Then let me sleep again," said the girl. "I haven't slept, I haven't dared to rest, for years and years. . . ."

"Oh, God," said MacTee. "What have I done, if she dies, Harrigan?"

"I'll tell you, MacTee," said Harrigan.

"Tell me, then," said Angus MacTee, "and curse me, Dan. Damn my heart black, because black it is."

"You're talking like a fool, MacTee," said Harrigan. "What's in a man has to come out of him. You loved her too much to want to see her turned over to a man like me, that's all. I'm not worthy of her. Neither are you. God pity her for coming into the hands of either of us, Angus. But God knows you're a better man than I am. If there's a black devil in you, there's a red devil in me."

"You're raving, Danny," said MacTee. "It hurts me to see you make such a fool of yourself. Stay here with her. Hold her life in your hands like a young bird, and I'll be back with a doctor to take care of her for you."

Instantly he was gone through the door of the cabin. The galloping hoofs of his horse went ringing up the valley and faded away into nothingness.

XIII

"OUT OF THE SHADOWS"

It was a long, long night for Dan Harrigan. He climbed the rock to the wooded mountainside above and broke off evergreen branches until he had enough armloads of them to make a bed. He beat them dry, built them soft and thick in the cabin, near the fire, and spread a saddle blanket over them. There he put the girl.

She merely groaned in her sleep as he lifted her. Another saddle blanket covered her. Harrigan sat beside her and watched through the hours.

Her breathing grew easier and more regular, and deeper. Another light than the red of the fire began to enter the cabin, and, turning his head, Harrigan saw the doorway brightened by the coming of the day. A greater hope came up in Harrigan at the same time. He went to the door and stared out at the dawn that was brightening the mountains above them.

"Dan!" called a voice behind him.

He whirled about and found her sitting up, braced on both arms.

"I've been dreaming," said the girl. "I thought that MacTee came."

"Hush," said Harrigan. "He came, and he's gone again. He'll never trouble us again."

He heard the clattering hoofs of horses coming down the valley, over the rocks. So he faced the doorway, and, looking out, he saw three riders, of whom the first was MacTee. As they came up, Harrigan saw that the other two were elderly men, frowning with grave thoughts and with the labor of their ride into the mountains. They dismounted.

"Two would be better than one, for what's wrong with Kate," said MacTee. "Here's Doctor Harden."

"She's better," said Harrigan to the doctor. "She's a lot better. I think the fever's dead in her."

The doctor gave him a rather biting glance, then entered the cabin. Harrigan remained outside with the other two.

"It's a strange business," said the other visitor, shaking his head. "What the law will say to this kidnapping in the middle of the night . . . what the law will say to that, you know as well as I do, Mister MacTee."

"Let the law be damned," said MacTee. "There are things above the law, I can tell you. And one of them is Harrigan and MacTee, just now."

The voice of the doctor spoke from within.

"She wants to see both of you . . . Harrigan and MacTee."

They entered. Her face was half white and half flushed. Eagerly she fixed her glance upon MacTee.

"Is it true, Angus?" she asked. "Are you the friend of Dan Harrigan, now and always?"

MacTee scowled at Harrigan, but he nodded.

"Was there ever a man made for a better friend than Harrigan?" he said. "I'll tell you this, Kate. I came up last night to find him and murder him. We fought it out. He could have choked the life out of me, Kate. He had my life in the tips of his fingers, but he wouldn't take it. And then the chance came to me. I had him helpless, and I couldn't finish him. There's a charm on us, Kate. We can't harm one another. And if you want him, you want the better man of us."

"Take his hand, then, Angus," said the girl.

81

"Here, Danny," said MacTee. He turned and gripped the ready hand of Harrigan. "I wish to God that I'd never laid eyes on you, Dan," said MacTee. "But now it's too late for such wishing. I hope to the same God that nothing will ever come between us again."

"Why . . . ," said Harrigan, "why, Angus, if we put our hands together, not even the devil could tear 'em apart. And there's my hand for life."

"Kiss me, Danny," said the girl. "God bless the two of you. This is the happiest day the world ever saw. Kiss me, Angus, too."

MacTee leaned over her.

"It's a way of kissing good bye to what I've wanted the most in my life," he said. "But there you are, Kate." He touched his lips to her forehead. "I've kissed one part of you good bye, but not the friend in you, Kate."

"No," she said, with sudden tears running down her face. "Never that."

"Come in here, now," exclaimed MacTee, rising. "I brought two doctors to make all well. I'm going to see an end of this damned business and get it off my mind for good. Come in here, Johnson."

The solemn face of the other stranger appeared in the doorway.

"Here's a sky pilot," said MacTee. "He'll tie your hand into the hand of Harrigan. I'm going outside till the trick's turned. Afterward, I'm coming back inside to see what Missus Danny Harrigan looks like, and how she wears her new name."

He strode out through the doorway.

"You must make him happier, Danny," said the girl. "Make him come back and be our witness. Can you lead him back in here?"

"Can I?" said Harrigan joyously. "Why, I could lead him

now with a silk thread. I could lift the whole weight of the soul of him on the tip of my little finger. For didn't you see, Kate? The blackness has gone out of MacTee forever."

The King of Rats

A Reata Story

Frederick Faust's original title for this story was "King of Rats." Street & Smith's *Western Story Magazine*, where it was first published in the December 9, 1933, issue under the byline George Owen Baxter, changed the title to "Reata's Desert Ride." This was the third short novel to feature Reata, who proved to be one of Faust's most popular characters among readers of this magazine, harking back to the enthusiasm that had met a previous, very different Faust character, Bull Hunter, in the same magazine a decade earlier. Like Bull Hunter, who was accompanied on his adventures by the stallion, Diablo, and the wolf dog, The Ghost, Reata also gains a mare and a mongrel, but they are very different from those found in the Bull Hunter stories. There would be seven short novels in all about Reata. The first, "Reata," appears in THE FUGITIVE'S MISSION: A WESTERN TRIO (Five Star Westerns, 1997). The second, "The Whisperer," appears in THE LOST VALLEY: A WESTERN TRIO (Five Star Westerns, 1998). The third story continues Reata's adventures after he has successfully accomplished two of his three labors for Pop Dickerman.

I

"THE MESSAGE"

Through the window, Pop Dickerman could see Reata reclining in the shade of the horse shed. It was the last place he should have been, because at any moment people from Rusty Gulch were likely to walk into the junk yard and rummage around through the assorted piles. Too many citizens knew Reata's face perfectly well, and too many kept remembering how he had sawed his way out of the jail. But Reata preferred the open air, even if it meant peril to his life, and Dickerman knew, by the increasing restlessness of that brown-faced young man, that he could not hold him very much longer at the junk yard.

The little dog, Rags, with his sleek body and fuzzy head walked up and down on guard, scanning every bird in the air, canting his head at every sound near and far, but his master seemed totally indifferent to the world around him. He had in his hands that lithe little lariat which was his one weapon and his principal diversion, and now he made it rise like a running snake, now coil like a snake about to strike. Seen from such a distance, the reata seemed no thicker than a piece of twine, even though Dickerman knew that it was strong enough to hold a horse.

Reata threw his knife on the ground and began to strike at it with the noose of his rope. The noose flicked in and out like a striking snake, and at the third try the knife was caught by the handle and snatched into the air, where Reata caught it.

A very neat little trick, Dickerman thought, not particularly showy, but useful in many a pinch. He continued to stare for some moments at Reata, his long, furry face wrinkling with intense disaster, for if Reata was typical of the lover of the open air, Dickerman preferred shadow and secrecy. However, Reata had twice been useful beyond price, and he would be useful once again before he was free from his obligation.

Yet Dickerman hated that young man. Wide-shouldered, slender of limb, totally relaxed now but capable of hand work swifter than mortal eyes could follow, it seemed to him that Reata was like a cat, a very king of cats. And he, Dickerman, had more use for the rat type. Just now Reata was useful to him, very useful. But he felt that in the long run nothing but evil could come of his connection with Reata.

He had got so far as the kitchen when he heard a beating at his front door. He paused a moment before going to answer that knock. Any summons from the street always gave him pause for an instant, and made his heart rise in guilty fear while he surveyed his actions of recent days. But always he was able to tell himself that, if he was a fence, he was such a subtle and secret receiver of stolen goods that the law would never get its hands on him. Even Reata, who now had worked for him some time, did not yet know the actual profession of his employer, no matter what he might suspect.

So Dickerman went on through the big room of his house which had once been simply the mow of the barn that he had converted to his own uses. No matter how often he went through that room, it was always a surprise and a comfort to him. In the piles of assorted junk that rose on the floor, in the bundles that hung by ropes from the rafters, his rapid eyes were always sure to find something that he had almost forgotten, as he saw now a good brass lamp hanging in a bundle of other lamps, great and small, and on the floor he spotted a tangle of half a dozen scythe blades, quite new and good, whose purchase he could not remember.

Whenever he saw these things, he was forced to remember the simplicity of other men, which permitted him to buy their possessions for a song. His only regret was that he sold these treasures from time to time, even if he gained tenfold on every transaction. Patience, patience was the golden key to unlock the safes in which the treasures lie. Other men, tired of effort in one place, moved and sold their goods for a song; they gave up the battle; they stared at the unapproachable stars and stumbled on their faces in the dusty way. But Dickerman, content with little trifles, kept adding them, one to one, to reach his million. He would have it before he died.

These were the thoughts that always streamed through his mind as he passed through the heart of his junk store. Now he pulled open the street door and found a rider dust-covered, sun-reddened.

"Are you Dickerman? Aye, you've got the look of him. This letter's for you."

Dickerman took the envelope, opened it, read the message. At the first words, he wanted to draw back into the shadow. He peered up in suspicion at this stranger who had in his possession news so precious.

"They paid you, eh?" said Dickerman.

"They paid me half," said the messenger. "I got ten dollars more coming."

"Here," said Dickerman. And he put a five-dollar bill in the hand of the stranger. There was a shout of rage. Dickerman slammed the door shut, and the voice was partly stifled by the stout partition. In the dimness, he was reading:

We can't find Bill Champion, but we've found his horse. He's left it in a safe place, and a place that keeps traveling. A gang of Gypsies has that horse in

charge. We don't know how to get at it. Gypsies can steal, but they can't be stolen from. Reata won't be of any help, because it's the same gang that knows him and hates him . . . Queen Maggie's outfit. We'll keep trying to snag the gray.

Bates

Reata would not be of any help? That was what Bates thought, but Bates had not had time enough to learn the qualities of Reata in detail.

There was heavy beating at the back door of the house. Someone was shaking the door violently, then giving it the weight of his shoulder. That would be the big, red-faced messenger, of course. He wanted his other five-dollar bill. But Dickerman preferred to part with blood rather than to give up dollars. Give a man half the price he asks, and in time he will be contented.

He went to the kitchen, and heard the voice of Reata call out: "Hey! Stop that racket, will you? I'm trying to sleep."

"You're *trying* to sleep?" shouted the big messenger. "Why, who are *you*, anyway?"

"I'm a sleepy man. Go on away and don't make such a noise, will you?" said Reata.

"What'll you do about it?" asked the big man. He went striding toward Reata with his fists clenched so hard that his elbows cocked out to the sides. "I wanta know what you'll do about it."

Reata rose slowly. He seemed to be weak and leaned a hand against the wall of the shed. But Dickerman laughed and then smoothed his furry face with his hand, still smiling.

"Go away and don't bother me," said Reata wearily. "I don't want to do you any harm. You haven't given me such cause . . . yet."

90

"How's this for cause, then?" shouted the messenger, and struck with the flat of his hand for that brown, yawning face. The hand beat against the empty air. Reata stepped forward and to the side. He made a little jerking movement with one foot and caught the arm of the other in a twist. It was done so leisurely that only the eye of a Dickerman could have estimated the real speed. And the husky messenger fell flat in the dust. Reata sat on his chest. He had the two hands of the messenger lashed together with a couple of turns of his inevitable lariat. With the pinch of two fingers he could keep the big fellow helpless now.

"You don't want to make so much noise," said Reata, yawning.

"Dickerman," shouted the prostrate man, writhing. "The robber, he. . . ."

"I don't care about Dickerman. I was just getting settled for a sleep," said Reata. "You want to remember that. You certainly ought to give a fellow a chance to have his sleep."

He stood up and turned the other loose. For an instant Dickerman hoped that the messenger would attempt to strike again, he loomed so much vaster than the taper outline of Reata. But second thought was stronger than temptation, and presently the fellow moved away, head down, dusting off his clothes as he went.

II

"KING OF THE RATS"

Dickerman went out into the junk yard, that outdoor domain of his wealth, and sat down beside Reata. Rags kept a space between them, growling softly. Nothing could make the little dog give up an instinctive hatred of the junk dealer.

Dickerman said — "Read this." — and gave the message to Reata. When it was read, Reata yawned again.

"Who's Bill Champion?" he asked.

"He's the thing that keeps Gene Salvio on the road," said Dickerman. "And Salvio's the third man you're going to bring back to me. You ain't forgot that, Reata?"

"No, I haven't forgotten. I thought he must be in jail somewhere."

"You got Quinn away from the Gypsies. You got Bates out of the pen. It's goin' to be harder to get Salvio away from Champion's trail, so he'll be free to come back to me."

"What keeps Salvio on Champion's trail, then?"

"You don't know Salvio," said Dickerman. "There's a gent that's all pride and fire."

"I saw his picture," said Reata. "He looked proud enough to rob a bank, all right. What's his pride got to do with Champion?"

"Gene was in a saloon one day," said Dickerman, "and he didn't like the looks of Champion. Nobody likes the looks of Champion, because he ain't got any. But Gene started to get more room, and Champion don't like to be elbowed. He elbowed back and knocked Gene flat, and then, when Gene pulled a gun, Champion kicked the gun out of his hand and threw Gene into the street."

"He's hard, is he?" said Reata. "I mean Champion . . . he's a hard *hombre,* is he?"

"He's as hard as they come. When Gene got a broken collarbone healed up, he went after Champion and finally met him again. And it's hard to meet Champion, because he's a crook that works all alone. He does his jobs in the West, but he lives other places mostly. He does a clean job . . . he does it all alone, and then he travels a thousand miles. He's got no cronies. He's got nothing behind him that the sheriff can lay hands on. The only thing folks know is that Champion always rides a gray hoss with four black stockings and a big white blaze between the eyes. Understand?"

"I follow that," said Reata. "He sounds like a sensible sort of a fellow, except that he's always got to ride one horse."

"Maybe he thinks that hoss is his luck," suggested Dickerman. "Well, I was saying that Gene Salvio met up with Champion again, and they had a fair break, and went for their guns, and Salvio's bullet took off the top of Champion's ear, and Champion's slug hit Salvio through the hip and laid him flat. And he stood over Salvio, then, and beat him up with a quirt, and some of the scars are still on Salvio's face. Understand?"

"Sounds like a fairly mean man," agreed Reata.

"That job spoiled everything for me," said Dickerman. "I had Gene Salvio so's I could use him whenever I had a hard job to do. I could pull him out like an ace and win any hand I wanted to win. There's a man, Reata, you wouldn't believe how useful he is. He can pick a pocket or a lock. He can fan a gun with both hands. He can ride anything that wears hair and some that don't. He can smell out a trail like a hunting dog, and he ain't afraid of the devil in the dark. But he's got one big fault. He's proud. And that's a devil of a fault, Reata. I'll tell you what it done to Gene Salvio.

"After he got out of the hospital the second time, when Champion had shot him up, I paid his hospital bill, and I fixed him up with a fine outfit, and I gave him a little job that was right up his street. But he wouldn't listen to me. He wouldn't do nothing. There wasn't nothing in the world for him, except a third chance at Bill Champion. He said that him or Bill Champion had to die the next meeting. And nothing I could offer would turn him off of that trail.

"I sent out Bates and Quinn, when I seen how things were, to snag Bill Champion and get him out of the way, so's business could commence again. But Quinn and Bates both got snagged. And then you come along, and you got the pair of them out for me. You've done two parts of your job for me, Reata. There's only one part of it left, and then you can forget about the way I pulled you out of jail that night. You'll be your own free man, and you'll have Sue to ride away on, wherever you please to go. Besides, I'll heel you with a stake in hard cash."

"All I have to do is to find Champion and kill him, eh?" said Reata.

"That's all you have to do," answered Dickerman.

"And I never carry a gun. You know that."

"You've got the reata, and you've got the brain. Brains can kill farther than bullets can. Don't say no to me, Reata."

"I'm a fool if I don't, but I won't."

"Good boy. Good boy," murmured Dickerman. He stretched out his hand to pat the shoulder of Reata, but the shrill snarl of Rags made the hand jump away to safety again. "They've spotted the horse, at last. They've located Champion's horse, and, sooner or later, Champion is goin' to come for that horse."

"And the Gypsies give it to him, and he rides away. What does that buy for you, Dickerman?"

"The Gypsies have the horse now, but they won't have it long. You're going up there to steal that horse, son. And when you got it, you and Quinn and Bates are goin' to go somewheres and sit tight, and wait for Mister Champion to come and find you."

"How will he find us?"

"He finds anything that he wants to find," answered Dickerman. "There ain't no way of pulling the wool over the eyes of Champion. He'd follow the scent of a hawk in the air, and he'd jump high enough to catch the hawk by the foot, if he had to."

"It's a kind of a ring around the rosy," said Reata. "There's Gene Salvio hunting down the trail of Champion, and Champion not giving a damn about Salvio, but getting ready to pull another crooked job, and coming back to get his lucky horse when he rides to work. And we slide in and catch the horse and use it for bait in the mantrap. That's the way of it, isn't it, Dickerman?"

"You understand me perfect," said Dickerman. "And when Champion's dead, Salvio will sure come back to me. I been a good chief to him, old son. I'm a good chief to all of them that puts some trust in me. Don't you forget that."

"Sure," said Reata. "The king of rats ought to be good to his tribe."

This remark stunned Dickerman. "Reata," he said mournfully, "you don't like me much."

"Not much," agreed Reata cheerfully. "Now go on and tell me about Champion. How will I know him? What does he look like?"

"He don't look like nothing," answered Dickerman, instantly forgetting his personal feelings in the pressure of business. "When he looks down, there ain't even eyes in his face. He had smallpox, or vitriol throwed at him young, or something like that. There ain't much face. There's only a slab, and, when he looks down, it's just flat. There ain't no eyebrows. There ain't no eyes. There's only a squash of a nose. But when he looks up, it's like something watching you from behind a mask. A bad mask, mind you. A mask like a kid could make with its thumbs out of wet clay . . . white clay . . . soft clay. Maybe you sort of foller me?"

"I sort of follow you," said Reata calmly. "I can see that this is going to be the rattiest job of the three."

"It's a lot the rattiest," agreed Dickerman.

"Tell me," said Reata, "why the devil don't I tell you to go to hell? Why don't I tell you that I've already done ten times as much for you as you've ever done for me?"

"Because you gave me your promise, son," said Dickerman gently.

"You'd break a promise like that quicker than a wink," said Reata.

"Sure," answered Dickerman. "What'd you expect from the king of rats?"

At this bit of naïveté, Reata broke into a frank and ringing laughter that made the little dog, Rags, jump happily up and down.

"All right," said Reata. "I'll go and try to catch the bait that'll catch the man without a face. This fellow, Champion, is he as mean with guns as you make him out?"

"So mean," said Dickerman, "that you'll never be able to beat him with a Colt. You'll have to use brains on him. Go on, Reata. Do this last thing for me, and I'll make you glad the rest of your life."

96

III

"THE GYPSY PARADE"

Far north of Rusty Gulch and Pop Dickerman's, Reata sat in a front bedroom of Glosson's Hotel in the town of Orchard Creek. Through the window he commanded a view of the central square of the town. As a matter of fact, Orchard Creek had hardly progressed beyond that central square. It managed to have houses and shops all around the plaza and a scattering of shacks along the irregular trails that wound into the town, but that was all. He could see the orchard, also, which had given the place its name — a wretched half dozen of crooked little apple trees that stood in the center of the square. Rags, from the feet of his master, watched the mindless gyrations of the reata that kept bobbing and twisting into strange formations out of the hands of the juggler.

Harry Quinn, walking restlessly up and down the room, also watched the gyrations of the lithe rope, and so did Dave Bates, who was crumpled up in a chair. He appeared to have no backbone. Even when he stood, he was small, and when he sat down, he was no bigger than a child. He seemed deformed, although there was no visible malformation. The patient malice of a cripple was in his pale eyes.

Quinn said: "Out there, they're goin' to give their show. You'll see Queen Maggie and the rest of the Gypsy cut-throats yonder. And to wind up the show, you'll spot Miriam doing her bareback trick with a big gray stallion that has four black stockings and a big white blaze between his eyes."

97

"You mean that she's given up the old gelding? You mean that she's trained the horse of Bill Champion for her tricks?" asked Reata sharply.

"Yeah, that's what she's gone and done."

"Doesn't anybody recognize the horse?" asked Reata. "Or is that part of the show . . . to let folks see Bill Champion's own horse?"

"Of course, it ain't any part of the show," said Dave Bates. "Champion's idea was like this . . . he don't want to keep coming back to the same place for his horse. So he leaves it with the Gypsies, and they're always wandering around, because that's the way Gypsies are. They're not hard to spot. He finds them, and then he can get his hoss. And there you are."

"But I've heard somewhere that Bill Champion's horse couldn't be handled by any other man," said Reata.

"Sure it can't," said Quinn. "But Miriam ain't a man." He chuckled, and added: "She's got that big hellion eatin' right out of her hand. She's got him so's he'll canter in the circle, and she can do her tricks on him like he was a circus hoss. It sure sets her off, though, the size and looks of that gray."

"And nobody recognizes the gray?" repeated Reata.

"How would they?" asked Dave Bates acridly. "They've all heard about Champion's stallion. They figure on seein' him jump across the mountains, from peak to peak, you might say, and here they up and find a hoss that jogs around like an old lady's pet. They wouldn't believe their eyes. Not if you was to tell them."

"But are you *sure* it's the right horse?" asked Reata.

"I seen Bill Champion once, and I seen his gray," said Dave Bates, "and what I see, I never forget. Will you stop playin' with that rope, Reata, and get down to business?"

Reata did not seem to hear this last portion of the remark, and the lariat ceaselessly wove and unwove patterns in the air.

He had a dreamy look as he stared out over the square, where people were already beginning to gather.

Harry Quinn said: "That rope *is* his business, Dave. It's likely to see us through."

"What way will it see us through?" asked Bates grimly.

"I dunno," said Harry Quinn. "It got you out of the pen, Dave. It got me away from the Gypsies. That's something, I guess."

"Well," said Reata, "if we can fetch the gray away from the Gypsies and take it off somewhere, Bill Champion is sure to find the gray and us along with it. Isn't that straight?"

"Champion would find things on the bottom of the sea," answered Bates, "if he wanted to."

"We steal the horse from the Gypsies, and we take it off into some faraway corner. And then we sit around and wait for trouble and Bill Champion to show up. Is that right?" confirmed Reata.

"Listen," exclaimed Dave Bates impatiently, "you know well that you can't steal from Gypsies. You can't steal from thieves."

"We'll have to try," said Reata.

"He stole *me* from the same gang," remarked Harry Quinn.

"Forget it," growled Bates. "He had one whale of a shot of luck. But now let's see what he can do. Reata, you get the big brain workin', and tell us what to do. Here comes the parade right now."

They could hear the shrilling of the flute and the thin whistling of the violins in the distance and then the shouting of happy children. Leaning out the window, Reata saw the procession come around the corner into the square. All in all, it was not a big affair, because the Gypsy crowd was not a large band, but it was enough of a sight to fill the eye of Orchard Creek. They were all on horseback, even the fiddlers, and riders and horses blazed with color. The music jigged into common tunes, or went wailing and whooping into strange interludes that brought sudden choruses of yelling from the Gypsies.

Queen Maggie passed, with big green glass jewels dropping from her ears and banging against her broad jaws. She had a crimson turban wound about her head and a sword at her side that her big hand looked perfectly capable of wielding. She was complete except for the long cigar that Reata generally had seen in her mouth in the other days.

And in the last group of the procession, with the entire swarm of Orchard Creek children yelling around her, came Miriam, the bareback rider. She was standing upon the back of a quiet gray gelding, a sheen of blue silk tights with a golden fluff of skirts around her middle. Her bare throat and arms were as bronzed as dull gilt. Reata looked at her laughter and tried to find the blue of her eyes, but failed. She seemed all Gypsy, just then. She led along, dancing at her side, turning his fiery front disdainfully toward the quiet gelding, as fine a stallion as Reata had ever seen, seventeen hands of might and speed, stockinged in black velvet to the knees and hocks, with a broad, white blaze between the eyes. He was girt with a surcingle; the reins of his bridle dripped from the hand of the girl, and he never drew them taut but, in spite of all his restless prancing, seemed to be ruled and checked by all her will more than her hand.

The whole of Orchard Creek, pouring out around the square, applauded this picture. The hair of Miriam was done in a chignon; there was a gilt crown of brightness on her head; and every twist and shining of that crown seemed to bring out fresh shouting and clapping of hands and whooping from the cowpunchers.

"That gal is pretty enough to make a pile of trouble," said Dave.

"She's walked Reata into guns a couple of times," answered

Harry Quinn. "Look at him now. He's kind of all out and senseless. You could kick him in the face, and he wouldn't know that you'd touched him."

"The fool's crazy about the Gypsy, eh?" Bates sneered.

"I wouldn't talk too loud," answered Harry Quinn, a grin on his broad face. "You've only seen her. You ain't talked to her, the way I done. It ain't her looks that poison you most . . . it's her voice."

Winding into the square, the Gypsies formed a wide circle. The music fell into different airs, and the entertainment began. There was jigging, sword dancing, and that performance of the grizzled old man who did the Cossack dance as though there were steel springs instead of muscles in his legs. Reata had admired it before. He admired it again, but dimly, always waiting.

The cat-faced strong man, smiling his prop smile until his eyes wrinkled almost shut, took the center and lifted weights and then balanced men in the air with his mighty muscles standing out as though painted.

"But Reata paralyzed that *hombre,*" said Harry Quinn to Bates. "Reata tied him up in knots. The same way that he can tie up anybody, if he gets close enough."

"The fool don't carry no guns," said Dave Bates. "That lets him out."

"He stalks till he's close," said Harry Quinn, "because he's the king of cats, old son. And don't you ever forget it."

Dave Bates made an involuntary, swift gesture beneath his coat and grinned a sour smile as he drew out his hand again. "Yeah, maybe," he growled. "There goes the girl. Lemme see how good she is."

At the close of the show — it had not been very long, but it had brought repeated cheers from the spectators — the gray stallion of Bill Champion was brought out by Miriam with his bridle reins tied back into the surcingle. He was not checked in

101

as an ordinary circus horse is reined up to make the neck bow as though in pride. There was no need to check the gray, because the very arch of arrogant might was in his neck, with the mane flowing in silver down from it. And he began to canter softly, but with a dangerous sweep to his stride, around and around in a circle.

The girl ran at him, leaped, struck with her soft slippers on the point of his shoulder and seemed to run up the sleek of the powerful shoulder muscles until she stood partly on his withers and partly on the working shoulder itself, slanting in at a sharp angle to balance against the speed of the circling stallion.

Orchard Creek, which knew a lot about plain horsemanship and something about fancy riding also, yelled at the top of its lungs, but the stallion was not startled. He simply shook his great head and went on at the same unvarying stride.

"By the jumpin' thunder," said Dave Bates, "that kid has got something in her head, or she couldn't 'a' trained the gray like that. Look at the way he keeps to his circle. Damn me, he seems like he enjoys it, sort of."

"That's nothing. She ain't started," said Harry Quinn. "Look at that!"

She had begun her dance in time with slow music into which the very movement of the horse seemed to be working with a perfect rhythm. Those perilous angles of her swaying threatened every moment to let her drop to the ground. One would have said many times that she was suspended by an invisible wire which supported her around the circle, regardless of the horse.

Orchard Creek began to grow hoarse with enthusiasm.

"Can anybody else handle that horse?" asked Reata, suddenly standing up.

"Nobody else," said Harry Quinn. "Nobody else can even lead it, without havin' a terrible fight on his hands."

"What happens at the end of this show?" demanded Reata.

"Why, she gets back on the geldin', and she leads the stallion away at the head of the procession," said Dave Bates.

"We're going down and get our horses," said Reata. "You fellows that wear guns, get ready to shoot . . . but do your shooting in the air."

IV

"REATA'S RUSH"

Dave Bates was ill content. As he went down the stairs, he said to Harry Quinn: "He starts right in and gives commands. He makes a boss out of himself. As if he had the right. The kid kind of makes me sick."

"Everything makes you sick, *hombre*," answered Harry Quinn. "Hold yourself down for a while, will you? I never seen Reata miss yet, and I reckon he ain't goin' to miss today. But the edge of a tall cliff is just like a sidewalk to him."

They had their horses in front of the hotel, with the packs already tied on behind the saddles. Quinn paid the hotel bill on the way out and then found that Reata was already in the saddle on Sue in front of the building. Dave Bates was just mounting. As Quinn tumbled into place on his own horse, he found Reata looking them over.

Reata said quietly: "You two fellows fall in behind me. The Gypsies are passing the hat now, and they're getting a lot of money out of this crowd. They're going to feel a little careless as the parade starts away again. But don't forget that they've all got knives, and a lot of 'em have guns. When I start working, you fall in behind me and pull your guns. Keep the crowd back, if you can. And have your spurs in your horses. You've got the best nags that Dickerman can give you. Use 'em. You'll need to."

With that, he rode straight off through the crowd, letting Sue pick her way gingerly through the press, while Rags stood upon the saddle bow and barked softly to clear a way.

It was easy to see Miriam leading the Gypsy parade as it began serpentining, for she stood upon the back of the quiet old gelding and seemed, as a matter of fact, to be drifting over the heads of the crowd that still cheered her, while she kept bowing and kissing her hand right and left.

Reata worked forward until he was out of the press of the townspeople and near the girl. Then a wild yell beat on his ears. He saw the cat-faced strong man leaping forward at him. The Gypsy jargon that the giant shouted was, of course, to warn the rest that the old enemy was on them. And once the grip of the big fellow was on the bridle reins of Sue, it would need the strength of four men to loosen his grasp.

Reata, jerking around in the saddle, slashed a four-fold coil of his lariat right across that cat-like face. The fellow howled and leaped straight up into the air, his hands clapped to his eyes. Reata, straightening, flung the snaky noose of his rope and snared Miriam under the arms, right around the waist.

"You fool! You fool!" she was screaming at him. "Go back, Reata, or they'll kill you! Ride for it! Ride for it!"

"Ride with me, then!" cried Reata. "Change to the gray and ride with me, or I'll try to take you on Sue!"

She pulled once, desperately, at the rope that held her. She looked back and saw the Gypsies rushing forward toward Reata. And then she made up her mind. She was off the gelding and onto the gray in a flash. The big stallion lurched away through the open gap down the street. Sue, sprinting with all her might, kept up.

Reata, as he looked back, saw the brandished guns of Harry Quinn and Dave Bates make the crowd reel back, shouting. There were other guns brightening in the air on either side of him. A bullet shaved the very back of his neck. But he heard one deep voice shouting: "Leave 'em! The gal wants to go . . . so leave 'em be!"

Perhaps that commanding voice saved the scalp of Reata for the first thirty seconds. After that, he was off the square and running full pelt with Sue after the stallion. Right to the very end of the lariat the stallion was leading, but long-bodied Sue, straining to her utmost, made the line slack, began to gain. The stallion ran gloriously; Sue ran like a low roan streak, and, as the last houses of Orchard Creek whirred away behind them, the mare was running level with the tall gray.

Then Reata loosened the noose, and the girl threw it away from her. She was sitting down like a jockey on the broad back of the gray. The slender brown arms stretched out straight to the reins, and the ruffles at her shoulders were blowing and shuddering with the wind of the gallop.

Behind them many horses pounded; leaving the rest comfortably, guns still in hand, came Dave Bates and Harry Quinn.

They had done their part well. They would do it still better, perhaps, if once they had to shoot to kill. But they were well mounted on the best horseflesh that Pop Dickerman could give them, and it was very doubtful if any of the riders from Orchard Creek could keep pace with the kidnappers.

No, now the crowd fell away. A few shots were fired. A dust cloud began to envelope the riders far in the rear. And still Sue and the gray drew away rapidly from Bates and Quinn, and the men of Orchard Creek were hopelessly last of all.

The girl began to laugh. She cried over her shoulder to Reata: "You're a crazy man."

"Sure I am," said Reata. "Bring that whale down to a lope, and we can talk."

She rated the stallion back. He moved with great, fluent bounds. Sue flowed smoothly along beside him.

"What did you want to see me about?" asked the girl. "Talk

fast, Reata. I've got to go back with the gray. Everybody will be wild. It was a crazy thing to rope me like that . . . it was just crazy. Talk fast . . . I've got to go back."

He looked at her with a faint smile. The ragged blues and browns of the mountains went storming up against the sky, just beyond them. The sun was turning golden in the west. Continents of wild space enclosed them, and through it rode the girl in her shimmering blue tights and golden ruffles, and with the false gleaming of the crown on her head.

He had been a fool to use the rope, with that threat of snatching her away on Sue, if she would not ride the gray on her account. He could see now that she would have come as readily, merely at a word from him. It was to save him from danger in the crowd that she had changed to the gray and made off.

"I can't talk yet," he said. "I want to look a while."

"You like it," said the girl. "Bullets . . . you like to hear 'em! While you're looking, take a slant at your hat."

He took off that good Stetson and saw the great rents where two .45-caliber slugs had torn through the strong white felt. That was preëminently a fair-weather hat from now on.

"You've got a pair through the tail of your coat, too," she said. "You *are* a crazy man, Reata. Now what have you got to say? I can't keep on."

"Keep on a little while," said Reata.

"You didn't need to do it," she insisted. "If you'd whistled from a window, I would have noticed, and somehow I would have come to you. Reata, they almost had you. The Gypsies . . . and most of all, the men of Orchard Creek. They didn't know. They thought it was a kidnapping. How were they to tell anyway?"

"One man knew," said Reata.

"I heard him bellow. I saw him knock down two or three guns that were ready to salt you away," said the girl. "Heaven bless him for that. Now tell me what it is, Reata."

He looked back. Far away, the dust cloud of those riders from Orchard Creek rolled small and dim, a golden mist under the sun. But close up came Bates and Quinn, their guns out of sight now, their horses at merely a brisk canter, with the dust funnels shooting back from beneath the beat of the hoofs and spreading out wide and high.

Then this picture was lost as the trail bore them behind the shoulder of high ground. They were entering the foothills. A deep valley, with one wall of gold and one wall of velvet black, opened before them, cleaving a way into the heart of the mountains.

Reata turned back to the girl. "Have you got a knife?" he asked.

"Yes," she said.

"Give it to me."

"Why?"

"I need it."

She produced from somewhere a vicious little icicle of a knife with the light dripping off its needle point.

"That's better," said Reata, taking it. "We can pull up here and talk. Because after what I say to you, you might want to put that knife into me."

They halted their horses. The dust came softly, slowly, up behind them. Bates and Quinn came swinging into view. Reata stopped them by lifting his hand.

"What is it?" asked the girl, frowning. "I don't like the way you're leading up to something, Reata."

"You'll like the something a lot less than the leading up to it," he assured her. "I'm going to ask you to take that gray horse off into the mountains. Just where, I don't know."

"Into the mountains?" she demanded, staring. "What do you mean by that?"

"What I say. I want to take that gray so far into the mountains that nothing but a turkey buzzard or a Bill Champion can find it again."

She cried out. There was no music in the sound. The soft velvet was rubbed from her voice that Harry Quinn had said was more poisonous to men than her looks. It made Reata think of nothing but the squall of an angry Gypsy. If she had had the knife then — well, he knew her just well enough never to be sure of what she would do next. This time she swung the big gray around as though she intended to drive the weight of the horse trampling over the smaller mare and its rider. She leaned out and caught Reata by the wrist and shook his arm savagely. Her whole face was savage, twisting with anger.

"D'you mean that you came for the horse?"

"And you, Miriam," he told her honestly. "I wanted to have a look at you. You know that. But I had to get the gray. It's fish bait, d'you see? And Bill Champion is the fish."

"Bill Champion!" she echoed. He was amazed to see the anger go out of her in one, sudden ebbing. Very pale, she stared at him.

"You . . . and the other pair . . . that thickhead of a Harry Quinn . . . you've come to trap Bill Champion? Reata, you fool, he'll kill you all!"

"He'll try," said Reata. "And we'll try. Or maybe I'll try alone. I don't like big odds on my side, because it takes the fun out of the game. And this is a game, Miriam. Straighten out the gray, and we'll start traveling."

V

"MIRIAM'S PLEA"

When she obeyed him, he could see that it was an instinctive re-action only. Her mind was working desperately. Her lips were parted. Words kept trembling in her throat for a time before she said, still half stunned: "Reata, you don't know Bill Champion. You can't know him. Tell me . . . did you ever so much as see him?"

"I never saw him," he admitted.

At that she groaned and struck her hands together and then against her forehead.

The stallion made a leap ahead. She, in an instant, was crouching forward, ready to send him speeding on his way, per-haps irrecoverably beyond the pursuit of the mare. But, with her backward glance, she saw the noose ready in the hand of Reata, and she surrendered to the coil of that almost living, snake-like presence.

Reata joined her, the mare jogging softly. They walked on into the gold and the shadow of the big valley. It was a huge thing. The trail wound along halfway up the steep side. Trees stuck out, angling from the wall of the cliff. At the bottom of the gorge, water boomed or sang with a hollow voice. And that despair which had come over the girl seemed to mate the big-ness and the wildness of the scene.

"You never saw him, but they raked you into this job . . . Quinn and the other one. No, I know the old devil behind all the trouble. Dickerman, the rat man. Dickerman! He's the one, Reata. Admit it!"

"Well, even suppose that I admit it," said Reata.

"But Bill Champion will eat you the way a cat eats a mouse. You don't know him, Reata. You've never seen his horrible face. You don't know anything about him. I've seen men. I've seen fighting men. I've seen blood. I've seen about everything, but nothing like Bill Champion. I've waked up at night and screamed, dreaming about him. Reata, it's not too late. Let me go. I'll go back to the band."

"Sure you will," agreed Reata. "You'll go back to the band, when we've hit a comfortable place to wait . . . out here in the hills."

"You're going to go through with your crazy scheme?" she asked him, beating her hands together.

"I'm going through with it, unless you know another idea that's a better one," he answered.

"I know a better thing for you to do," she declared. "It's for you to let me go back, and you never stop riding till you've put a thousand miles between you and this neck of the woods, and you never come back here for a year or so, till Champion has a chance to forget that there's anybody like you in the world. And every day of the year, get down on your two skinny knees and thank God that you're still alive."

"He must be quite a noise, this Bill Champion," said Reata ironically.

The irony did not affect her.

"Once," she said, "I was walking along through the woods . . . that was weeks ago, near the place we were camping. And something came over me. A chill, you might call it. A chill in the pit of my stomach. But it was a hot day. And I turned around, wanting to get right into the hot of the sun, and there, behind me, I saw Bill Champion leaning a hand against a tree and just looking at me, and I couldn't move. My knees began to sag. I yelled out . . . 'Bill, go away! Go away!' I screamed it out. His face moved into what he might have called a smile. His face stretched a little at the sides, and he went out of sight through the trees. But I kept on wanting to scream. I got out into the sunshine, and for an hour I couldn't feel the heat of it. There was a darkness that kept welling up inside of me."

She paused, her eyes closed, her hands gripping the flowing silver of the gray's mane.

"Well," said Reata when he could speak, "there are a lot of men who are pretty good hands at scaring the girls."

"Bah!" she snapped at him. "Don't tell me that you think I'm a squealing, silly, fainting, rattle-headed dummy, like other women. I'm not, and you know I'm not!"

He knew it very well. "You're not like the rest," he admitted. "But just because Champion has a funny-looking face, he's got on your nerves."

"Nobody could tell you," she sighed, shaking her head. "But I'm going to find some way. Somehow I'll find a way to tell you what he's like, and then you'll let me take the horse back. Listen to me."

"I'm listening, and I'm looking, Miriam."

"Don't look. If you keep seeing my fool of a pretty face, you won't hear what I have to say. Ah, men have no brains. Because I've got red lips and blue eyes and a body hitched to them, you can hardly follow what I'm saying. But I'm talking life and death. Reata, listen to me. Look ten years of wrinkles into my face and ten years of scrawniness into my body. Then let me tell you that I've seen Bill Champion take hold of a bar of iron bigger than you'd use to hammer out the shoes for a work horse. And I've seen him bend it."

"That's a good trick. Your man that looks like a cat, he could do that, I suppose."

"Reata, listen to me! I've seen him take the hand of our

112

strong man . . . and he *is* a real strong man . . . and in half a second our strong man was down on his knees, groaning, his bones almost breaking in his hand. Does that mean anything to you?"

"Yes," admitted Reata. "That means something."

"He's lived with guns all his life. He doesn't do tricks. He shoots what he wants to eat. But he likes small birds. You hear, Reata? He likes to get a mess of small birds to fill his stomach, and he shoots the birds. He doesn't trap them, but he shoots them. I've seen him shoot them on the wing."

"Just nips off their heads, eh?" Reata smiled.

"Reata!" she cried aloud.

He shook his head. "It's no good," he told her. "I believe everything that you're saying, but it's no good. I've started this trail, and I've got to come to the end of it."

"He'll kill you!" cried Miriam. All at once she began to sob, though her face was fierce, and she kept beating her hands together or grabbing at her face with them. "Reata, he'll kill you, he'll kill you. That's why I had the horrors when I saw him. That's why I wakened at night and screamed till the whole tribe came running to my wagon. It's because I knew that he was the man who would kill you, Reata! And you . . . like a fool, you sit there in the saddle, and you sneer, and you smile, and you shrug your shoulders . . . and I hate you! I hope he does kill you! I hope he puts his hands on you and breaks you like a stick. I hope that I'm standing by, and I'll laugh! I'll cheer him on. I'll tell him to go ahead, slowly, so that I can taste the screaming better. That's what I hope!"

He kept watching her, smiling a little still. He could not tell what part of her was woman and what part of her was cat.

"Well," he said aloud, "what part of you is woman and what part of you is cat, Miriam?"

"I don't know," mourned the girl. "But if I'm a cat, you're

113

the king of the cats. Reata, tell me honestly . . . aren't you afraid after what I've just told you?"

"I am," he admitted. "I've got the chills up my spine."

"When you have a chance to think it over, you'll see that you don't need to be ashamed," said the girl. "Nobody needs to be ashamed for running away from Bill Champion. Any more than a man needs to be ashamed for running away from the devil. Reata, let me go back now. Please, please, please let me go back now."

He said nothing. The softness went out of voice and eyes as she demanded suddenly: "What do you think that you could do if you ever met Bill Champion? What do you think he'd make of your silly reata? He'd break it with his hands. He'd bite it in two with his wolf's teeth. And he'd laugh as he got at you. What would you do, even if you had a chance to meet him?"

"I don't know exactly," said Reata. "But the more I think about it, the more I think that I'm going to enjoy killing him."

"You're what?"

"I never wanted to kill a man all the days of my life," said Reata. "Not even Dickerman, and that's a strange thing. Dickerman ought to be killed, but I've never wanted to. But Bill Champion seems mostly beast, and I'm going to choke the breath out of him one day."

She started to make a savage protest, a scornful laugh beginning on her lips. But after a moment she began to weep instead. "You know what it's like," she managed to say through her sobbing. "It's like a silly pet rooster that's bossed the barn yard for six months . . . it's like that silly little fool of a rooster flapping up into the air to meet an eagle swooping out of the middle of the sky. Well," she cried, angry again, "find him, then! Find him! And I'll have the burying of you. But I won't cry over your grave. I'll laugh. Because that's all that a fool ought to get out of

114

life . . . just laughter . . . just laughter! You hear?"

They were deep in the valley. The sun no longer fell around them but only shadow, yet the light was glowing on the upper eastern slope. The voices of the stream in the bottom of the gorge called faintly about them. It seemed to Reata that he was riding in a dream, or that his ghost was here, come back from the other world after being killed by the terrible hands of Bill Champion.

But that was not entirely bravado, that speech he had made to the girl. He began to smooth the head of Rags with the palm of one hand. He began to remember the horrible description of Bill Champion that he had heard from Pop Dickerman. And he had a very sure foreknowledge that he and Bill Champion could not live much longer in this world. Another thought came to him.

"Miriam," he said, "you loath big Bill Champion, eh?"

She shuddered for answer.

"And the fact is," said Reata, "that the brute left the gray with you. It wasn't because he really needed to leave it with the Gypsies. It was because he wanted to please you. Eh?"

She said nothing.

"He showed you some ways of making friends with the gray, and you've gone on and found others. But the fact is that he likes you pretty well, eh? That's why you screamed when you saw him behind you that day in the woods?"

She put up both hands and covered her eyes. She said nothing. She did not need to say anything.

115

VI

"THE PERFECT SPOT"

They traveled straight south out of the big valley, through the foothills, through the first range, and out of the day and into the night they followed beneath the stars whatever fortune might bring them, until at last they came to what all three men agreed was a perfect spot. It was a smooth valley laid across a soft hump of brown hills like a gun barrel's indentation across a sack of wheat. One end of the valley pointed at the mist of the western desert. The other end pointed at the big mountains through which they had passed.

They were very tired, because it was after midnight. They could hear the thin murmur of a little creek; they could even, after they dismounted and got away from the breathing of horses and the creak of saddle leather, hear the faint slapping of waves on the shore of a tiny lake.

The girl was so tired that she threw her arms up over the back of the stallion and leaned her face against the surcingle. Her whole body sagged in.

However, the gray devil would not let a hand touch him except her own. When Reata came up, he tried for the head of the man with his teeth, with his striking forehoofs, and then, whirling, with the long drive of his hind legs, like a pair of Long Toms. Reata had to order the girl three times to get the surcingle off the stallion and put the bridle up and hobble him out, since he could not be tethered to a rope, having the habit of throwing himself headlong back against any restraint.

116

She stripped the surcingle and the bridle from him and put the hobbles on. Then she slid down into the grass and lay with her face on the cross of her arms.

The three men went on making camp. Every instant, as they could examine the ground more carefully under the starlight, they were better and better pleased with their choice. When the great Bill Champion found them here, he would have to come at them through the open, where rifles tell against might and main. There was a bit of woodland pouring darkly out from between two hills on the left, giving them wood not fifty yards away, an easy distance to drag fuel with a willing horse and a strong rope. They had water. They had with them, in their packs, plenty of food, besides what accurate rifles would bring down for them in this virgin country. Altogether, they could hardly have chosen better with all the brightness of the sun to help them. There was even a scattering of small brush near the shores of the lake that they could tear up to make tinder for their fires. Out of this, in fact, they built their fire for that night. They fried bacon, they made coffee, of course, and they had hardtack.

When the food was nearly ready, Reata got out of his pack the change of shirts and the pair of overalls that he carried with him. She could furl these things and get into them. He went over to wake her up, but, even when he shook her shoulder, she still lay like one dead. So he put Rags down to watch her and returned to the fire. He was through with a bacon and hardtack sandwich when the yipping of Rags summoned him, so he took a cup of the hot coffee over to her.

"She ain't so dead as she seems, if you just know how to wake her up," said Harry Quinn.

Reata patted her shoulder, for he found her lying exactly as before.

"You're awake," he told her. "Rags has been telling me all

about you. Wake up, Miriam."

She lay like a log. When he shook her, her whole body wobbled. He got hold of her and sat her up and made her head spill over against his shoulder, since it had to spill in some direction.

"Listen," said Reata. "If you won't stop this pretending . . . if you won't wake up . . . I'm going to put this coffee to your mouth, and, if you don't sip it, it'll burn you, it's that hot. I'll keep right on pouring till it blisters your mouth for you."

He put the hot tin against her mouth, and she winced her head away. She rolled her head back on his shoulder and looked up at him.

"All right," she said. "I was trying to think while I lay there. I couldn't make up my mind whether I loved or hated or laughed at you most, but I guess I do all three together. Give me the coffee. It smells pretty good. Give me a hand up, and I'll go over there and toast some of the dew out of me. The dew falls pretty thick in this neck of the woods, doesn't it?"

He half lifted her to her feet. She sighed again. The fatigue seemed to have run out of her, and the new strength was filling her.

"I'll go over there and get some bacon under my skin," she said. "It's making my mouth water."

"Put on this shirt and these overalls," he commanded.

"Yeah? Why should I put on a pair of old overalls and a shirt of thirty summers?" she asked him.

"Just because I tell you to," said Reata.

"Miriam," she said, "you're not modest enough. The trouble with you is that you don't take enough trouble. That's the trouble." She shuffled the shirt over her head. Then she stepped into the overalls. "Where do I take in the reefs?" she asked him. "Give me that coffee again. I need a drink. The old ship looks like it needs a wind, doesn't it? 'Why, you look perfectly all right . . . you look perfectly proper now,' he said. Say, how proper are you, brother?"

"Quit it," said Reata. "How are those slippers? I can't lend you boots."

"I'd go roughshod, if you did," said the girl. She walked to the fire with an ambling stride. Cup in hand, she scowled down at the two men. "Hullo, Harry," she said. "How's the old boy? The last time I saw that red neck I thought a rope was going to stretch it the next day. How does it feel to be sitting up and swallowing coffee and bacon like a real man instead of a ghost?"

"Hello, sister," said Harry. He stood up and held out a hand, which she shook cordially enough. He grinned at her. "Every time I swaller, I say to myself . . . 'Reata done it! Reata done it!' What do you say?"

"He done it, all right," she answered, nodding. "Introduce me to your friend."

"This is Dave Bates, Miriam. Miriam what, I dunno."

Bates got up and shook hands in his turn, silently, staring.

"I haven't got a headache, doctor," said the girl. "No use giving me the long look. Wait till I furl these sails, and I'll sit down and be one of the boys."

She sat down cross-legged. Reata gave her hardtack and bacon. She began to munch contentedly.

"That was a pretty good song and dance back there at Orchard Creek," she said. "Who thought it up?"

"Reata done the thinking," said Harry Quinn.

"He would," she answered. "That idea had Reata all over it. It was so crazy that it rattled. It rattled so much that I knew it was Reata, and so I came along to keep him from getting the spot he stood on all red. All that saved you two was the crowd having him to shoot at, and all that saved him was luck and a long chance. If Reata was a poker hand, it would take a poker-faced bluffer to lay a ten-cent bet on him. But here we

119

are, boys, out under the stars, waiting for Bill Champion. Nice and cozy, isn't it?"

"Listen to her," said Harry Quinn, grinning. "You know Bill pretty good, don't you, Miriam?"

"I know the chills of him, but you fellows are going to know the fever," she answered. "You boys have read too much. You've read about Jack the Giant Killer, but when you get a little older, you won't believe everything you find in print. I keep seeing Bill walking across the mountains, so to speak. There's only one danger ahead of him. When he sees the three of you waiting for a fight, he may laugh himself to death."

"Yes, she knows Bill Champion pretty good," said Dave Bates. "She's a help to have around, too."

"The way you boys throw away good advice, you must be great spenders," she said. Then she stood up suddenly, having finished her bit of the food. "Why don't you all turn around three times and make a wish, and wish yourselves home in bed? You have no right to be out here in the open with all the trouble walking around waiting to find you out. Listen, Reata, when am I allowed to go home, or do I have to stay here to make the gray horse feel at home?"

"You're too tired to go home tonight," said Reata. "You can start in the morning. I'll take you through the hills. You can ride one of the horses . . . Quinn's, maybe."

"Hey, hold on," said Quinn. "How do you get that way? She rides my horse means I walk how far?"

"There's always the gray for you," said Reata. "Besides, when Bill Champion comes, he'll have a horse under him. I'll break up some of that brush and build you a bed, Miriam."

He cut down a quantity of the brush with a small axe that he always made a part of his pack. On that soft and springy bedding he rolled down a blanket. The girl sat on the bed, sinking deeply into it.

"How do you make sure that I don't slide away from you during the night and get onto the gray?" she asked, studying Reata by the starlight.

"I put Rags here to watch you."

"He's a fine big guard dog," she said.

"He'll bark every time you so much as lift a hand," said Reata.

"I'll have him quiet enough after a while," she said. "I'm an animal tamer, Reata. Look at the gray."

"You train the wild ones . . . you're no good with the tame," he replied, smiling at her.

"This is about the last time I'll ever have a chance to say good night to you," said the girl. "The most I'll ever see of you after tomorrow is maybe a finger bone that Bill may be wearing for a watch charm the next time I meet him. Well, the sooner it's said, the sooner I'm asleep. Good night, Reata."

"Fresh, ain't she?" said Harry Quinn when Reata went back to the fire.

"Sure she's fresh," answered Reata. "And the best of it is that she's not going to spoil in our company. You boys get that?"

They got it, staring steadily at him.

He had given his blankets to the girl. So he made a heap of the soft brush, burrowed into it, and went to sleep.

VII

"THE FAREWELL"

It was a broken sleep. He wakened twice out of frightful dreams in which he was seeing a faceless man with eyes that seemed to be staring through a scar-tissue mask. Each time he sat up and made sure that the girl was in her place, with Rags beside her.

A third time he wakened, not because of a dream — at least, there were no floating shreds of the sleep images left in his consciousness — but because something seemed to have plucked at him from the outer night. He stared wildly around him, his heart thundering, and braced himself to see the silhouette of a man coming toward the single red eye of the campfire.

But he saw nothing of that. Instead, he made out Rags coiled in perfect slumber near the bed of the girl, and from those empty blankets a slinking form was stealing away toward the gray stallion.

Reata stood up and called softly: "Before you can get the hobbles off him, I'll be able to reach you with this rope, Miriam."

She did not turn at once. She simply stood, facing the horse, and gradually she turned.

He walked slowly toward her, and she said: "Where do you keep the extra eyes, Reata? You were snoring, soft and low, a while ago."

"I keep an extra ear for Miriam," he told her.

She had a way of coming up close to people and looking them up and down. She did that now to Reata. "All right," she

122

said. "You notice that Rags is still asleep, eh?"

"I notice it," admitted Reata. "You can train them, wild or tame. But you haven't trained me yet."

"I didn't have time before Bill Champion came and got him," she answered. "So long, Reata."

She went back to her blankets, but Reata knew that there could be no more sleep for him. Once a fugitive instinct had touched and wakened him, a second time it might fail, and she would be gone, and the trap for Bill Champion would be sprung before he entered it.

Luckily the dawn began a little later. The big mountains turned black against the east, and then the soft color began all around the horizon. He forgot Bill Champion and the girl and the two crooks who completed the company at that camp. For a little while he was alone in his own country, then the day commenced more brightly, and the voice of Dave Bates shattered the time of peace.

They had for breakfast a pair of mountain grouse that Harry Quinn gathered in by the briefest of walks up the slope of the eastern hill. The meat was broiled on the ends of wooden spits. They had coffee and hardtack again with it, and everyone voted the meal prime. Afterward Reata started at once with the girl.

Quinn made no real difficulty about his horse. He gave it up with a shrug and a squint.

"How do I know?" he asked. "Maybe I ain't ever goin' to ride out of this here place anyway. Maybe Bill Champion is goin' to show me a way to go down a longer trail."

The girl shook hands with the two men rather solemnly. "After he's gone, you'll have a good chance to get out," she said to them.

She went cantering down the trail with Reata. They were over the eastern ridge of the valley before he pulled up Sue and said

123

to the girl: "You understand, Miriam. I turn you loose because you promise not to make any trouble for me in this job?"

"What sort of trouble could I make?" she asked him.

"If you've got the devil in your mind," he answered, "you could do anything to stop me. You could even let the sheriff at Rusty Gulch know where I am, if you'd rather have me in jail than dead. But you're promising, word of honor, that you won't make any trouble."

"Sure, I promise."

"Word of honor?"

"A Gypsy's word of honor . . . that would mean a lot," she said.

"I want your word of honor," he commanded, "or we turn about and go back to the camp."

"You can't do it!" she argued. "You can't hold me out here in the hills . . . a girl and three men."

"I'm doing what I have to, not what I want," said Reata.

"It's what you want. It's what you're crazy enough to want," she told him. "You *want* to meet Bill Champion. It's like telling a fool of a young horse wrangler about an outlaw horse. He can't wait till he's had a go at it and got himself a broken neck. That's the way with you. You want to show Bill that *you're* the champion!"

"I'm waiting for our promise, on your word of honor," he told her.

"Oh, well, take it, then."

"Give me your hand with it."

She obeyed gloomily.

"Look at me," he directed. "Now say it over. You promise on your word of honor."

"All right, I promise," she said.

He released her hand.

"A lot you trust me." She sneered. "You'd rather trust Rags

124

. . . even if he does go to sleep in the middle of things, the way he did last night."

"I trust you," said Reata thoughtfully. "I don't know why. But I trust you, all right."

"Tell me how you trust me?" she asked.

"Well, in the last pinch . . . if there were life or death in a job . . . you'd risk your neck."

"For you?"

"Yes, for me."

She made no answer to this, and smiled steadily for at least two hours as they rode into the east. They were not going north, toward the town of Orchard Creek, because he wanted to get her out of the rough hill country and onto the flat, where he could leave her and return. For there were more habitations there on the flat, and he would feel safer about her. He offered her his Stetson to keep off the sun.

"I don't want your hat," she said. "I don't want anything of yours."

"You'd rather have sunstroke?"

"I swore that no man would ever do what you've done to me . . . kick me around like a dog!" she cried at him. "I hate you, Reata! You're not even a man. You're not even half a man. You're only a skinny runt. You're only a slavey that Dickerman sends around to do his dirty jobs. But you've been man enough to drag me around by the nape of the neck. That'll make you proud. That's enough to set you up for the rest of your life."

There was nothing to say to this. He had to set his teeth and endure. And suddenly she broke out: "I'm sorry, Reata. I didn't mean that last."

"It's all right."

"But why don't we go north, straight off?" she asked. "That's the shortest way to Orchard Creek."

He repeated his thoughts. "I want to get back to the camp as

125

soon as I can. I suppose it's too soon for even a Bill Champion to get on the trail, but I can't be sure. I want to get back there before trouble starts. And the best thing that I can do is to take you out of the hills into the flat. There are more ranches there. I'd feel safer about you."

At this she insulted him with loud laughter. "Chaperoning me, eh, Reata?" she said. "You drag me in the dirt and then you chaperone me, eh? That's pretty good."

Rags turned his head suddenly as he ran ahead of the horse, and snarled over his shoulder at her. The thing struck Reata heavily. It was as though the dog sensed evil in her.

"You might as well worry about a hawk in the sky as about me," she insisted. "What's the matter with you, Reata?"

"I don't know," he said. "Maybe I'm being a fool, all right. But this is the way we go."

She softened again just after that and tried to be friendly, but he was overcast with a gloomy doubt.

They came through woods to the top of the last ridge, and below them lay the plains, dotted with cattle, and with ranch houses, here and there, awash in the heat waves that the sun struck off the ground.

He pulled up Sue, dismounted, loosed her cinches, took off her bridle, and turned her out to graze and rest for a short time before he started the return journey. It was already past noon.

"There's the way for you," he told her. "You head down into the flat, and then you pull gradually north, and you'll hit Orchard Creek in the eye . . . and you'll be at home with Queen Maggie and the rest again."

She felt the grimness underlying his words. "Tell me something, Reata," she asked. "You've been fond of a lot of girls. A whole lot."

"Yes," he admitted.

126

"Since you were a little kid you've been falling in love and out again?"

"Yes."

"It's the practice that counts," she said bitterly. "And what a man learns the easiest is the falling out."

He, staring at her, tried to think forward to that time. He wanted to have it come soon. He wanted to shake off the thought of her quickly, and never let his mind go back to her. They could never get on together. He kept telling himself that.

"This time it won't be easy," he said. "Not for me. But what about you, Miriam? If I've looked at one girl, you've looked at ten men."

"And let 'em pass," she said.

"Sure," he said ironically. "I'm the first man that ever meant a thing to you."

"You are," said the girl. "The first one that ever meant a thing." Then she added: "Ask me to say that on my word of honor, too."

But in his bewilderment he knew that what she told him had been perfectly true. He was still stunned as she waved him a brief farewell, and, without another word, rode her mustang down the slope of the hill toward the flat country beyond.

Even Rags stood up on a rock to watch her go.

VIII

"A POSSE"

The girl, as she went down the slope, kept her teeth locked hard together in order to master the trembling of her lips. She had done everything wrong, she felt. She should have poured out tenderness on him in this last meeting. She should have showed him clearly how completely he dominated her world. Instead, she had left him on a wrangling note. Would she ever learn to check herself and express only the pleasant thing which men may care to know? No, there was a savage in her that made her burst out against the things she loved the best.

What did she love? she asked herself then. Well, she loved to sway and dance on the back of a horse with plenty of people looking on, applauding, finding her beautiful, and all the men, and even the little boys, with half-mournful eyes as they stared at an unapproachable thing. She loved to lie in the grass and look up at the sky through the brown and green branches of a tree, while the Gypsy music hummed and throbbed somewhere not too close. She loved to look over the Gypsy crew and know that even Queen Maggie could not rule them as she might do by the mere crooking of her small finger. She loved a good horse, and sandy ground, and to ride against the rain. She loved these things, but last of all she loved Reata, and most of all. He was neither magnificent nor handsome. He was not rich. He had none of those qualities of fairy prince about which she had daydreamed. But he had an eye that washed her clean.

Those two men who were back at the camp, they were formidable enough to have been picked out of any crowd. They were dangerous fellows, dangerously trained, but they were nothing compared with Reata. As she thought of this, an agony came over her. There were two mighty forces in this world, and one was Reata, standing for the right, it seemed to the girl, and one was Bill Champion, standing for all that is foul and dark. And the evil would conquer the good. Surely, if ever they met, Reata could not stand against that monster. It would be like asking a child to stand against the devil.

The devil in every way was Bill Champion, and most of all in that secrecy which he had maintained so perfectly that there were hardly a dozen men in the West who knew about his majestic or his revolting crimes. A sheriff or a federal marshal here and there patiently and steadily searched for that master devil among men. The others knew little or nothing about him. And his deeds were so monstrous that they were quickly forgotten, like nightmares that dissolve from the mind in the brightness of daylight.

She alone, in this world, was able now to stretch out her hand and make a gesture to protect Reata, yet she had given her word and her honor that she would not do such a thing. Word? Honor? Suddenly such things were breath to her. Reata was already saddling the mare behind her, no doubt. Reata was already turning back toward the camp on Sue, and the little dog Rags was scampering ahead of his master, happily running down every attractive scent that crossed the trail.

Something had to be done. It was in her hands. It seemed to the tormented girl then that the voice of Reata himself had told her the proper thing. Her word and her honor? She waved them away. It was for the life of Reata that she would have to struggle.

Reata had told her that the sheriff of Rusty Gulch would be glad enough to ride long and far to put hands on him. And, of course, that was true. Men knew how Reata had carved his way out of the jail at Rusty Gulch after he had been lodged there for a very trifling offense, indeed. And, of course, the sheriff would welcome him back. Then, it seemed to her, settling her mind of all doubt, that fate must have chosen the course in which Reata had ridden. For the way had been around a corner toward Orchard Creek, to be sure, but it had been almost on a straight line for Rusty Gulch.

She gave over her thinking. The thing to do, it seemed to her, was to make her horse fly to Rusty Gulch as fast as she could, and then start the sheriff galloping back toward the spot where Reata would be waiting, and his two companions beside him. Let Reata curse her and rage at her. It would be better, far better, to have him resting safely behind bars than to have him stretched out as food for the buzzards. Those were the things that she kept rehearsing to herself as she urged her horse on. And she nursed its strength and saved its wind on the steep slopes and even dismounted and ran up the hardest climbs so that there would be a greater power in the horse for taking the level stretches.

Then, at last, the miles fell away from before her, and she saw the sun flaming on the windows of Rusty Gulch. It was late in the afternoon already. But, by twilight, if the sheriff could start at once, they could be up there into the mountains in full power. They could find Reata and close on him, and hold him fast in the great, safe hand of the law.

So she stormed into the main street of the town. The sheriff? He was at his house. His house was down there on the corner — and look! She could see the sheriff himself sitting out on the front porch in his carpet slippers. She spurred the mustang cruelly, till with a switching tail it raced that remaining small distance, and she flung herself down in front of the fence of the sheriff.

130

Lowell Mason had what a sheriff needs in his face. He had a sense of humor, too. And when he saw the girl in those flapping clothes of a man, he smiled a little. He wiped the smile away as she raced up the steps to him.

"You're the sheriff?" she said.

"That's my job," he said.

"I want you. Come fast. Reata!" she called to him.

"Reata? What about him?"

She had turned away to the steps again, burning in haste. Now she paused and stamped with impatience.

"Reata . . . you want him here . . . he broke out of your jail, didn't he?"

"Yes," said the sheriff, unhurried, casual, watching every detail of her.

"Well, I can show you where he is. I can lead you to him. But you'll need men. Will you come, or are you just going to sit there and stare?"

"A girl like you," answered the sheriff, keeping well inside his maddening calm, "would never sell Reata. Never to the law. Not for money, either, I take it."

"I tell you, I can show you where he is!" she cried.

"What sort of a put-up job is this?" asked the sheriff. "You'd be more likely to fight for him than to sell him like this . . . without a price, either. Come on, now, and tell me the straight of it."

This calmness of his seemed to her like a vast, metal monster. But she had to be reasonable. Suddenly she saw that it was necessary for her to tell the truth, incredible as that might seem. "Did you ever hear of Bill Champion?" she demanded.

The sheriff leaned forward. Then he stood up.

"What are you talking about?" he asked sharply.

"Bill Champion, you know about him?"

"Aye, but you don't . . . you can't . . . ," said the sheriff.

131

"I'm wasting time . . . *you're* wasting time," she cried desperately. "But he's up there in the hills . . . Reata's up there . . . and Bill Champion is coming for him. Do you hear that? Does that mean anything to you? Oh, if you want to get famous . . . maybe you'll get Bill Champion, too. Will that budge you?"

Budge the sheriff? It made Lowell Mason walk up to her and stare fixedly into her eyes, as though he thought she might be mad, and that he had to get at the inner truth in some way like this.

"I'm tryin' to understand and believe what I hear," he said. "There's sure a spur drove into you. You say Bill Champion is comin' into the hills to meet up with Reata?"

"He's going to meet Reata . . . they're going to fight . . . Reata will be murdered! Does that mean anything to you? Will you come? Will you come? Will you get men and come?"

"And Reata's going to be a lot safer in jail, eh? Is that the angle? I can foller that, all right," said the sheriff.

"Are you going to do anything?" she cried at him.

"Oh, aye! I'm going to do something. I'd take a trip around the world on my hands and knees, if I could lay hands on Bill Champion! You know the way, you say?"

"I can take you there . . . I could take you in the dark. But will you start?"

"As fast as I can get hosses and men," said the sheriff. "Because I ain't fool enough to think that this here is any one-man job."

"One horse for me!" she begged. "One fresh horse for me!"

The sheriff, once he was in motion, moved very fast. He had a horse ready at his hitch rack. He flung himself into the saddle on that horse and galloped up the street. Here and there and again he checked his mustang and shouted — men came to doors, listened, and then flew into action in turn.

The sheriff was quite right when he said that it was not a

132

one-man job, but neither did he intend to take an entire crowd with him. Men are willing enough to volunteer for posse duty, but they are also likely to make such a noise that they would frighten away the eagles from the mountaintops, to say nothing of the hunted criminals. What Lowell Mason got for this work was a small party of six men. Every one of them was a fellow able to ride and to shoot and to follow a trail. Every man of them had proved his nerve in more ways than one, but above everything else with guns.

It was not a pretty party, at that. Old Lem Oliver was sixty-two, but his tough rawhide and whalebone would still stand a hundred-mile ride in a day. Young Terry Craig was a fat lad of eighteen whose swollen, red face made him look as though he were about to burst into laughter every moment, but he was as good a shot and as brave a man as rode with the sheriff that day.

And the girl, as she swung into the saddle on a strong, fresh horse, looked over the faces of those men, read them beneath the skin, and was content.

"BILL CHAMPION"

Back at the camp beside that small lake in the valley, Bates and Harry Quinn did not spend a peaceful day. The trouble was that Quinn chose to boast about the prowess of Reata, and this boasting hurt his companion to the quick, for the nature of Bates was such that he could not endure to hear another man praised.

"I told you what he would do, and he done it," said Quinn. "He went in, and he grabbed the hoss, and he took it away, and he brought it out here."

"You heard the girl say . . . Reata . . . he rattles, Reata!" Bates sneered.

"Yeah, the girl was only kidding. What did she say about you, *hombre?* 'Doctor,' she called you . . . poison face is what she meant."

"Did she?" said Bates. "Me, I wouldn't waste my time on no Gypsy. I got sort of principles, now and then."

"Yeah, and I bet you have," agreed Quinn. "You wouldn't steal after no Gypsy, maybe, because the Gypsy wouldn't leave nothing behind."

"The way I was raised," said the poisonous little man, "I wouldn't go and chuck myself away for no black-headed, black-eyed Gypsy gal, like you and the kid would."

"She ain't got black eyes. She's got blue eyes," said Harry Quinn. "You oughta look twice before you talk. The trouble with you is that she let you pass so fast that you been seein' black ever since."

134

"She didn't linger none over you," remarked Dave Bates.

"Me? What claim would I put in? Not with Reata around. That *hombre* has to come first, and I've got sense enough to know it. But a gent like you, Dave, you wanta see yourself first, or you don't want to see yourself at all. It'd choke you to see the facts about what folks think of you. But my throat's too big to be choked. I know what they think, and I swaller it and have another drink."

It was well on in the afternoon as they chatted in this jolly vein, and the gray stallion, by this time, had wandered, in spite of his hobbles, rather close to the edge of the woods that spilled down from between the two hills. The pair had watched him fairly steadily all the day — not that they expected Bill Champion, to be sure, but because the great horse represented to them a focal point on which danger would at some time be directed.

They were so busy with their argument now that they did not see the shadowy form that moved among the trunks of the trees, stealthily and soundlessly as a hunting cat, a huge being who strode, and paused, and shifted from one shadow to another.

For Dave Bates was saying: "The trouble with this gent, Reata, is that he's all wide open and lookin' for a sock on the chin, and he's goin' to get it. You seen the holes in his hat? Well, they might as well 'a' been a coupla holes in his head. Is that brains? No, it ain't. He's ripe to get punched, and, when he gets it, it'll be a hole that'll spoil the ticket. He'll ride only one way, and there ain't goin' to be no return."

"I tell you," said Harry Quinn warmly, "that the only thing to it is the luck that he's got, and he knows how to ride it like a damn' jockey."

"Wait a minute," muttered Dave Bates. "It looks to me like the gray was steppin' along without those hobbles. I think he's broke the rope."

For, a moment before this, the knife of the man in the woods had slashed the rope that made the hobble. And he had stretched out his vast arm from behind a tree to grip the mane of the stallion.

It was at this instant that, as the horse turned his head, pricking his ears, Dave Bates had a glimpse of the white slab of that face, and he screeched suddenly: "Hi! Harry . . . it's him!"

There was a rifle not two steps away, and Dave Bates knew the importance of accuracy in dealing with that monster, but he knew the importance of speed, also.

Harry Quinn, gaping, paralyzed by the suddenness of the danger, dragged out his own gun slowly. And he saw a huge man leap out of the woods onto the back of the gray stallion — a man so big that the gray horse looked as small as an ordinary mustang. As he sprang, a snarl issued from the beast face of the creature. He could have drawn back among the trees to safety, but, seeing battle, the sudden lust for it had mastered him.

He had sprung onto the back of the gray, and now, with the gigantic pressure of his knees alone and the sway of his body, he turned the head of the horse straight toward the men by the lake and charged, his spurs gouging the flanks of his mount.

He had a Colt in either hand. Fast as Dave Bates had been on the draw, that charging monster was faster still with his bullets. The first of them struck Harry Quinn and hurled him violently back against his companion, so that both went down, and only that fall prevented the second slug from the guns of Bill Champion from flashing through the brain of Bates.

A howl came out of the throat of the giant as he saw the victory already almost accomplished. That howl gripped the whole body of Dave Bates with cold. He knew what was coming. He strove to wriggle from beneath the pinning body of Harry Quinn, so that he could use his guns, but Bill Champion dived from the back of his halting stallion and hurled himself on the two men. He knocked the wits from the head of Harry Quinn with a back-handed stroke. He picked Dave Bates up by the throat and stripped the Colt out of his grasp as though it had been in the fingers of a child.

Then Bill Champion sat down on the rock beside the ashes of the dead fire and began to laugh. It was not a real laugh, in fact, but a brooding chuckle, long continued, and the sun played on the scar gristle that made a flat of his face as though on the quicksilver of a mirror. The eyes seemed deeply buried behind that mask, looking out through profound holes.

Bill Champion, in his hands, held the scrawny body of the gunman, and turned it this way and that, curiously, as a monstrous ape might have done.

"Why," said Bill Champion, "if it ain't the friend of the gent that eats fire. It's the friend of little Gene Salvio, ain't it?"

Dave Bates, half strangled, made no effort to reply, but the giant added suddenly, gruffly: "Talk, you fool!"

He got Bates by the hair of his head and easily bent back his head and forced him to his knees.

"Yeah," gasped Bates. "I'm a friend of Gene Salvio."

"It's a kind of a funny thing that I'd bump into you up here," said Champion. "What I'm wonderin' is could I cut the scrawny neck of you clean off with one swipe with the old Bowie knife. What do you think, eh?"

Bates said nothing. Being about to die, he gathered his nerve. He did not look into the frightful face of Champion for fear of going to pieces.

Here Harry Quinn recovered enough to sit up with a groan. The bullet had struck him through the body, and he was sick with the pain of the wound, and gasping for air.

Bill Champion kicked him deliberately in the face and knocked him flat and senseless again.

"Went over like a ninepin, all balanced fine," said Champion, grinning. "Now, you . . . what's your name? You big enough to have a name?"

"Bates," he answered.

"Bates, eh? First name?"

"Dave."

"Dave Bates. A little wizened runt like you, and yet you wear two names, just like a real man. Dave Bates, tell me something. There was another gent in this job, they tell me. And he grabbed the gal, and he grabbed the gray at one wallop. What's become of him?"

"He's gone," said Bates.

"Sure, he's gone. I ain't a fool. I can see he's gone. But where's he gone to?"

"He took the girl away," said Bates.

"And is he gonna bring her back?"

"I dunno. I guess not. I guess he took her back to Orchard Creek."

"You lie. I come down by Orchard Creek way."

"Then I dunno where he took her."

"She went free and willing with him, did she?"

"Yes."

"There ain't a woman in the world that's worth anything," said Bill Champion. "All that they can see is faces. They ain't got brains enough to look behind faces and see facts. They can't see no heart and soul. Am I right?"

"By thunder," exploded Dave Bates, "you *are* right."

"You agree with me, do you? A lot it means to me to have a monkey like you say that you agree with me. It sure makes me a lot happier. Now, tell me something. When does this here Reata get back to the camp?"

"I don't know."

"He's coming back pretty soon, ain't he?"

138

"I dunno," said Dave Bates. "Maybe he's not coming back at all."

"You wouldn't lie to me, would you?" asked the giant, freshening his grip on the hair of Bates until it almost came out by the roots.

Suddenly the little man, in his agony, smiled. "I might lie to you, you gristle-faced baboon," he said.

Bill Champion closed his eyes. When they were closed, it was not even a semblance of a face that he wore. It was a deformed stone rather, horribly white with the sheen of flesh.

"Say it again, kid," said Bill Champion. "Damn me, but I sort of like to hear you."

"I've said it . . . I'll say it again. I might lie to you, you gristle-faced baboon," repeated Dave Bates.

"Good," said Champion, opening his eyes and his formless, crooked slit of a mouth. "Plenty good! Why, I been hearin' about men with the real nerve, but I had to find a monkey before I could find anybody that would talk like a man. You know what I'm goin' to do to you for this? I ain't goin' to take you apart bit by bit. I ain't goin' to unravel you. I'm just goin' to tie you up and throw you in the lake, and there you'll choke peaceful and *pronto,* and go wherever apes go. Maybe there's a special heaven for the runts and the half-faced monkeys that wear clothes . . . and two names, just like men."

X

"THE HORNET"

Champion wound the entire length of a forty-foot rope around Dave Bates, saying: "Look, Bates. This is kind of a big honor that I'm doin' you, wastin' the whole of a pretty good rope on you. I could tie you up with twine, and that would do all right, but damn me, I don't mind what I spend on a good man and a real man like you."

Bates, to this compliment, merely answered: "If you're goin' to throw me in the lake, go and do it, but if you ain't hurryin', put my hat back on my head. I hate the sun in my eyes."

Bill Champion bit the corner of a fresh plug of chewing tobacco and spit out the loose shreds of the leaves. He was gap-toothed. The teeth of upper and lower jaw looked to Bates as though they would fit into one another like the teeth of a shark. He munched his tobacco quietly, considering his captive. His lips seemed stiff and uneasily compressed; they kept pushing in and out as he chewed.

"Yeah, yeah," decided Bill Champion, "I kind of like you. I'm near sorry to drown you. I gotta fix up your sidekicker, and then I'll talk a minute to you." With that he tied Quinn securely. "I wanta know something about this Reata," resumed Bill Champion. "Why not tell me something about him? It'll give you a little time on dry land."

"Reata? Don't you know about him?" asked Bates.

"No," said Champion.

"Yeah, you know about him," answered Bates. "Everybody knows about him."

"I'm telling you straight. I never heard of him till the other day." Champion spit and folded his vast hands, prepared to listen.

"Aw, well," said Bates very seriously, "I dunno what I could tell you. You wouldn't believe it, because he ain't so big."

"That's what I hear. That he ain't big."

"Not more'n a hundred and fifty pounds, maybe. So you wouldn't understand."

"Why wouldn't I?"

"You wouldn't know what he could do. You wouldn't believe it. But maybe you've seen a hornet and a tarantula?"

"What you mean? Sure, I've seen 'em."

"How much bigger is the spider than the wasp?"

"Why, I dunno. Three or four times."

"Yeah, or five or six. But the hornet gets the spider into the open, don't he?"

"Yeah. I've seen that. And then tackles him, and the damned tarantula don't seem to know what to do. Pretty soon the hornet stings him, and he turns into a wet rag, and the hornet drags him away."

"You know what happens then, Champion?"

"No, I dunno, then."

Harry Quinn began to groan. He would still have fought back those groans, if he had been aware of them, but he could hear nothing. With every breath he drew, the groan shook his body. Bill Champion canted his head to listen and to grin.

"I'll tell you what the hornet does with the big spider. Drags it off to a hole in the ground and lays an egg onto it, and the egg hatches into a worm. And that spider ain't dead. It's only chloroformed, like you might say, and the worm pitches in and starts eatin' the spider for days and days, and gets bigger and

141

fatter, and the spider feels every bite, but it can't move, because its legs and its mouth are all paralyzed. It has to lie there, and finally the worm, it takes and feeds on the vitals of that tarantula, and that's the finish of the spider, and the grub is ready to turn into a hornet."

"Damn me, but that's a good idea. Where'd the wasp come to think about an idea like that?" asked Champion, full of admiration.

"That's what you wanta watch out for," said Dave Bates. "Don't you let Reata get you into the open."

"Why not?"

"I'm just tellin' you," said Bates. "Don't you let Reata get you into the open, is all I'm telling you. Because he'll paralyze you, like the wasp paralyzes the spider. You stay in a hole in the ground, if you got any sense."

"What does Reata do, eh?" asked Champion.

"You wouldn't understand," said Dave Bates, shaking his head. "He'd sting you numb so fast you wouldn't know nothing."

"I can sting 'em now and then," said Champion, tapping one of his big Colts.

"Sure. You're all right," said Bates. "But I was telling you. You're big and you're fast, and you can shoot pretty straight. There ain't many like you. You're one of the best that I ever seen. And you got strength enough to bend iron. I've seen that, too. Only . . . don't you let Reata get a hold on you. Understand?"

Bill Champion frowned. He spread out his huge hands and looked down at them.

"That's right where I live . . . in the hands," he said. "Why wouldn't I wanta let him get a hold on me?"

"I'm tellin' you," said Dave Bates.

"But he ain't so big," said Bill Champion.

"The hornet's a lot smaller than the spider, too. But you

know what happens. I just been tellin' you."

Bill Champion scowled, but in thought rather than in anger. Men who are about to die tell the truth, and there is even an old proverb to say that they tell it. Bill Champion had a belief in proverbs, now and then. But what could the mystery of Reata be?

"Well," said Champion, "that's all you can tell me, eh?"

"That's all you'd understand," said Dave Bates.

"You think I'm a dummy, eh?"

"No, you're bright enough. But ordinary gents like you and me, we don't understand. I seen him work, and even then I couldn't understand. You take a gent that rides right in and takes a gal and a hoss out from a whole crowd . . . could you understand that?"

Champion pursed his frightful mouth and said nothing.

"I couldn't hardly understand, neither, but I seen it. Maybe it's hypnotism. But there ain't any use for gents like me and you. We don't know enough. We couldn't understand."

"The devil with him," decided Bill Champion suddenly.

A little chill had run into his blood, into his nerves. He stood up and took a breath, to make himself realize his own size and strength a little more vividly. Then he picked up Dave Bates.

"Got any last requests, son?" asked Champion, beginning to sway the burden back and forth, ready for the toss.

"Not me," said Dave Bates. "This is as easy as any way. That's why I been givin' you the good advice. That's why I been tellin' you to get into a hole, when you see Reata comin'. So long, Bill."

"So long," growled Champion, and heaved the weight of the body far out in the water. It struck, threw up a crystal flash into the slant sunlight, and then the body of Dave Bates disappeared.

Champion, content, turned and leaned over Harry Quinn

143

for a moment. The mouth of Quinn had sagged open; his eyes were popping.

After that, Champion saddled the gray, took Dave Bates's horse, plundered the camp of the food that he needed, threw the rest into the lake, and then mounted and rode down the narrow valley toward the end that pointed out at the hot mist of the desert beyond. He did not look back till he was on his way, and then he scanned the horizon with a certain doubt in his mind.

The tarantula, to be sure, is bigger than the wasp. Also, dying men tell the truth.

A little shudder of cold ran again, swift as quicksilver, through the blood of the giant. He turned back and put the gray into a strong gallop, because he wanted to get from the view of that valley as quickly as possible.

Dave Bates, as his body cleft down through the ice of the water, knew that he had come to the end of his way, but instinctively he had drawn his breath, so as to hold it when submerged.

Falling, his shoulder struck the hard ridge of a submerged rock. He could see the vague, sloping shadow of it rising toward the sunlit brightness of the surface. The lake was very shallow. If, perhaps, he could manage to roll his body up that inclined surface of the rock he might be able to project his nostrils and mouth into the sweet heaven of life-giving air. He could not move hand or foot, but he could roll, and he could twist and thrust with his entire body like a half-frozen serpent. So, stifling, his lungs bursting, a fist opening in his throat, he worked his way patiently up the rock — and slipped off it to the slimy bottom.

He tried again. A last long effort, and he gained a distance up the rock. He sat up, and the air burst from his lips above the

144

surface of the water. He drew in the sweetness of the air, incredulous. His life had been given back to him — but for how long?

There was a decided current flowing down the lake. It moved against him. It threatened, every instant, to buoy him up and swing him away from his perch of safety.

In the distance, he could hear Harry Quinn groaning more huskily, more faintly with every breath.

XI

"GENE SALVIO"

Reata was two thirds of the way back toward the valley, with the sun rolling red in the west, when he saw a horseman swing over a hilltop and drive suddenly down into the hollow where he was traveling. The rider saw Reata, and swung instantly toward him.

Even the weariness of his mustang could not prevent this stranger from showing an essential dash. His style in the saddle was straight without stiffness. He seemed to be all lightness and strength. His hands and his head moved with unusual quickness. There was a decision and a certainty about him. If he had ridden up in a group of a hundred cowpunchers, one could have picked him out in the distance. Even a novice would have said: "That fellow is a real man!"

As he came up to Reata, there was another thing worth noticing, and that was an air of perfect poise. He seemed ready to drop the reins and ride with his knees only, leaving the hands free for other things. And as he came, driving, with the wind of the gallop furling up the brim of his white Stetson and his bandanna fluttering out behind his neck, Reata thought this stranger one of the finest sights he had ever spotted in all of his days.

A moment later, he recognized the dark, handsome face which he had seen in the photograph. It was the third and the greatest of Pop Dickerman's men. It was Gene Salvio, who twice had gone down before Champion, and still clung like a savage hawk to the chase of that greater bird of prey.

Once, Reata had seen a swift duck hawk dropping again and again from the dim zenith at a wide-winged eagle, making the huge king of the air flop over on its back to wait clumsily, foolishly, with talons and beak prepared for the attack. Still the hawk kept swooping and shifting at the last moment from the grasp of those deadly feet, so they had flown out of sight into the horizon.

And Reata thought of that now, as he looked at the lithe, strong, swift body of Gene Salvio. For all his good looks, the savage showed in him, and the wild freedom. He said, as he came up: "Hullo, stranger. What's the good word?"

"The goose hangs high for somebody," said Reata. "How's things for you?"

"I'm looking," said Salvio, "for an *hombre* with a gray horse . . . a whale of a stallion, and a whale of a man on the back of him. He oughta be over in this direction somewhere. Have you seen him?"

He fell in beside Reata. He was nervously alert. With his high head, he seemed to disdain all things around him. He seemed to be wishing to rush over the thin mist of the horizon into a new view of the world. He kept his horse prancing and dancing uneasily, for the spurs, which on the heels of Reata were rather an ornament than a tool, were useful instruments to Gene Salvio. There was a red, round spot in the tenderness of the flank of his good gelding. Pain and fear and labor had widened the nostrils of the horse, and its eyes were red.

Reata looked hastily up from the horse to the man. He hated to give pain, and he hated to see it given. That doubt which he had first felt when he looked at the fine face of Salvio in the picture returned now with a fuller strength. But what could one expect of the men of Dickerman? Keenness and courage and strength, one could hope to find in them, but that was about all. In Harry Quinn, also, a certain faithfulness, perhaps.

147

"I don't know where Bill Champion is," said Reata. "But I can show you the gray, Salvio."

Salvio, thus recognized, jerked about suddenly in the saddle, and could not help darting a hand down to a holster beside him. He kept the hand there, staring at Reata.

"Steady," said Reata, smiling.

"Who are you? I never saw you before," said Salvio.

"Not even in a crowd?" asked Reata, still smiling.

The bright, black eyes of Salvio flashed over him. "No," he said. "I'd remember you. You're easy to remember."

"I never saw you, matter of fact, except in a picture," said Reata. "Dickerman showed you to me."

Salvio tossed back his head with an air of instant understanding. "Dickerman, eh? Old Pop Dickerman, eh? You're with him?"

"I'm with him on loan," said Reata. "My time's about up, I hope."

"What were you talking about . . . Bill Champion and the gray . . . what's the meaning of all of that?" demanded Salvio.

"We've got the gray. We're waiting for Champion to show up on the trail of it. Quinn and Bates and I have the gray, and we're doing the waiting."

The facts went home behind the eyes of Salvio, and at last he brightened with understanding. "All right," he said. "I see the idea. You grab the horse . . . that's bait for Bill Champion . . . and when you have him . . . well, I'm free to go home to Pop. Is that right?"

"You've got the idea," agreed Reata.

"Brains," said Salvio. "Pop always shows the brains, when it comes to punches. How far away is the gray and the camp?"

"There'll still be red in the sky," answered Reata.

Salvio rode hard, but the long roan mare flowed easily along over the ground behind him, while little Rags sat up before his master and squinted his eyes into the wind of that ride. An extra strap gave Rags a foothold for his forepaws, and he balanced himself like a circus dog.

That was how these two men came swinging up the narrow little valley, with the blue gleam of the lake still tarnished by the last of the sunset colors.

"They're gone!" exclaimed Reata. "They've pulled out, Salvio!"

"Maybe they're in the trees," suggested Salvio anxiously.

"In the trees? Where Champion could get 'em in the dark? They wouldn't be fools enough for that. They're gone!"

Silently the two increased the speed of their horses and rushed to the stain of ashes on the ground. Beside it they saw Harry Quinn stretched out in the welter of his own blood; he was still groaning feebly.

It was Salvio who got to the ground first and slashed the cords that were torturing Quinn. It was Reata who heard, before he dismounted, the voice of Dave Bates that called weakly from the cold waters of the lake.

He rode Sue straight into the pool, and carried out Bates to the shore. Even when the ropes were cut, Bates was helpless for a time. But he made no complaints. When he could use his hands, he started massaging his numbed body.

He merely said: "Get a fire going, and work on Harry. He needs you a lot more than I do . . . or else he don't need you at all."

Salvio and Reata worked almost silently. Each knew what had to be done, and there was no need for orders to be given or advice asked. They had Harry Quinn stripped to the hips in no time, and a fire burning to give light and warmth. They washed the wound. And when Reata saw the location of the bullet hole, before and behind, his lips pinched hard together. It looked hopeless. It looked as though even help given at the first moment would have been useless in the end. But they bandaged the wound and stopped the bleeding. They gave Harry Quinn water, and water again, and more water, until the thickness of his tongue was lessened, and his eyes popped out of his head less horribly.

He was out of his head, at first. Only gradually sense came back to him, and, when he made out the voice of Reata, his wits cleared up almost at once. He made a reaching gesture, and Reata gripped his hand.

"You got back," muttered Harry Quinn. "Things'll be all right then. I didn't think that you'd ever get back, but here you are. Reata, it's good to have you around ag'in. It makes things sort of safe, I'd say."

Salvio, at this, looked sharply from the face of the wounded man to that of Reata. He knew Harry Quinn perfectly well and, therefore, his respect for Reata suddenly climbed to the top of a very high ladder.

A good drink of coffee and then a short whiskey poured a bit of strength into Harry Quinn. He kept his eyes closed, and he kept on smiling.

Salvio said to him, rather brutally: "You're hit pretty bad, Harry. This might not turn out very good."

"You think that I'll be cashin'?" said Harry Quinn. "Ain't you got any sense, Gene? It's a joke . . . that's what it is. Bill Champion comes and slams me and pegs me out to die, and I don't die. There wouldn't 'a' been any sense of you fellers comin' along, if I was to die. There's a meanin' and a purpose to everything, Gene. But you're too young, and so you don't understand. Besides, Reata, he knows how to pull a gent through a tight fit."

"Aye," said Salvio thoughtfully. "He must know a lot . . . because Dickerman liked him well enough to give him Sue to ride." A sudden flash of jealousy gleamed in his eyes. "It's more than he ever done for me," he added. Then he said: "Bates, can you talk now?"

"It's easy," said Bates. "We sit here, watchin'. Champion comes out of the woods, near where the gray is chewing the grass. He jumps the stallion and rushes us. He bowls over Harry, and Harry falls into me, and we go down in a heap. And then up comes Champion and picks me out of the heap by the neck. He ties Harry up, talks a bit to me, and then swaddles me up in a rope and chucks me into the lake. I manage to roll myself up the side of the rocks and hitch onto the fresh air ag'in. Then you *hombres* arrive, and there you are. How much nearer are you to Bill Champion than you were back there in Rusty Gulch, Reata?"

"I'm nearer," said Reata. "I know the trail the gray leaves. Where I see it, Rags can smell it. I'm going to find Champion!"

"All by yourself, eh?" asked Gene Salvio critically.

"Your horse can't keep up with Sue," explained Reata.

"That," said Salvio, "is why I'm goin' to ride Sue. This here is my job, partner. And I'm goin' to have the hoss that'll gimme a chance to catch up with Bill Champion. Right now he ain't ten miles away. Bates, you must 'a' seen which way he rode."

"Out straight at the desert," said Dave Bates.

"I'm off!" exclaimed Salvio. "Take care of Quinn, you two. And luck to you!"

With that, he sprang into the saddle on the back of the roan mare.

151

XII

"THE LONG TRAIL"

There was the snaky length of the lariat which could have pitched Salvio out of the saddle in an instant, but Reata did not wish to use it. Instead, he merely whistled, and the good mare answered the spur of Salvio by suddenly rearing, wheeling, and coming down facing Reata.

"You whistled that mare back to you?" shouted Gene Salvio, in a rage. He controlled himself a little. "Maybe you've done a good job, Reata. But here's where your job stops off! Here's where I begin. Champion's my meat, and you know it!"

"Why be a chopping block?" asked Reata. "He's cleaned you up twice already. Get off that mare, Salvio!"

"You mean it, eh?" asked Salvio.

"I mean it."

"Why, then, the devil with you. Come on, Sue! We're off!"

The lariat shot from the hand of Reata, almost invisible in that dim twilight. The underhand flip was hardly a threatening gesture, even, but the narrow, hard coil of the noose struck over the shoulders of Gene Salvio and the binding grip of the rope suddenly imprisoned his arms at his sides.

"Let me go!" yelled Gene Salvio. "I'm goin' to cut you in two for this, Reata!"

He leaped from the saddle, springing down with wonderful lightness in spite of the fact that he could not help himself with his hands. But there was sufficient play in his forearms to enable him to twitch a revolver out of a thigh holster that hung

152

low on his leg. In the madness of that instant, Salvio would have used the gun, too, but he stepped at that moment into a flying coil of the reata and tripped forward on his face.

Reata stooped over him, took his guns and knife, and loosed him from the rope. As he worked, he talked to a face that was frozen with incredulous rage. "If you want to fight for the mare, you can fight with your hands, Salvio," he said. "There's no use shooting each other up for the sake of taking the first crack at Bill Champion. Likely, there's enough of him to go around for both of us, or two times both of us. There you are. Now you can have all the fighting you want."

Gene Salvio, springing like a wildcat to his feet, balanced an instant on tiptoe. He was bent forward, his crouched body ready to hurl at Reata. But something in the quiet expectancy of Reata — not aggressive in the least, and not at all inviting trouble, and yet calmly ready for anything that might happen — something in this fearless and quiet attitude worked so on the mind of Salvio that he broke off to exclaim: "I'm a dummy! I start fighting the gents that have come out to help me, and I'm a fool. Take the mare then. I'll take my own nag. He's got some good work left in him, and I'm goin' to have it out!"

He flung into the saddle as he spoke, and rushed the gelding straight down the valley toward the desert night beyond the hills.

Reata waited for a short time. He took the bridle from the mare, led her to the lake, and gave her a few swallows of water. Then he brought her back, and, opening one of the canvas saddlebags, he gave her a small feed of crushed barley. She devoured it greedily, then started to graze. Reata, lying flat on his back on the grass, paid no heed to her. One would have said that nothing was farther from his mind than the pursuit of Bill Champion, now riding far away on the gray stallion.

But Dave Bates said: "It's brains that wins the race. You

got the brains, Reata."

"He's got the brains," agreed Harry Quinn softly.

"How d'you feel, Harry?" asked Reata.

"Better. Better, and sleepy. I'm goin' to sleep. I'm goin' to get well. I'm goin' to get so well that I'm goin' to be able to laugh. I'm goin' to . . . laugh . . . hard. . . ." His voice trailed away.

Reata smiled at the stars. The coolness of the grass was soaking into him, and the fever of the sun was soaking out. The stars burned down brighter and closer. Under the vast arc of them, the girl was rounded in. She was back at Orchard Creek, by this time. She might be looking up at the same stars, hating him calmly and steadily. Or, perhaps, she was looking up at them and forgiving him. That was more like it. When people have been through many things together, they are more apt to forgive, and distance softens resentment. If he lived, he would come back to her. He would find her, somewhere, and take her away. If he had her and the roan mare and Rags to find a way through the world — well, there would be nothing but happiness. And he, Reata, would reform. He made that resolution almost sleepily, so complete was the relaxing of his body.

At last, he sat up and lighted a cigarette. Dave Bates silently offered him coffee, but he refused it.

"I can live on the thought of Bill Champion," said Reata, inhaling a cloud of the smoke and breathing it out slowly. "What he did to Harry Quinn is better than food and drink to me."

"You're right," said Bates. "And when you catch up with him, you're goin' to find that he expects something big."

"How big?"

"Big as a hornet is to a spider. I put some ideas in his head. But watch yourself, Reata. If he lays hold on you with one finger, he's goin' to smash your bones."

"Thanks," said Reata. "I've been guessing that."

154

He stood up and saddled the mare and bridled her. Then he took Rags and, by match light, picked out the bigger hoof marks left on the grass by the stallion. The little dog sniffed at those prints until he filled his tense, sleek body to trembling with the scent. Then Reata put him upon the saddle and prepared to mount. But first, he kneeled by Quinn and took the cold hand of the sleeper for a moment.

When he stood up, Bates said: "It's a funny thing. When a gent is down, you get to thinkin' about the good side of him. I never knew that Harry had a good side, till now. He didn't do no groanin' till he was out of his head. He put up a good show, Reata."

"There's something right in him," agreed Reata. He held out his hand. "I wish I could have you along with me."

"There's no place where I'd rather be," answered the other earnestly. "But maybe I'd only make a bigger spot for Champion to see. Mind you, Reata, he's got everything. He's big, but he's as fast as a cat. He's as fast, almost, as you are. And he can't miss with a gun. He had his hoss at a full gallop when he slammed a slug into Harry Quinn. And nobody's shootin' straight off the back of a runnin' hoss. Nobody but Bill Champion."

"I'll go after him," said Reata cheerfully, "with both my eyes wide open. So long, Dave. Be seeing you later, I hope."

He mounted. He did not put the mare into a canter. Although he rode on that long trail to catch Bill Champion, he let the mare drift down the valley at an easy trot.

XIII

"THE DESERT"

A loping horse will catch a blooded racer; a trotting horse will wear down the one that lopes; and the walking horse, if the distance is great enough, will surely finish off all the others.

Reata knew the span of that desert into which the valley had pointed like a gun barrel. He had not crossed it, but he knew the look of it from the surrounding mountains and the width of it on the map, and he could judge it by its fellows. The result was that he kept the mare at a trot, and out of the valley they passed into the desert itself.

There he swung down from the saddle. The ground was not firm. A lot of it was the sort of blow sand that shifts like mercury under foot and kills the heart of man or beast. Ten minutes of running will kill a cowpuncher in his ordinary riding boots, but the boots of Reata were as supple as kid and made for running as well as riding. So he struck out at his own dog-trot and took the killing burden of his weight off the back of the mare.

He grew tired. His legs ached. His very arms ached at the shoulders from the constant swing. But he stuck with the work like a day laborer who knows the pain of extended effort.

He had a mare that already had covered a great distance that day. He was pursuing a man on a powerful and fresh horse. And if he were to wear Bill Champion down, he would have to use every device known to him, and in every way supplement the strength of Sue. He had one element fighting for him, and that was the weight of the gray horse on these treacherous sands, and, above all, the crushing burden of Bill Champion himself, which must be killing the stallion. In order to take advantage of this factor of weight, he had to keep traveling, not fast, but steadily. There was time. By the brightness of the next dawn they would be among the painted mesas on the farther side of the desert, and after that they would get into the mountains. Before the mountains were reached, he hoped to be at Bill Champion.

Mile by mile, the desert flowed slowly behind him. In the painful illusion which came to him, it seemed as though the earth were in motion beneath him, bearing him back on a vast treadmill. But he had strength to draw upon in various ways. He could remember old Pop Dickerman's description of the frightful face of Champion. He could remember how the girl had covered her face at the thought of him; he could remember, last of all, how he had carried Bates like a drowning rat out of the lake, and how he had taken the cold hand of poor Harry Quinn in his and seen by firelight the gray death invading the face of the man. When he thought of these things, they did not oppress his spirit. They gave him power which he could translate into more miles.

They crossed the shifting sand and gained, at once, a firmer footing and a belt of greater heat. It seemed as though the fierceness of the sun had soaked deeper into the ground here, and, therefore, it was radiated for a longer time. The soil was more rocks than earth, but little Rags rarely had to drop his muzzle to the surface. He could read the scent as easily with his head up, and his small feet kept twinkling on.

The moon rose. Its silver light seemed to be bringing the suffocating heat down through the windless air, but it showed the way to Reata's own eyes for the first time. He could see, here and there, the big imprint of the hoofs of the gray horse.

And he knew that Rags was running true.

Thirst began to parch his throat. Well, they would have to come to water before long. The bigger Bill Champion was, the huger his horse, the more need there was of water for them, and their trail would touch at water holes. Reata had filled two canteens before starting. He made a brief halt now, and took a swallow out of one canteen. Then he held it at the mouth of the mare. She took hold of it as though she were trained in drinking from a bottle, and swallowed down the contents. That was fuel against the time to come, and the mare needed that help not long after, when they came again to soft sand.

Reata had ridden across the firm ground; he forced himself to go on foot again, when they came to the soft. He was still very tired. His left foot was chafing badly. There was blood in that boot, or else he did not know the meaning of pain. But small things like that had to be taken for granted. If his whole body were roasted in fire, it would not keep him, he knew, from going forward.

Then he saw a strange silhouette before him. It grew clearer. He made out a man seated on the prone body of a horse, and he knew what that meant. It was Gene Salvio, who had rushed into the desert thinking that his horse could live on the red of the spur. That horse was dead, and Salvio was there with his head in his hands, grinding his teeth, cursing life. There was nothing to be done for Salvio, and, therefore, Reata called Rags in and took a deliberate detour to the side.

A shout challenged him before he had gone far. He looked and saw that Salvio was on his feet, running, waving his hands in wild gesticulations, and calling out, again and again: "Reata! Reata!"

Reata swung into the saddle, snatched up Rags, and put the mare to a canter. He knew that Salvio was desperate, but he was not prepared for what followed. Salvio dropped to one knee, steadied his revolver with a rest, and fired a bullet that whined in the air right across the face of Reata. That was it. For the sake of a better chance at Bill Champion, Salvio was ready to murder any friend.

The mare did not need heel or hand. She was instantly running like the wind, that wire-strung body of hers stretching out as straight as a string. Another and another shot followed, all whirring frightfully close. And then the shooting ended.

Looking back, Reata saw Salvio throwing up his hands into the air, and then running like a madman to overtake the horse. In a sense, no doubt, the man *was* mad. He was one of Pop Dickerman's poisonous rats, cornered and savage for the fight.

But Gene Salvio dropped away in the distance, and again Reata was on foot, driving ceaselessly forward. The heat was so intense that already he was beginning to have the water dreams. Little moments like sleep overcame his weary body and his brain, and he found himself starting back to full consciousness with a sound of water in his ears, not the faintly musical trickling of a little stream, but the chiming and gushing outpouring of whole cataracts that cooled the winds and gave a delicious savor of wetness to the air. Always, of course, the hot, narrow horizon of the desert closed in upon him again, and yet again the delirium returned and brought him one high-hearted instant of hope, insane hope, to be followed by the realization of the truth.

Then they found the first water at which Bill Champion had stopped. Rather, it was not water but seethed mud. For Champion, after watering himself and his horse, had ridden the stallion around and around the banks of the hole and trampled the alkaline soil into the water. It was fouled and spoiled. And that was murder. Men might come to this place on their last legs, their blood and their brains on fire with desperation, and they would find a slimy mess instead of life. Reata trembled with hot anger. But he was almost glad, because Champion had to die and he was the appointed executioner.

He poured from his last canteen, a bit of water on a clean bandanna, and with it he swabbed out the mouth of the mare. He parted her teeth and reached far back and washed off the scum and the grit from her tongue and the roof of her mouth, and then he cleaned the nostrils as deeply as he could. Afterward, he poured some of that precious fluid into the palm of his hand. At the touch of it, a frightful desire came to dash the liquid down his own throat. But he set his teeth and grinned back the temptation. He lowered his hands, and Rags whined with delight as he drank. Again, and again, he emptied the hollow palm of that hand. Then Reata stood up and poured the rest down the throat of the mare, and he struck on again through the desert.

It had been right, he felt. Without the strong legs of Sue, without the faultless nose of Rags, he would be a useless wanderer along this trail. And as for himself, no matter if the fire were mounting out of his throat and into his brain, he had human thought and invention to feed him and to give him drink. So, through the endless soft of the sand, he kept plugging along at his work, remembering what he had heard an Indian say, that the way to keep breathing is to keep the chin tucked down a little. Let the chin rise and the head begins to fall back, the throat muscles strain, the whole body bends and labors, before long. So, no matter how he felt his strength giving way, he jogged on with chin down, breathing deeply of that acrid air.

After all, there would have to be another water hole before very long. Bill Champion would never take a trail that he did not know by heart. There would be more water, and Champion, of course, would not spoil the second drinking place. He would depend upon the fouling of the first one to discourage any hunters who might venture along his trail — not even a Bill

160

Champion, beast though he might be, would venture on ruining two water holes in the parching middle of the desert!

That hope kept Reata swinging along in his stride, until they reached a firm footing once more, and he climbed dizzily into the saddle again. He picked up Rags to rest the little dog, also, since it was certain that Rags could not endure this pace forever. Rags kept shuddering, as though in pain. It was the pain of terrible thirst, Reata knew, that tormented the poor little dog.

So they crossed the desert to the second water hole and found — that it had been destroyed, exactly like the first. In the vagueness of his mind, in his desperation, Reata drove his hands to the wrists in the mud. It was warm. It would have been as hot as blood. Aye, and it would have meant the blood of life to them. Champion had done his work again. If he had killed men before, he had killed treble the number now, for men who trusted the second water hole would die of sheer despair when they came to the place and found it ruined.

But Reata did not die of despair. His throat and mouth were so dry that he could have bitten his own arm and sucked the blood like that fevered wretch in the poem. But he sat cross-legged and put his chin on his hands and made himself swallow and wondered how long it would be before the swelling of his tongue forced him to open his mouth to the air.

If the sun had been shining. . . . Aye, but under the sun there is always a brighter hope and a wider horizon, with new visions always rolling in upon the mind. But here, the moon radiating in a small circle through the misty air of the desert, it seemed to him that he was traveling in the very country of death.

Rest was the next best thing to water. He rested, therefore, lying on his back, his arms outstretched. And little Rags came and sat down beside his face with his tongue hanging out, shuddering back and forth with the rapidity of his panting. And now and again, as though on a drawn breath, Rags moaned with the greatness of his despair. Only the mare seemed brave and hopeful. Queer cartoon that she was, she kept her ears pricked as though she knew good things about the future, and Reata loved her for her courage. He could remember now that Dickerman had promised her as a gift, a great bonus, if the three men were actually brought back to Rusty Gulch. Well, he would have her. The thought poured a bit of new strength into him.

He got up and resumed the way, not walking, but always at a shambling run. For walking would not overtake the great Bill Champion in the width of this desert. He put up Rags on the saddle, only taking the little dog down, now and again, to solve some riddle in the disappearing trail. The nose of Rags had become the second most important thing in the world.

XIV

"THE GOLDEN STREAK"

Sometimes it seemed to Reata, as he went on, that this was the fire of torment that purified mind and soul as metal is purified before the forge hammers begin their play — he would have the hammering, too, before very long.

Time went out of his mind. There were ways of measuring it, however. He could count his burning footsteps to a hundred and then another hundred. He could tell himself that he would mount the saddle after another hundred strides, and then another hundred, and then another. Or he could listen to the thudding pulse in his temple that plainly told of an over-worked engine. Queer crowds of words and thoughts and memories bumped roughly into his mind, each thing repeated to the verge of madness. He had to keep his chin down and run. He had to keep his chin down and run. Chin down — run. Chin down — run. Chin down — run. That was the way phrases took possession of him and beat out the words slowly in his mind, one for every stride he took.

Then he found himself running open-mouthed, babbling the words, and staggering as he ran. This frightened him back to soberness. He mounted the saddle and told himself grimly that he would see how long the mare could last. But there was no wearing Sue out. She kept on with her wire-strung body, her gaunt, swinging legs as though she did not know what fatigue might mean. Dickerman had once said that she could get fat on thistles. Fat — thistles. Fat — thistles.

Well, why not? A fellow could chew the green stalk of a this-tle, and the sap would be like water. It would be better than wa-ter. It would be better than wine. The green sap of thistles would be life. Thistles — life — thistles — life.

And then they struck soft going again. He slid from the sad-dle. His knees sagged when his feet hit the ground, but he be-gan to run. Those refrains that had been maddening him were now a help, a comfort, a strength to lean upon. He welcomed them into his mind, and suddenly he found that the words would come no more. All that he could think about was the twinkling feet of little Rags as the dog made the way sure, and the sliding crunch of the hoofs of Sue behind him, and the pain of breathing. He was sure that the membrane was peeling in-side his throat, inside his lungs.

He saw Rags stumble, recover, stumble and recover again. Rags was going out. Rags was near the limit. But the little dog always recovered and went on with a suddenly fresh spurt. He realized, in a golden burst of feeling, that they were both heroes — the mare and Rags. Not beautiful, but heroes. They knew nothing about the goal toward which he was driving them so re-morselessly, but they were sticking to their jobs, blindly, with-out complaint.

The going began to be firmer once more. He pulled himself into the saddle again, and this time, not only were his knees nearly numb, but there was so little strength in his arms that they shuddered and shook under the weight of his body, which he was pulling up. This was a thing to worry about. This was a frightful calamity — if the strength went out of his arms and the cunning out of his hands. For all that he had was the strength of those arms — worthless, almost, against the brute force of the great Champion — and the cunning of his hands.

Brains will win. That was what Bates had said. Yes, but brains will not win without hands to serve. And his hands were

164

going. They trembled, even when he rested them folded on the pommel of the saddle.

Sue carried on, while the head of Reata bobbed sleepily. The mare went on like a ship of the desert, carried by winds, without effort. It was for this that all flesh was stripped from her. She was simply heart and lungs mounted on wire-strung legs that would not fall.

Well, Champion had a big start, a long start, but how far away could he be, even now? At that, Reata looked up, and suddenly he saw what seemed to him the mighty parapets of heaven, with all the gates flung wide and dim, gold shining out. His staggering mind realized, in a moment, that he had come to the verge of the great painted mesas at the foot of the mountains. And this was the golden dawn that was pouring out through them, gilding the cañons. It was beautiful. He told himself that only a man near to death could realize how beautiful it was. And then he remembered another thing. Through these cañons, men said who had traveled through the desert, small streams of water ran and passed a little distance into the desert, and there were drunk up and wasted.

He glanced to the left. There ran a streak of faint gold far out into the desert for miles and miles. In a moment, he realized that it was water, with the dawn color reflecting from it. Water that he had been running so near all this time — that he could have had an hour ago, a sweet eternity ago, perhaps. But he had stuck to the trail. He began to laugh, hysterically, and then he was aware, like the old illusion that had haunted him so often during this nightmare of a journey, that there was a sound of gushing waters. No, it was no illusion, but the mighty truth. There, at the entrance to the first cañon, making its last leap down from the mountains, there was a little crystal cataract — and both his own will and the trail of Bill

165

Champion led straight for that point.

It grew bigger. The mare was cantering of her own will, stretching out her head. If that brilliance of flinging water had been composed of fine diamonds, it could not have been half so beautiful, so bright, so invaluable. Reata flung himself out of the saddle. He plunged his face into the water — and he could not drink. He was merely stifling himself, but he could not swallow a drop. He had to sit up and take the water in his hand and let a bit of it flow into his mouth and so trickle, little by little, into the burning heat of his throat. He could swallow then. He gathered handfuls of the water, laughing crazily, and drank from his hands.

What was that story in the Bible about those soldiers being chosen, who, in the water famine, when they came to the river drank like men from their hands, and not with lowered heads, like beasts? Somehow, he found an omen in that. Bill Champion was a beast, and Reata would have to play the part of a man. And always there was that shaking laughter in his breast.

Afterward, he sat up, dizzy, and looked around him at the unreal beauty of that world of the dawn. He stood up. Strength had returned to his body and steadiness to his hands. Actually it was as though he had been drinking, not water, but the very blood of life.

The canteens were not filled. There was no need for them in a world of many waters, a blessed mountain world. There was no need of anything now, except to hope that the nose of Rags would be able to follow the sign of the gray stallion over the naked, the iron-hard trails that wound along the sides of these cañons. The big, flat-topped mesas stood out against him with a degree of scorn, forbidding him to carry his petty hopes and his malice into their great domain. But presently, he was traveling up a sharp slope along a narrow, jutting trail, with Rags, head down, working hard on the sign of the gray horse.

166

The way wound upward dizzily. And still Rags kept true where the trail forked at the coming in of a greater ravine. They turned down the side of a very narrow valley, its walls of red rock with the gold of the dawn dripping over the polished surfaces. Above them was the sky, golden, too. Beneath them the waters of the creek that had carved out these rocks was gilded, also. Heaven help the man for whom existence was blotted out in a world so beautiful.

The trail wound steadily. He had a glimpse of a place where the creek had tunneled through the base of a giant wall, on the face of which the trail crooked back and traveled again across the opposite side of the ravine, hardly twenty-five or thirty feet away. That was when he heard the clang of the rifle, monstrously loud, and felt the sting of a bullet that drove through his left thigh cleanly.

He fell forward on his hands and his right knee. Even in falling, he had snatched out the reata from his pocket, but it slithered out of his hand and dropped not over the edge of the cliff but down a ragged gap in the floor of the trail. He was helpless, and from the other side of the ravine a vast, beastly, booming voice was roaring down at him.

XV

"THE LARIAT"

He turned his head slowly. He was seeing clearly through this trick of fate, which brought him gloriously across the desert, gloriously into the presence of his enemy, and then let him be blind. Why, fool that he was, had he not realized that Bill Champion must be very close? For how else would Rags have been able to follow a scent over those rocks of red iron? If there had been half a wit in his head, he would have known that he was on the very heels of his quarry.

Then he saw the man. The gray stallion was there, also, a weary horse with a downward head. If only he, Reata, had been in the saddle when that rifle spoke, instead of saving the mare by taking the steep of that strong incline on foot, she would have carried him swiftly past danger of rifle fire around the corner of the next rock. And, after that, wounded as he was, he would have been able to shift for himself.

Little Rags came whining back and stood upon his hind legs to lick his master's face.

Reata merely muttered: "Fetch it, Rags! Down! Rags! Fetch it, boy!"

Rags jumped back and canted his head to one side. How would the poor dog be able to understand that his master wanted that slenderly coiling snake of a lariat back in his hand?

So, calmly, despairingly, Reata looked up, and across the ravine at the face of the rifleman. Even death was made more horrible by the sight of the featureless slab of gristle. It was like standing half in hell and half out to confront the monster.

Bill Champion was laughing, but not enough to shake the arm of the rifle at his shoulder. It was hardly a sound of laughter so much as the snarling of a happy wolf. It was not the look of laughter, but a writhing of the face only.

"Hi, Reata," said Bill Champion. "I'm glad to see you, boy."

"Hi, Champion," said Reata, "I'm seeing you, too."

"How does it feel?" asked Champion, behind his rifle.

"Like a hammer stroke . . . with a wasp sitting in the center of the bruise. Sort of numb, Champion."

"That's a pretty good description," said Champion. "That's what a bullet through the leg feels like. I wasn't sure that I'd sock the slug through your leg, at first. I thought that I'd put it through your head. But I didn't want to have only one mouthful of you. I wanted to *see* you die, Reata."

"That's natural," said Reata. "What made you doubt your rifle, Bill?"

"A fool of a dead man," said Bill Champion. "He went and talked you up like you was somebody. And when it comes to travelin', you are. You're a travelin' fool, all right. I didn't think that nobody would show up on the trail behind me, as fast as this. And then I seen you. And I had to laugh, Reata, when I seen you ridin' right up, blind as a bat."

"Yes, I was the fool," said Reata.

"You was the fool, all right. I spotted you by the little dog that I'd heard about from the Gypsies."

"They told you about me, eh?"

"Not Queen Maggie," said Champion. "Damn me if she ain't sort of fond of you. The others, they talked plenty. But Queen Maggie, she held back. She wouldn't talk none. What would she see in a sawed-off runt like you, eh?"

"Women are queer," said Reata.

"That's a true word," said Bill Champion. "But bust loose and tell me something. Damn me if I don't always learn something from my dead men."

"What'll I tell you?"

"Why, the last dead man that I left behind me, he told me that you was hell on wheels, and he told me to keep in a hole, when I seen you coming. Well, I kept in a hole, all right. I pulled in out of sight, and just looked over the rim of the rock to slam you. But there ain't nothin' to you. You ain't no kind of a fightin' man. Reata! Bates, he's as sure a liar as he's sure dead."

"All right," said Reata. "You'll have to choke that one down, because he's not dead."

"He's as dead as water can drown him."

"He's not dead. He wormed his way up in a rock in the lake. That lake was only a shallow pool, Bill. If you'd had good sense, you would have made sure of that. You want to drop a man out of his depth before you are so sure of drowning him."

"I ain't got good sense?"

"You're too big to be very bright, Bill," said Reata. "All you big beefy boys depend on your hands, instead of your head. That's why you don't have a chance in the long run."

"A chance? What sort of a chance have *you* got?"

"I'm not dead yet."

"You're goin' to be, and *pronto,* too!"

"I'll believe that when the lights go out," said Reata.

As he said this, out of the tail of his eye he marked the fuzzy head of little Rags appearing out of the gap in the floor of the trail, with the end of the lariat gripped between his teeth. Reata had it instantly in his fingers.

How much would Bill Champion see? In that beautiful but uncertain golden light of the dawn, how much could he see? Reata raised the hand that now held the end of the thin lariat and knotted it swiftly inside the stirrup leather that hung down close to him. For the mare had halted in place and remained there, motionless. Now the rope was anchored. Without motion of his arm, with the working of his dexterous fingers only, he began to gather in the sleek, meager coils of the reata.

"How long, brother, you think you're goin' to live?" asked Champion, his wide mouth actually gaping.

"Why, I don't know," answered Reata. "There are a lot of things that can happen to you, Bill."

"Are you bleedin' a lot?" asked Champion eagerly.

"Not a lot. A rifle bullet doesn't tear up the way a Forty-Five caliber slug does."

"You would 'a' used a revolver, would you?"

"No. I never carry a gun."

"You never what?" shouted Champion. He stepped forward to the edge of the rock, with the perilous drop down the cañon wall unheeded at his toes. "You mean that you never carry a gun? What you talkin' about?"

"I'm telling you the truth. Now and then it pays, Bill."

"How would you 'a' done anything to me, if you *had* caught up with me?"

Anything to keep the monster occupied, while that forty feet of line gradually retreated into the hand of Reata, gradually gathered in, as a spider gathers in its longest thread of silk with rapid claws.

"Didn't Bates tell you what I could do?" asked Reata.

"No. He didn't tell me. Hypnotism, or some fool thing like that, he talked about. You might as well try to hypnotize one of these here cliffs as to make a dent in me with your eyes, Reata."

"That's right," said Reata. "A fellow has to have a brain to work on."

"Look here," complained Bill Champion — and Reata could almost have smiled as he listened — "you think that I'm some kind of a wooden dummy, do you? You don't know

171

nothin' whatsoever about me, do you?"

"Oh, I know enough," said Reata. "You've got hands big enough to break a neck or two, now and then. That's all you have. And you're willing to shoot from behind. That's why you've killed your men."

"Did I shoot Gene Salvio from behind?" shouted the giant.

"That's what Salvio told me," lied Reata smoothly.

"He told you that? The . . . why, the sneak! He won't give me no credit, eh?"

"Why should he," asked Reata, "when you're running away from him all over the lot?"

"Running away? From him? Who said that he was after me?"

"He's back there in the desert now, and you know it," replied Reata. "And that's why you humped across the desert so fast and even smashed in the water holes on your way. You're afraid of Salvio. Why don't you make yourself easy and tell the truth?"

"The truth? It ain't the truth! It's the worst lie that anybody ever wriggled his tongue around. Why, I was kind of sorry, almost, to step on you after you come so fast across the desert after me. I was goin' to ask you how you managed to come through that hell without no water for two whole stages . . . but the way you yarn, and lie, damn me if it ain't goin' to be good to sink a chunk of lead into you and finish you off."

"Now?" asked Reata.

"Yeah, right now."

"I'll take it standing up, then," said Reata.

He had gathered in the subtle coils of the lariat, by that time. He had spread, with the magic of his fingers, a sufficient noose. And all he wanted now was to stand erect for a single instant. So he grasped the stirrup leather and pulled himself halfway to his feet.

The rifle clanged. A bullet slid like the thrust of a hot needle

172

through his right thigh, and the numbed leg let him down with a thud on the rock. He sat up and stared at Bill Champion, and, with a gesture, pushed the coils of the slithering rope behind him. His right hand hungrily fingered the noose.

Champion was shouting: "I'll learn you to try to move before I want you to! I wish that I could make you die the way Quinn died! That'd do me a lot of good, to tie you up like that and let you stare at the sun till you died!" He added: "Are you ready?"

"I'm ready any old time," said Reata. "But don't think that you killed Quinn. He's a tough *hombre,* that Quinn."

"Dead! I got him right through the body."

"That's what you think. The bullet just kind of glanced around his ribs, that's all, and then came out his back."

"What you mean?" roared Champion.

"I mean he was sitting up with coffee in one hand and a smoke in the other, when I last saw him. Does that sound dead to you?"

"By thunder," muttered Champion, and even that muttering wakened a sullen echo up the wall of the ravine. "I pretty near believe what you say."

"You ought to. The truth ought to be pretty fine for you to hear, Bill."

"Would you take and swear on your word of honor that Quinn was alive at sundown?"

"I'll swear that."

"And Bates, too?"

"I'll swear that."

"What's the matter with me?" exclaimed Bill Champion. "I dunno what's the matter today."

"You don't understand," said Reata. He had struck on a sore chord.

"Don't understand? What don't I understand? First Bates talks about me not being able to understand, and then you begin to yammer like a fool at me about not understanding. What don't I understand?"

"There's not much good explaining," said Reata. "It's too deep for you, Bill. It's one of those things that a big, beefy fellow like you wouldn't be able to understand. Didn't Bates tell you what it was that was too deep for you?"

"Bates? What would Bates know that might be too deep for me?"

"He didn't tell you, eh? Why, Bill, it's hard to explain. But everybody knows, the minute you've said two words. . . ."

"They know what?"

"They know what's wrong with you, Bill."

"I've got a mind to come around there and wring it out of you. Talk out! What you mean, Reata?"

"You've never seen people laughing at you?"

"Laughing at me? I'd tear their hearts out!"

"Think back, Bill. You're not very bright, but you ought to be able to remember. You've walked past people, and felt 'em smiling behind you?"

Bill Champion seemed stunned.

"I dunno," he muttered, the words carrying dull and thick to the ear of Reata. "I dunno what's behind it all. Maybe they've smiled. But why would they smile at me?"

"You ought to be able to see. It's why I'm smiling now, Bill."

"You're goin' to stop laughin'," shouted Bill Champion. "You're having your last laugh now! Rifle bullets don't mean so much, eh? I'm goin' to chop you up with slugs out of a Colt. I'm goin' to whittle you away, Reata, little by little!" He turned, as he spoke, and wrenched a long Colt out of the saddle holster on the gray stallion.

It was for that moment that Reata had talked and worked and waited, with the sharp agony of the wounds growing momentarily greater. Now he swayed his body forward until he

174

pitched up onto his knees, the torn legs shuddering under the weight. And with a wide, underhanded sweep, he hurled the noose of the rope. It carried like a flung stone. He thought, for a moment, that the noose would not open, that he had hurled it too flat, but at the last instant, as though a snaky brain worked in the thing, it spread out and dropped as the big man turned.

It seemed to Reata that there was not even time to let the coil settle. The instant it was over the head, he snatched the grip of the running noose tight around the throat of Bill Champion and with his wrench on the line made the monster totter on the verge of the abyss.

That moment would have been the end of Champion, but grasping wildly back, the gun falling from his hand, he caught the gray horse by the reins, and that pull steadied him.

"Sue!" Reata screamed, and slapped her with his hand.

His own strength of both arms was a mere nothing against the power of Champion. With his one free hand, the monster snatched the line quite out of the hands of Reata, and then jerked the noose open. He was free — no, for at that moment the trotting mare brought the line tight. The noose jerked hard in, imprisoning the one hand of Champion. He was thrust forward by the pull. Still, with his other hand, he gripped the bridle of the gray and actually brought the stallion slithering forward and down the shelving surface of the trail until the gray, as though disdaining fear, as though familiar with frightful needs in following its master, suddenly rose and leaped far out into the ravine.

The two bodies dropped out of view. Reata then heard the sound of the body of the hanging man as it thudded against the side of the cliff. Next, he heard the crash of the horse beneath. And faintly, out of strangled throat, Reata halted the mare with a word.

175

XVI

"BACK AT RUSTY GULCH"

He had to loose the lariat, when he had dragged himself to the mare, from the stirrup leather. And he heard the second sound of the fall of Bill Champion on the red rocks of the ravine below. After that, he had to make the bandages for his wounded legs. Finally, there was the need of pulling himself up into the saddle. He managed that, his body limp as a sack, his legs quite useless. Balanced in the saddle, he turned the mare down the old Spanish trail and passed to the bottom of the ravine, then up beside the foaming waters until he reached the place where Champion lay.

It was hard to loosen the reata, it had sunk so deeply into the thick of the neck, but he managed it with weakening hands. Afterward, from his saddlebag, he got out the ration of hardtack and raisins, and slowly munched them.

The pain from his feet was much greater, even now, than the pain of his wounds, which were merely a dull, numb ache. He worked off his boots and dipped his raw and bleeding feet in the cold water.

His shirt and undershirt had been torn to bits to make the bandages for his wounds. And that was the way they found him, sitting with his back to a rock, calmly smoking a cigarette and looking up toward the bright sun that was now flooding that narrow street which the edges of the cliffs fenced through the morning sky.

The yipping of Rags, when he heard hoofbeats, was what had called the attention of the sheriff and his men, but, as they came up the ravine, a haggard set with their horses staggering under them, Miriam fled before them, galloping her mustang among the boulders.

She was on her knees when the sheriff came up. She was babbling out things that had not a great deal of meaning, and Reata was smiling up at her in a curious, detached sort of way.

The sheriff looked at this scene with a frown, as though he derived great pain from it. Then he went to the body of the gray horse, and last of all stood with his three men — all who had managed to keep their horses going across the desert — and looked down at the last of Bill Champion. The mark of the reata was around his neck, sunk in deeply, marked with red and purple.

"It ain't possible," said the sheriff. "The way I see it, Champion was able to sink two bullets through him. And yet he was able after that to shake that reata around Champion's neck . . . and do this. It ain't possible . . . but here's the dead man laying!"

He went back to Reata and leaned over him. "The hoosegow for you, son," said the sheriff.

"I have to lie up for a while, anyway," answered Reata.

"Don't talk to him," pleaded the girl. "Not till you've told me if you forgive me, Reata."

"Why, all that anybody can do is his best," said Reata. "You did your best and brought along the sheriff, and the sheriff wants to take me where I can find a doctor and stretch out long and lazy, till I've got two good pins under me again. What could be better than that? You knew I'd need an ambulance, and I wouldn't want a better driver than ol' Lowell Mason."

In fact, Reata was "stretched out long and lazy" in Rusty

Gulch, but not in the jail. They put him in the hotel, instead, while letters and telegrams poured in on the governor of the state. A federal marshal spent forty minutes telling the governor a few details concerning the life and crimes of Bill Champion, and after that a free pardon came down for Reata.

It must be admitted that he enjoyed his convalescence immensely. His visitors ranged from the sheriff up and down through various degrees of the community. Salvio came in one day and stood turning his hat in his hands and staring at the wounded man, and asking his forgiveness, and getting it. Then Salvio gave one keen, bright flash of a look at Miriam, and went out.

"What did that look mean?" asked Reata.

"It means that I'll see him again. He knows that, too. It means he'll have some trouble . . . and that he *doesn't* know," said the girl.

Reports came in that Bates was still caring for Quinn, who was progressing very favorably.

And then, one day, two strange personalities met at Reata's bedside — Queen Maggie and Pop Dickerman. They walked in at almost the same moment, and Reata introduced them. He used phrases that had been in his mind long before.

"Maggie," he said, "I want you to meet Pop Dickerman, the king of the rats. Pop, this is Queen Maggie, the queen of the cats. You two ought to know each other."

They did not make a foolish gesture at shaking hands. They merely stared and grinned.

"How come you wasn't hanged a long time ago?" Maggie asked.

"They wouldn't bother," said Pop Dickerman. "They been too busy lookin' for you." And he stroked his long, furry face.

"Get out and leave me talk business," said Queen Maggie.

Pop Dickerman got out, grinning, for he felt that he had had the best of the encounter, and Queen Maggie sat down and put her spurred heels on the edge of the table. She lighted a thick, oily Havana and closed her eyes during the first few, sweet puffs. Then she said: "Things is all gone bust with the tribe, Miriam. The boys are gettin' out of hand. They get drunk . . . the police slam 'em in jail . . . and there ain't any Miriam to talk 'em out again. We give our show, and we get pennies instead of dollars, because Miriam ain't there to give us a cymbal crash at the wind-up. Honey, why don't you come back to the easy life?"

"There's the reason," said the girl, pointing at Reata.

"A rotten reason," said Queen Maggie. "Listen to me, Reata. Ain't you a rotten reason?"

"Sure I am," said Reata.

"He knows he is," said Queen Maggie, puffing around her words thick clouds of strong tobacco smoke. "You wouldn't have no kind of a life with him. It'd be marriage, wouldn't it?"

"That's what it seems like," Miriam answered.

"He'll keep you toeing a chalk mark," advised Queen Maggie. "Wouldn't you, Reata?"

"Yes," said Reata.

"In his house there'd be only one boss. Wouldn't there, Reata?"

"Only one," agreed Reata calmly.

"He's been around so much that he knows things, and you couldn't cut no corners. Miriam, it'd be a bust. Can't you see that?"

Miriam said nothing.

"And ain't there no cravin' in you for Gypsy stew and Gypsy days and Gypsy nights, honey?" asked Queen Maggie. "Don't you kind of hunger a bit to hear old Maggie cussin' around the camp and watchin' the pots over the fire?"

"I hunger pretty bad for all of it," said Miriam, "and the

tights and ruffles and . . . and the flounces and the people yelling. But I don't know. I guess I'll stay here while I'm wanted."

"Hi!" shouted Queen Maggie, leaping to her feet. "You mean to say that you've found your boss? You found your master?"

"It looks that way," said the girl. "It's mighty hard, but it looks that way. I'm going to be a sick cat a lot of the time, but it looks as though I've found my boss."

"I see it in your eyes," said Queen Maggie heavily. "You used to be a wild young heifer cutting up capers. But I can see the heavy look, the cow look, all over your eyes. Reata, treat her fine, but don't keep sharp knives in your house."

The Gauntlet

"The Gauntlet" under the byline George Owen Baxter first appeared in Street & Smith's *Western Story Magazine* (11/12/21). Frederick Faust was intrigued by the way in which human beings come to choose what they believe is an ideal mate. In the fairy tale, "Aschenputtel" ["Cinderella"], recorded by the Brothers Grimm, the prince, of course, goes in search of the one woman in all the kingdom whose slender foot will fit into a glass slipper. In this story, Larrimee imagines his soul-mate to be the woman whose hand will fit a certain glove. She is known only as "Lady." It remained an intriguing notion that Faust would later incorporate into one of his finest novels, first published as a six-part serial titled "Galloping Danger" by Max Brand in *Western Story Magazine* (7/14/23 - 8/18/23). In book form it appears as THE QUEST OF LEE GARRISON (Circle Ⓥ Westerns, 1998). In "The Gauntlet" this notion has a very different, if no less striking, outcome.

I

"A MAN MADE FOR MINING"

"When making a long and difficult trail," says the book, "the pack should, of course, be lightened as much as possible; it should contain only essentials for the preservation of life and health; and, under no circumstances shall nonessential articles be admitted. Remember that an extra pound carried twenty days is equal to twenty pounds carried for one day."

Now, Joseph Stillwater Larrimee, better known in that district of the Rocky Mountains as plain Larry, was wise in the ways of trails, and yet he carried on his back an extra burden of needless weight. He had carried it well over a hundred miles, and he would have carried it a hundred more, if need be, for the extra weight was a heavy yellow metal, and the value of it ran up into the thousands.

It represented, on the face of it, some nine odd months of labor, digging and blasting and washing; in reality, it meant three or four years of patient drudgery, spent in prospecting, then working for wages until another stake was accumulated, then another splurge, wandering among lonely places and tapping rocks. But, in the joy of the weight that now tugged down against his shoulders, the long work, the long waiting for a reward seemed to Larrimee only a moment's space; and the gold was like a gift of Providence. Moreover, there was more of it in the district adjoining his strike, and, when he returned, it would be with a fine outfit, men to work under his directions, and the prospects of making a clean-up.

He paused on the top of the hill to readjust his load and to scan the distance. He could make it out distinctly enough, the scattered village tucked away under the horizon. That was his immediate goal, and his eyes brightened as he saw it.

He would make up for that. When he struck the town, the report of his coming would be an explosion resounding for miles around. "One large, long, rounded-out party" was the way Larrimee phrased it to himself.

Lowering the hand which had been screening his eyes, he looked in detached surprise at the back of it. Once it had sun-burned to a fiery red which then deepened to coppery-brown, but now it was more coppery-black. Continual exposure to sun, which had no mercy, had given him the color of an Indian — and not a light-colored Indian at that. When he smiled, as he did very often, even when he was alone, his teeth were glistening white against the darkness of that skin.

Beneath the ragged clothes the lines of his body suggested a strength as durable as that weathered skin. He was not overly tall; he was not ponderously broad; but there was an impressive gathering of bulk about the shoulders and a tapering toward the waist which, since the beginning of time, have meant the maximum strength and the maximum activity combined. One can tell of some men whether they are meant for mere physical labor day after day, or for endurance in walking, or for sprinting, or for handling weights, or, perhaps, for the boxing arena. But no one could place that all-round type of Larrimee. Now he was gaunt from excessive labor. His cheeks were drawn, and his eyes were buried in shadow, but the leanness merely served to make the imposing lines of his body thrust out more distinctly beneath the masking clothes.

At length he adjusted his pack with a shrug of his shoulders and, as the familiar weight settled into place, began the descent of the hill. He would make that town if he could. It was not the decision of a wise and temperate man, but Larrimee had never been distinguished for either temperance or wisdom. This day he had already covered an incredible distance with his crushing load, and a sensible fellow would have camped for the night on the brow of that hill, with wood and water, the two great essentials, conveniently to hand. But there was a chance of reaching the town before his strength was entirely exhausted, and Larrimee was determined to take it. Perhaps there was a dash of the Celt in his make-up.

Coming down the slope went well, but, when he struck the level, he discovered that the town which, from above, had seemed so near was in reality many a long mile still ahead of him. Instantly he knew that it was impossible for him to reach the place at this stage of the journey, but he kept struggling on sullenly, in spite of the knowledge. It was very foolish, of course, but Larrimee was a foolish man. Besides, he had dreamed all that day and all of many days before about the party he would have when it was possible once more for him to put his legs under a table covered with a white cloth and be served by the hands of another.

Sometimes he grew so impatient that he even growled at the weight of the fortune which he was carrying on his back. In reality it was more than fifty pounds of gold; in the eyes of the world it was fifty pounds of respect.

For Larrimee was a failure, a rank failure. To be sure, he was as clean as a whistle, from head to foot, and his life was as free from any blemish of cruelty or cowardice as his body was free from weakness. Yet he was a failure. In him two long lines joined and culminated, and the two long lines, in their mutual estimation, had produced a man not worth his salt. When Charles Larrimee married Agnes Stillwater there was every expectation that the offspring of such a marriage would be a person to be wondered at, but the offspring was one son, and that son was a black failure.

He did nothing right. He should have stepped into the paths of finance, where the large tread of his father and grandfather and great-grandfather had beaten down so wide and smooth a trail. But it was characteristic of him that he cared not a breath about the past of either his father's or his mother's people. "I'll tell you what," young Larrimee had said, "every man is born only once, and he only has one life. If I don't live my own life this time, I won't get a second chance."

He carried into college a good classical education, and then he wasted it, in the unanimous judgment of the entire family, by taking up mining. A Larrimee as a mining engineer. It would have been a thing for laughter, if it had not been so completely a thing of blushes and a hanging of the head. A Larrimee in overalls, perspiring and bossing a gang of sweating laborers, what a prospect. In vain they took him out of college and sent him into the mellowing atmosphere of London and Paris and Rome for a year. He learned all about French vintages, but otherwise it was wasted time. He wrote characteristically from Paris to his revered father:

With all due apologies for my ignorance, I'd rather hear a glee club than a symphony playing Beethoven; I'd rather see a touchdown than the Venus.

His father sat for an hour with his head buried in his hands, then he wrote a letter bidding Joseph Stillwater Larrimee to return instantly. He returned, reëntered college, took up mining, and graduated not actually at the foot of his class, but remarkably near it. "You see," he said to a saddened family, "I have a good many pounds to carry about, and you know that heavy things sink to the bottom." That was the worst of all. He was the first Larrimee, the first Stillwater that failed to take himself seriously.

But there was hope even in mining. There were large firms, great offices. Calluses were not absolutely necessary — by any means. Then came a fresh shock. "I'm not going to be a parlor miner," said Larry — this being the disrespectful nickname that his college mates had given him — "I'm not going to mine behind a desk. I want to get the feel of a drill sinking into hard rock. I'd like that sort of thing. Working with your head is all well enough, but I'd rather be using some of my muscles at the same time. Otherwise, why was I given muscles at all?"

What could be done with such a fellow? The family followed the example of Pilate and, having washed its hands of him, allowed him to go West. Thereafter, they spoke of him only when direct questions were asked, and then their answers were given with bated breath. People began to feel that all was ended with Larry, except the inscription to be placed on his tombstone.

But how would they feel when they learned that he had taken five or six thousands out of a soil that promised to yield him ten times that sum in a very short time? He had a shrewdly founded suspicion that the pride of the Larrimee and the Stillwater families was based upon dollars and cents. He could see his father prick up his ears; he could see uncles and aunts say: "After all, inheritance will tell."

"And murder will out," declared Larrimee, when he came to this point in his reflections.

In the meantime, the pack had grown to be a more crushing weight. He kept on, while the afternoon turned yellow with age, and then the flaring sunset burned up across the western sky, straight ahead of him, with the squat outlines of the village outlined in black against it. Then came the quiet pastels of twilight. And, last of all, the stars of night burned steel-blue above him. He was temptingly near the village now, but his strength was absolutely gone. He had covered the last five miles on nerve alone. His legs were numbed from the hips down and swung with only an instinctive rhythm, and there was a warning ache at the back of his neck.

Still, when he sat down to rest beside the trail, that had now widened to the dimensions of a comfortable road, Larrimee had not given up. He firmly intended to rise again, but, in order to crowd the maximum of rest into the minimum of time, he threw himself flat on his side, without removing the pack.

The instant he relaxed sleep swept over him, reached his brain in a stunning wave, and his eyes closed heavily. However, in his dreams, he seemed to have risen strangely refreshed after that moment of rest, seemed to have almost run the rest of the way into the town, and there. . . .

At this point he awakened and found above him a sky pink with morning light.

II

"BELLE CHANGES MASTERS"

Another man would have been so cramped and muscle-sore that he could have moved only with the greatest difficulty; but Larrimee was used to working in the mine until he almost dropped with exhaustion, and he slept in the first position into which he fell on the hard boards of his cabin floor. Now it needed only one or two incidental gymnastics and a round of vigorous expletives directed at his own foolishness. After these muscular and vocal experiments Larrimee was able to swing down the road and lift his voice in a ringing song.

For he had one of those cheerful dispositions that actually irritate ordinary folks. Indeed, there is nothing quite so exasperating as a man who sings before breakfast, and that was Larrimee's habit.

Unconsciously he carried his head so high that it was only by the merest chance that he saw a long, slender gauntlet glove lying by the side of the road. At such a time, in such a mood, with his nine-months-wished-for-goal so close ahead of him, it was a wonder that he paused for so trifling a thing, even after he had seen it. But the glove lay palm up, and the fingers curled a little, so that there was almost a human appeal for help in it.

Chuckling at his own folly, Larrimee raised the glove. It was only buckskin, but it seemed to him that it was the softest buckskin he had ever touched, with a velvety surface, an extreme pliability. It was a right-hand glove, and, therefore, it was very little worn and blackened by the touch of reins, but, apparently,

189

it was used for riding. There was little to distinguish it from other gloves of the sort — it had the usual fringe, worn away in places and shortened in others, and on the back there was a diamond pattern stamped in green ink. No doubt one could buy the partner of that glove in any one of a thousand country stores.

But who was it that had ridden this way and lost that glove? What man had passed him in the night? No, it was not a man. He tried the glove. Not three of his broad fingers could be wedged at the same time into the body of it. A boy, then, had worn it. But it was not usual for the children of that hardy country to wear gloves. The men were tough specimens enough, but the boys were all leather of the hardiest grain. One who wore gloves would be the laughingstock of his companions, a sissy, most despicable of the despised. Not a man, then, not a boy — unquestionably it must be a woman.

Yes, now that he looked more closely, striding along the road while he studied the glove, he wondered that the truth had not come to him sooner. The leather had been molded about slim and tapering fingers. It was a woman who had ridden past him that night, while he lay a shadow among the shadows, oblivious. It made him think of a parable in a schoolbook of the old days, something about the sleeper and opportunity, that travels only once on every road, hurrying by. For some reason, the heart of Larrimee sank.

Of course, it showed the excitable, the foolishly imaginative nature of the man. Dreamers like this, indeed, are the only ones who will devote the cream of their lives to tapping rocks in the hope of finding gold. Behold, he was now drawing her picture, and he proceeded in some such wise as this — the possessor of such a hand was not overly large. The print of the hand in the glove was rather long for its width. She was a slender, willowy figure, no doubt. A gentle nature, too, for see how little wrin-

190

kled the glove was, and those wrinkles not the deeply creased ones which tell of strong, impatient gripping of the hand. A gentle temperament, a quiet soul, no doubt. What else could be read in the glove? Well, she who possessed this lovely hand was likewise beautiful in person. For had he not marked a thousand times that the hand is, in small, the index of the whole body, a sign pointing out the truth. With that daintily proportioned body it would be blasphemy to think of other than a lovely head to crown it.

What a great progress was here. The owner of the glove, then, was young, of average height, of a slender build, and, above all, with a beautiful face. Moreover, there was more to be learned. The gentleness of the hand implied more things. Surely it did not mean a black and flashing eye, for these black-eyed girls, said Larrimee to himself, are ever quick and vigorous in their movements and their gestures. Not black, then, but probably blue. The blue of mid-ocean with the sun on it — those were her eyes. And for her hair — well, what manner of hair went best with such eyes? Yellow hair, no doubt. Yes, golden hair was what she had. Larrimee now balanced the glove on the palm of his hand, with as much care as if it were a separate individuality. It seemed almost capable of hearing and understanding. Lest he should be suspected of being a complete idiot, let it be remembered that for nine months he had not laid eyes on "human face divine."

Then he went on, before him a pleasant picture of a girl cantering somewhere ahead, lilting in the saddle, as perfect riders do, with an eye blue as blue, with a wisp of yellow hair blowing beneath the brim of her hat. To tell the truth, the foolish heart of the miner leaped at the imagined picture, and his step was longer and lighter, as he entered the little town.

There the realities came to shatter dreams. First he dined, and the old proprietor of that wayside hotel tells to this day of

191

the mighty inroads which Larry Larrimee on that morning made on ham and eggs and hot cakes. Thereafter, he soaked in a hot tub and came forth clean, then he shaved, and next he sat in the barber's chair and had his hair trimmed. He had kept it short by occasionally sawing off chunks of it with his penknife.

After this, with the first tailor-made cigarette in nearly a year in his lips, he went forth to clothe himself and appeared again in supple riding boots, blue silk shirt, and a sombrero. His mother, poor lady, would hardly have admired the outfit, but young Larrimee had fallen so far away from his old standards that he even liked the dress of his adopted mountains. He came back to the hotel to plan his party at leisure.

During the greater part of that year he had turned a hundred thoughts of it back and forth through his brain. Now he had to make selections, and he did not care to follow the moods of the moment. He wanted something that he would appreciate at second-hand, so to speak, when he was once more isolated in that mine among the distant hills. First he must plan this party, and he would execute it with a vengeance. Then he would set about hiring men and buying horses and mules and wagons and equipment in order to return and work his claim as it should be worked.

While he turned over in his mind various plans, he absently pulled the lost glove from a hip pocket and began to draw it carelessly through the palm of his hand. The proprietor, who had been loitering nearby, watched him with amusement.

"Kind of a small-sized glove you're wearing, partner," he suggested at length.

Larrimee looked up with a grin and found that the old fellow was ready to grin back, his honest old eyes alight. The rest of his body had aged, but the eyes remained wonderfully keen. It was easy to look deep into them, and it was easy for them to look deep into others. Larrimee liked him instantly, and for the

192

moment party and business alike were forgotten.

"What I'm wondering," he said at length, "is . . . did a girl, with blue eyes and yellow-golden hair, come riding into town, last night or this morning?"

With a start he remembered that she was not a reality, only his dream built around a glove. But the proprietor was answering.

"Her that had the five gents along with her?" he asked.

Larrimee was stunned. Had there, indeed, been such an arrival in the village last night? By some miraculous power had he built out of the mere glove the true picture of its owner? A superstitious chill struck through him. Then he looked the hotel man steadily in the eye and, controlling his voice and making his face grave, he went on, delving into the picture that he had conjured up under the morning sun, as he had walked down the road into the village.

"She's about five feet five and a half," he enlarged, "and she weighs . . . maybe a hundred and twenty-five? She's got long, thin hands, mighty pretty . . . blue eyes, very big and dark . . . yellow hair and piles of it . . . and a face that's easy to look at. Is that she?"

The proprietor was smiling in the manner of one who has formed an opinion that he does not wish to expose. "I guess you've had some practice describing her," he said. "I couldn't improve on what you've just said."

Larrimee lowered his glance to the floor. He was afraid that the wise-eyed old fellow might see the actual terror that was beginning to take hold of him. What did it mean? He had heard enough weird tales of ghosts and such things since he came West. Every mining camp was full of odd legends of the ghosts of miners dead and gone and returned to haunt the premises; but the duplicate of this queer daylight experience he had never heard. He was on the verge of confessing the truth and asking the opinion of his companion, but he feared that his sanity

193

might be doubted. He compromised with a halfway admission.

"I don't know her," he declared. "I was just putting out my camp for the night near the road, and I saw her come by, her and the five fellows with her."

"You don't know her?" said the hotel proprietor, showing a new interest at once. "She's a beauty, right enough, but it sort of give me a shiver to see her riding around the country with such five bad lookers like them that were with her. Didn't you feel the same way?"

"That's why I asked about her," lied Larrimee. "After I saw that hard-looking crew go by, with a flower like that among them, I stayed awake half the night, wondering how it came about."

"And me," replied the other. "I done the same fool thing. It ain't many girls that gets under the hide of an old codger like me, but she had a way about her, sort of trusting and willing to please and be pleased . . . well, you don't find it none too often in girls the way they're brought up nowadays. The five of 'em treated her nice enough, but, when I brought the hot water up to her room, I come near asking questions, which ain't my way with most, and you can lay to that!"

"I believe it," said Larrimee.

"But I didn't," continued the other, "and I've been sort of sorry ever since. That gent with the broken nose was sure a bad one, if I ever laid eyes on a crook in my life. Don't you think?"

"I'll never forget the look of him," answered Larrimee glibly. "It was the contrast between his face and hers that got most on my nerves. Besides," he ventured further, "he looked dangerous."

"Dangerous! I should say so! I ain't a kid, and I ain't been raised in a garden, but, of all the fighting faces I ever seen, his is the worst. Reckon if the sheriff had clamped eyes on that flat mug, he'd have placed it quick enough."

"I guess perhaps he would," agreed Larrimee.

"Though, when you come right down to it, for straight ugliness he didn't touch the tall skinny gent, with the face like a hawk's."

"Another bad one, all right," said Larrimee, his attention growing more keen, as this ill-favored gang was described, one by one. "But I noticed the flat-faced fellow most of all."

"Maybe that's because he seems to be the one that runs the bunch. He gives the orders, and he does the paying . . . he certainly has a choice bunch. The two twins, the young fellows, I mean, ain't so bad, but the prize fighter was another beauty."

"I had only a glimpse, as they rode by," said the crafty Larrimee. "I couldn't pick out every face."

"He was a prize fighter, all right," said the host, "and he had a cauliflower ear and all. His nose was puffed up from a lot of pounding he'd got in his palmy fighting days, I guess. For that matter, he'd be a hard one for a man to tackle right now. Got shoulders as wide as that door yonder. Well, sir, I've been thinking all day about that girl and that pack of yeggs. If they mean any good by her, I'm weak in the head . . . that's what."

"What were their names?" Larrimee asked hopefully.

"I used to keep a register," said the other, "but it wasn't no drawing card in these parts. It caused more cussing than you could listen to, so I threw it away after a while. Ain't been a name signed in this house these five year, pretty nigh."

The arrival of a new guest drew him away and left Larrimee in a brown study. Party and plans were forgotten now. His whole impulse was to find that girl whom he had drawn in the air as a dream, and who had now become, by white magic, so it seemed, a reality in the flesh. She was so vital to him that the thought of her filled him with a tingling joy, that peculiar joy which arises from the contemplation of people whom we know and love. His impulse was to find her and her ominous escort.

What was she doing with them, or what were they doing with her? Why were there five men about one young girl?

The three questions came one after the other, and Larrimee rose and began to pace the floor. He needed more room and walked out onto the verandah. Here he paced at greater freedom, until a noise among the horses, tied at the rack beyond the watering trough, drew his attention. It was a buckskin mare who was lashing out with her heels at the nearest of her neighbors. Larrimee centered his attention on her for the moment and decided that she was well built. There was not much daylight under her, the hocks were well let down, and the canon bone reasonably short to match them. Her length of neck and leg did not promise great speed, to be sure, but the ample girth of the cinches promised staying power, and every item of her build suggested weight-carrying ability. She was not a pretty animal, but she had points of honest quality that pleased Larrimee.

"Who owns the buckskin?" he asked of the idlers who sat on the verandah, their chairs tilted back against the wall.

A little dark-skinned, cross-eyed fellow spoke from the farther end of the line. "Me! Why?"

"Wondered how much she was worth as she stands."

"Standing or running," said the other, "she's worth two-fifty, if she's worth a cent. She'll do you a hundred miles a day and come through it fresh as a daisy, pretty near."

"That's stretching it," said a neighbor.

"Not a whole lot. I say, standing or running, she's worth two-fifty, but she'd a pile rather buck than do either. I've fought her since she was three, and she's six now, and she don't show no let-up about wanting to fight. Curse her eyes!"

"Saddle and all," asked Larrimee, "how much is she worth?"

"Why?" queried the other again.

196

"Because I've got to take a trip, and I haven't a horse."

"Well. . . ."

"You say she's worth two-fifty without her bucking habits, but the bucking cuts her price down fifty, eh?"

"Well. . . ."

"Partner," said Larrimee, counting coins hastily out of his money belt, "here's ten twenty-dollar pieces, two hundred dollars for her and her whole outfit, minus the rifle, there, of course."

Larrimee had sold some of his gold for cash at a mining camp, after leaving his own strike, and the present circumstance justified his foresight.

The other needed no time for thought, and he choked with his eagerness. "Take you!" he said, as he advanced with outstretched hand.

Ordinarily men would have been made cautious by such readiness, but Larrimee dropped the money into that brown hand and instantly stepped from the verandah.

"Mind you," said the cross-eyed man shrilly, "I didn't ask you to do no buying. I told you she bucked. But now you've paid for her, you can keep her. I guess that's business. I ain't your guardian."

Joseph Stillwater Larrimee turned on his heel and glared at the other, with a look that would have shocked his staid mother to the gasping point — it was that glint of eager fire that one sees so often in a bull terrier held on a leash, and the leash was his sense of the difference between his size and that of the cross-eyed man. Without a word of answer he turned again and untied the buckskin. She had become suddenly quiet, looking at him in a whimsical manner, one ear cocked forward and one ear cocked back.

"How d'you call her?" asked Larrimee.

"Belle."

197

"Now, Belle," said Larrimee, "you've got a pretty quiet name for a bad-acting mare. Matter of fact, I don't blame you for your reputation. I've never known a bad horse that wasn't made bad by the men that rode it. I'm going to treat you as if it's true, anyway. And so" — he caught up the reins and swung into place on the saddle — "here I am ready for the fun!"

Fun, he was certain, there was sure to be, for the men on the verandah were standing up, smiling in anticipation. As for Belle, she backed away from the rack, shaking her head in bewilderment. A careless bit of riding, when she was broken, a too-free use of spurs and quirt and cursing, and she had been launched on her career as a bad one. Now she was distinctly bewildered by the fact that she had not been either cursed or spurred, the moment this new rider got into the saddle. Neither did he put his whole weight against the bit, but kept only a reasonable pressure. In the middle of the road she waited. There was not a move.

Tentatively she reared and pitched heavily down on her forefeet again. The new rider gave easily with the shock, but, instead of the stream of profanity for which she was waiting, the wrench at the cruel curb, the biting of the spurs, there was only a pleasantly softened voice murmuring above her. She gave an outright test by bolting for fifty yards. That brought yells, indeed, but the shouts came from the spectators, not from the man in the saddle. And, realizing this fact, there was less than the ordinary vim in her leap at the end of the run, not quite her usual famous stiffness of leg, as she landed. It was a severe jar, at that, and Larrimee felt his temper rise with its customary mercurial quickness, but he curbed it sharply and spoke once more in his ordinary voice.

She had stopped with forelegs braced. Now she turned her head well about and sniffed heavily at his knee. Her ears were back, her nose wrinkling in expectancy of the blow with the

198

loaded quirt handle across her face. Men were such idiots that they did not realize that it was absolutely necessary for a horse to take the scent of a rider as well as a sight of him. This time there was no blow; there was not even a withdrawal of the knee. Instead, a hand came slowly down and stroked her face, and the touch was tinglingly pleasant.

Then she was urged forward, but only with a pat of the hand on her flank. It was a pleasure to follow such a bidding. She was turned, not with a wrench that tore her mouth, but with a gentle rein across the neck. It was a pleasure to wheel under this guidance, to be brought again to the hitching rack, to allow this man to get out of the saddle and rub her nose. Moreover, for the first time in her life, a man had turned his back on her, while he was still within biting distance. This unexpected incident recalled old, old days — the sun-flecked pasture, the brown-legged boy who used to gallop her bareback and feed her apples. That was before strangers had come and clamped a heavy saddle on her back and slashed her with fierce whips. She nuzzled curiously at the shoulder that was before her.

"Partner," Larrimee was saying to the former owner, agape in that row of astonished men, "my advice to you is to fight men, not horses."

III

"LARRIMEE TAKES THE ROAD"

It seemed to Larrimee, as he walked into the hotel again, that he was still walking in the happy daylight dream that had begun with the glimpse of the glove on the roadside. Fate, he felt, had picked him up and hurled him into the adventure, whether he would or no. Thereafter nothing could stop him. He went straight to the proprietor who began to compliment him on his riding, but Larrimee cut him short — "My friend, I have a lot of gold in my room."

"And no guard?" asked the other in astonishment.

"No guard. What I want to do is to have you write out a receipt, saying that you have the money. Then I want to put that money in your safe and ride my way."

"But suppose you should never turn up again?"

"Wait a year or two," said Larrimee seriously, as if there were, indeed, a possibility of this, "and then the money is yours."

"But you don't know me."

"I know you better than you think. I'll be down in a minute."

Presently he returned, carrying a canvas sack in one hand, while the other held his rolled pack, ready for strapping behind the saddle. His host had already prepared the receipt. "Looks to me," he said, "that I might make some easy money."

"Partner," said Larrimee, smiling, "if I don't turn up, you'll be more likely to give that money to charity than to keep it yourself. You see, I really know you very well."

Then he deposited the money on the counter and walked out, leaving the old fellow behind him blinking and rubbing a forefinger across his nose, so deep was his thought.

Once in the saddle, he wheeled Belle into the road and let her take a rapid pace through the street of the village and into the open country beyond. He was afraid that, if he ever paused for thought, he would give up the trail and so ride out of the dream. Only a canter could keep him in it, he felt.

It may seem that Larrimee was a very eccentric fellow, indeed, but it should be remembered always that he was still under thirty, an age at which a modicum of foolishness is permissible and even desirable, as very old men are apt to admit. Moreover, he had just come down from nine months of bitter loneliness, and the very thought of a girl was like music heard over water, to say nothing of this blue-eyed, golden-haired beauty of whom he had dreamed — a dream that had almost immediately turned into a living reality. Truly his heart sang within him, as Belle pricked her ears into the morning and rocked smoothly along.

In five miles they had established a close *entente*. He could control her by the sway of his body and the pressure of his knees, without the use of reins at all, save for quick maneuvers. It seemed strange to Larrimee, but how could he know of the little bare-legged fellow who, years before, had instructed her in just this manner? But Belle? Ah, she remembered very well, and, when Larrimee leaned in the saddle and stroked her neck under the flying mane, it was like the act of a kindly ghost.

Odd fancies held the brain of Larrimee during the long ride of that day. There were a dozen times when he was about to branch off and give up his quixotic journey, but, at other times — and these were more frequent and lasted longer — he felt that fate, which had revealed this nameless girl to him, had en-

201

abled him to work for her and win her, by giving him this blind trail to follow.

At any rate he kept straight on it at a stiff pace, and Belle stood up admirably. During the morning he thought her quite an ordinary traveler, but, after he stopped and cooked and ate at noon and resumed the journey, his admiration grew. There seemed no wearing her out, unless he strove to urge her beyond her normal gait. It was one well established. She struck a slow, rocking lope and held it without variation, hour after hour, breaking to a trot, going up a slope, and to a gallop, going down, but always coming back on the level stretches to the standard lope. That was the way, he knew, to wear out the miles. He had forgotten to ask about the horses of the party of six that preceded him, but he was reasonably sure that, unless they were mounted on whirlwinds, the bulldog tenacity of Belle would eventually run them down.

What he would do when he came up with them — that was another story — and he did not care to dwell on it. Fate, which had launched him on the expedition, would teach him what to do, what to say when he reached the object of his quest. Would he ever overtake her? From this main road many a trail branched off, and, although he scanned them all for signs of a party of mounted people, he struck several, but there was such a mingling of signs that he could not pretend to decipher the puzzle. He kept to the main road chiefly, in the hope that the riders would continue the straight line of their journey. That same straight line, in due time, carried him to a crossroads jumble of huts which could not be dignified with the name of a village. It was, as Larrimee said to himself, merely an accident. The store, hotel, and blacksmith shop were all grouped under one roof, and not an extensive one, either.

It was mid-afternoon, and Larrimee paused, unsaddled, and gave Belle, in the shed behind the hotel, a rack full of fodder.

Then he returned to the front of the building to hunt for news. He found the blacksmith seated on his anvil, smoking a pipe, and the rusty anvil looked as if no work had been done on it for many a mortal day. His arrival brought a grin of welcome and a chatter of talk from the lonesome smith. It was very easy for Larrimee to insert his inquiry into the flood of talk.

"I was camping out down the road this morning," he said, "and I saw a party of six come by . . . or was it five? Have they come through here?"

"Party of five?" asked the blacksmith, turning up his eyes in thought.

It gave Larrimee a thrill of suspicion. Certainly everyone in the little group of houses would know if any such cavalcade had come through, within the last week or more.

"Come to think about it," said the smith, "there was. Dropped through about noon. Five men and a girl, maybe you mean?"

"Didn't notice a girl," said Larrimee, in order to seem truly noncommittal.

He was rewarded with a sharp side glance that stung him. He was a fool to have made the last remark. Naturally any man would instantly notice a woman in this part of the country, particularly such a girl as she whom he followed. "I was back from the road," he said hastily. "Couldn't make out anything very clearly."

"I see," said the other, without pronounced enthusiasm. "Sun might have been in your eyes, too."

At once he began to talk of other things, but it was with an entire lack of interest. In spite of his endeavors to cover his false step, Larrimee began to feel an air of restraint. But why should he? Why was it necessary to mask an inquiry about six people who rode the highway? And why should the first hint of them bring such pronounced caution?

"The old woman," said the blacksmith at length, "is taking a nap. She asked me to wake her up about this time. Done a big washing this morning, and it sort of played her out. Ain't been the same since she had rheumatism last winter."

Excusing himself in this manner, he sauntered through the side door, which communicated with the main portion of the house, and Larrimee, very much perturbed, walked about to the front of the hotel. He had come a cropper, he knew, but how much of a one it remained to be seen. And then, glancing to the right, he was able to look through the window of the hotel and see the dark profile of the blacksmith, speaking animatedly into a telephone receiver.

Larrimee shrank back, as if from a blow, and then turned and hurried back to the shop, where he resumed his old seat on top of an upturned barrel. It was quite plain. Alarmed even by this most casual inquiry the blacksmith had hurried to the telephone. How there happened to be a line connecting with this little village could only be explained by considering it a link directly in line with two more important centers of life. Evidently the smith had telephoned ahead, along the course of the six riders, and was warning them that a pursuer was on their trail.

Something, obviously, was wrong with the mission of the riders; something was decidedly wrong, or they would not have planted behind them such spies as this blacksmith. In the meantime the first problem was to discover which road the fugitives, for such they seemed to be, had followed. Two roads led out of the village, one southwest, the other directly west, the latter, presumably, the course taken by the six. Could he gain this information from the suspicious smith?

The latter returned at this point. The old woman, he said, had refused to get up.

" 'But it's about time to start dinner,' says I to her.

" 'Let dinner cook itself,' says she. 'I'm plain fagged, and that's enough. You can cook as good as me. Many's the time you've said so. Now let me see some of your proof.'

"That's the way with women," concluded the grieved blacksmith. "They always got a way of putting you in the wrong. Why, there was a minute or two when I pretty near come to agreeing with her and telling her to rest easy and get well of the rheumatism, while I fixed up a snack for tonight. But I come to myself after a minute and told her where to head in. They's only one boss in my house, and that's me. I ain't one of these modern husbands, I tell you . . . not me!"

Larrimee could not but admire the fluidity of the fellow's lies and the unsuspicious dullness that he kept in his eyes. A few more minutes of talk, however, and Joseph Stillwater Larrimee felt that his temper might begin to get the best of him. He asked bluntly: "Which road is most traveled out of town?"

"Mostly west," said the blacksmith. "The south road leads around the same way, pretty much, and you can cut back from it, straight onto the west road. It takes you a little more time, but you get better going, and it saves horseflesh a pile."

"Did the six ride south?" asked Larrimee.

"Nope. They listened to reason," said the blacksmith without hesitation. "They wanted to keep right on west. Seemed sort of hurried. I dunno why." His glance lost its dullness for a moment and bored into the eyes of Larrimee.

"Well," said Larrimee, "I'll follow reason, too. I don't want to be hard on my nag. So long . . . and thanks."

He paid for his fodder in the stable, saddled willing Belle, and trotted out of the village on the southwest road, the blacksmith standing in the door of his shop, smoking the pipe and following with his eyes.

Straight down that road, for a matter of two miles, rode Larrimee. He was convinced that the smith had misinformed him, but he was also convinced that the moment he was committed fairly to the wrong course, the spy would telephone again and tell them that the pursuer had been thrown awry. If those five men were not forewarned, they would not be half so formidable for a single trailer to follow.

At the end of the two miles, riding through a country of broken willow groves and marshland, Larrimee dropped over a ridge of hills. When he reached this shelter, he turned Belle and headed across country for the west road. After all, the little maneuver would not cost him more than an extra mile of travel, and, if it served to throw the six horsemen off their guard, it would be richly worth the added distance.

Half the distance back toward the west road he had covered when an impulse made him rein sharply to the right and come cautiously up, until his head was just above the ridge of the hill. Nothing was to be seen among the willows of the lowland, and he was about to turn back to his route, satisfied, when he saw a horseman dart across an open space, on a rapid flight for the village. Even at that distance he knew it was the blacksmith.

The shrewd fellow had suspected and scented the ruse of Larrimee, and this was his parry. No doubt that telephone would ring again, and this time they would be informed that a determined and crafty enemy was following to run them to the ground.

IV

"IN THE MIDDLE OF THE NIGHT"

He was riding now on the trail of enemies whom the old hotel proprietor had evidently thought extremely dangerous, and dangerous they most indubitably were. But the fear of what they might accomplish against him worried Larrimee far less than his brooding over the girl. What could she possibly be doing in company with such rough villains as these? He recalled unsavory stories of pretty girls who had entered gangs of thieves, co-operated with the hardest criminals, even become leaders among them. What if his blue-eyed lady were one of these?

But he revolted against that thought. The wise-eyed seer at the first hotel had spoken tenderly of her, and, even more than this, that preconception of her, that he was beginning to feel now must be the truth in all respects, admitted no such possibilities in her. All that was pure, all that was gentle, all that was femininely noble must be this dream, this illusion which had turned into reality, only to flee from him.

And still the doubt returned. It was like the shadow that slid noiselessly beneath Belle, an impalpable, inescapable thing. It saddened him, because he could not tell the cause of his sadness.

Sunset, twilight came and passed, and, as the stars stood out, one by one, then in dim groups, the gallop of Belle became more pounding. She rolled a trifle in her lope, and Larrimee, good horseman that he was, knew that even her stout legs and brave heart were reaching the limit of strength. And, where the trail wound into the first grouping of lights, another tiny village, he stopped to find quarters for the night.

How many miles he had put behind him that day he could not tell, but he knew that Belle had kept a steady pace almost the entire time, and it would be rare, indeed, if he had not traveled three miles to the two of the six riders. For no group, as he was perfectly well aware, is faster than the very slowest of its members. Even if the mounts of the six included five that were better than Belle at distance work, which was more than doubtful, one slow nag would bring them back to her. It might even be that he had actually overtaken them at this stage of the journey.

Putting up his horse in the shed behind the hotel, he made sure that the six were not in town. A Negro, too dull to be a hired spy, assured him that no group of six had come that way from any direction, particularly no girl had entered the village. So he walked back to the hotel, having seen Belle well tended, and leaving directions that she should not be watered until she was cool.

Under the stars he took stock of the landscape beyond the little town. The sunlight had kept him riding with lowered head, unobservant of distant objects. Now he saw that he had come right in under the western mountains that had been merely a haze in the morning. It was a startling proof of the ground he had covered. Big and dim and black the heights pushed up among the stars. By noon tomorrow he would be among the foothills, but the steep grades, no doubt, would be easy for the strongly-built buckskin.

It was a dull time, apparently, in the little hotel. Only one man was in the combined lobby and parlor, and this was a fellow sleeping in a chair, with his wide sombrero pulled down over his face. Larrimee caught only a glimpse of a disfigured ear, as he went by in search of the kitchen and food. The cartilage of the ear had grown into a thick mass, so that there was only a small opening to the eardrum. It was what followers of the ring call the cauliflower ear.

He gave that disagreeable sight only a side glance and passed on. For food he could get only the cold remains of the evening meal, but there was a hot cup of coffee to flank the platter, and his appetite was sauce. He ate hurriedly and, tired and sore from the long ride, went immediately to his room.

Weariness overcame him the moment he lighted the lamp. His eyes remained open only long enough for him to drag off his clothes and put out the light, and, before the welcome chill had worn off the sheets, he was fast asleep.

Ordinarily he was not a long sleeper, but this night he wakened suddenly to find the dim gray of the first dawn in the room. In his mind was an uneasy consciousness of having heard an unusual sound in the room, like the soft closing of a door, the cautious turning of a key, with a faint, scratching sound. He was about to dismiss the illusion and compose himself for another nap, before getting up, when he heard, and this time unmistakably, the creak of a footstep on the floor.

Larrimee was instantly bolt erect in the bed, but he was far too late. Bulking large in that unsatisfactory light, he made out a shadowy figure, a misty shape, save that in the hand there was a gleam of steel. Then a murmur, that was barely louder than a whisper, said: "Sit tight, bucko! Sit tight and shove them hands up over your head."

Larrimee calculated swiftly. His gun and belt were where he had flung them, over the back of a chair. That was one lesson he would not have to be taught a second time, if he were ever lucky enough to get his hands on them again. But to reach them now and under that gun was impossible. Besides, he was no trained gunfighter, as this fellow probably was. Even if he reached his gun before he was shot, he would probably do very poor execution with it in the uncertain light. He pushed his hands above his head and sat quiet.

"I know why you're after me," he said at length, as the other made no effort to move or speak. "You're on a cold trail, my friend. I've cached my money a good many miles from here. It's in a safe, in fact. But, if you want some spare change, I'll tell you where it is . . . look in the money belt on the inside of my cartridge belt, on that chair beside you."

"Huh?" asked his nocturnal guest. "Free and easy with your coin, ain't you? I'll have a look at you, beauty. Here's some matches. Light that lamp beside the bed, yonder. Mind you don't turn it up more'n a glimmer. I don't want any bonfire in here, so's it can be seen from the horse shed."

His box of matches fell with a rattle on the lap of Larrimee. Larrimee hesitated. What if this were a maneuver to throw him into an unprotected position so that the thief could stun him with a blow over his head.

"Hurry it up," said the other impatiently, "and don't try no reaching under your pillow, old-timer. I'm watching close. I don't aim to have to shoot twice, if it comes to a pinch."

Larrimee submitted and lighted the lamp with due care. Its nearness blinded him for a moment after he sat up again in his bed, with his hands raised to their former position. Eventually he made out a man whose face was completely covered with a black mask. The fellow was in the act of taking Larrimee's revolver from its holster, on the chair beside him.

"You can put your hands down in your lap, son," he said. "Only mind you never move 'em jerky. I'm nervous with this gun, and I'm sort of sympathetic, you see. Minute a gent moves quick, my finger comes down quick on this trigger. Bad habit of mine, but I don't seem to get over it, no ways."

The grim humor of the speech failed to bring a smile from Larrimee. The robber approached the bed, even made himself comfortable by sitting on it, with his back braced against the footboard.

"And here we are," he said, and Larrimee could guess that the rascal was grinning behind his mask. "Here we are, all comfortable and cozy and ready to hear you tell a story. So start in, son!"

"Story?" asked Larrimee. "Story?"

"You know what I want, right enough. Come out with it, partner. I'm treating you plumb easy, the way I figure it. No rapping you on the head, no tying of your hands . . . just let you sit comfortable and give you a tip to talk. You ain't got no appreciation, kid."

He shook his head mournfully at this lack of gratitude, and, in the gesture, Larrimee, for the second time that night, caught sight of a cauliflower ear. Then, for the first time, he harked back to his earliest information about the girl and her five riders. Had not one of these been described as an ex-pugilist, with exactly this deformity? He could have cursed his stupidity aloud for not having perceived the whole thing the minute he glimpsed the sleeper in the room downstairs. The blacksmith had warned the fugitives, and they had dropped behind them one efficient member to destroy the trailer. Certainly he was a smoothly efficient worker.

It seemed that the masked man had followed his thoughts in some measure. "I thought I was a goner for a minute," he said, "when you walked in on me downstairs. It sure give me a start, son. I figured you wouldn't be along till midnight or tomorrow morning. You must have got hold of a traveler for fair, or did you change horses?"

"No. I rode the same one."

"Must be a whirlwind, then. I'll take her along with me when I say good bye to you this morning, kid. Now let's hear you talk."

211

"And what," said Larrimee, "do you want me to tell you?"

The other leaned forward, and his voice became a snarl. Even the outjutting of his jaw was perceptible through the mask. "Look here, bud, I like smooth ways . . . but, when it comes to being rough, I'm the roughest you ever seen. Trouble-raising comes nacheral to me. Everything else was learned, and it don't take me long to unlearn it. But I'll go slow and easy. I'll ask the questions. How come old Wheeler sent you out alone?"

Larrimee cast about in his mind for the proper line of action. It would by no means do to antagonize this fellow, and it was dangerous to attempt to act a part. But he was irresistibly tempted to tap this source of information and learn what he could about the girl. As for telling the man the truth about how he actually came to be on the trail, that, of course, was impossible. Who could old Wheeler be? Evidently he was the force that the fugitive dreaded.

"Don't waste time thinking up lies," said the other. "You'll save my time and yours by talking straight. Besides, it keeps me from getting my dander up, and that'll be a saving on your hide, my boy! How come he sent you alone?"

"I expect that he wanted to save money."

The other growled and nodded. "The old rat!" he exclaimed. "That's him . . . that sounds like him. To think that one like the lady has got some of the same blood in her that's in him, why, curse his no-good heart, I don't believe they's two drops of man fluid in him!"

One word of that speech thrilled Larrimee mightily. "Lady," he had called her, and it needed no interpreter to tell him that she was the blue-eyed girl on whose trail he rode.

"Him and that brat of a kid," said the masked man. "Think of the skunk trying to make that kid lock up to lady, will you? Makes me cold inside. I'd wring his skinny neck before I'd see it!"

"Well," ventured Larrimee cautiously, "is what you're bringing her to any better?"

"How d'you know what we're bringing her to?" asked the other sharply. "Has the old fox smelled out even that? Then he's more devil than man. I always knowed it about him, the minute I set eyes on his little pig eyes! He knows, does he? Well, kid, I don't mind saying that Tucker ain't the best in the world, from my way of thinking, but he'll make a better looking pair with her than Wheeler's yaller-hearted brat would! He'll look the mate for her, even if he ain't. Besides, she likes him, and that's half the fight."

Vaguely Larrimee was fumbling toward discoveries that were leaden to his heart.

"She likes him," he said, still guessing at large. "But she doesn't love Tucker, and, when she's been married to him a month, she'll loathe him."

"And what d'you know about him?" inquired the other sharply. "Has she talked this stuff over with you, maybe?"

Larrimee shrugged his shoulders. The masked man went on to answer his own question, in a measure. "He'll be good to her . . . he ain't plumb bad. But . . . here I am doing all the talking. S'pose you start in?"

"I'm breaking my back this way. Let me pull up my legs and get comfortable, will you?"

"All right, but no funny business, kid!"

Larrimee nodded and drew up his long legs, locking his hands around the knees.

"You're a cool enough one," said the pugilist. "But how come Wheeler sent one man on Lefty's trail is more'n I can make out. How d'you figure it yourself, son? What you been? What you done to make a name for yourself? Who've you cleaned up on? Looks to me like you've handled it pretty rough, talking clean out and out to Bud Younger, the way you done

213

this afternoon, and then walking right over me tonight and not noticing who I am. Where did you get enough rep to make Wheeler want to buy you and sic you on a rough one like Lefty, let alone some that Lefty has with him?"

"I'll tell you the truth," said Larrimee. "I'm not on this trail because Wheeler sent me. I'm on it on my own hook. You understand?"

"I sure don't. What you aim to get out of it?"

"Can't you guess?"

"Nope. It's past me."

"It begins with a glove," said Larrimee, "and it goes on to what you might call a hunch, and then it takes in a horse . . . and. . . ."

"A glove, a hunch, a horse . . . say, son, are you kidding me, or are you just a plain nut?"

"Sometimes," said Larrimee, smiling broadly, "I think that I'm just a plain nut."

"Well," answered the other, "you better get your brains working right again. I want answers, and I want the right ones. First off . . . how many has Wheeler sent off besides you?"

"None," said Larrimee boldly, but feeling that it was impossible to tell the true story to this practical mind that had probably never dreamed a dream, to say nothing of following one. "Not a single man."

"That's lie number one," said the other without heat, "and a boy's-size lie at that. Think I'm fool enough to be took in like that? Loosen up, son, and talk straight. I know four names of them he's sent, but I want to know where he's headed them, and what roads they're going to follow."

"I don't know," said Larrimee. "I give you my word of honor, since you insist on saying that Wheeler must have sent me, that I haven't the least idea what else he has done."

"And yet you're his right-hand man? You're the one he sent

all by yourself to trail Lefty? Bah! Not know his plans? You know 'em well enough, and I'm going to know 'em before I'm through with you. They's ways of getting it out. Suppose I put a cord around your head and start twisting it up with the barrel of my gat, son? What you think happens?"

The perspiration poured out on Larrimee's forehead. "Well?" he queried.

"First it gets tight as trouble, and then tighter. Soon the cord cuts through your skin, not slow, but all at once . . . zip! Then something begins to run down all over your face, and that ain't very funny. I know all about it. Bunch of greasers got me once, and they showed me that trick." He pointed toward his forehead, and there, above the edge of the mask, Larrimee made out a white streak.

"I'd have told 'em anything they wanted before they was through," said the masked man, "but they wanted me to stamp on a scrap of an old American flag they had, and it plumb went ag'in' the grain! Well, kid, I don't want to try that trick on you, unless I have to. I like the nervy way you sit there and look me in the eye, but work is work, and, if I go back to Lefty without the news, he'll. . . ."

In his earnestness he had allowed the muzzle of his revolver to sink well below its original level, and Larrimee saw not a real chance, but the ghost of a chance. The sheet and thin blanket were a very slight encumbrance to those active legs of his. Suddenly he kicked out with all the strength he could muster.

There was a startled oath from the other, but, as he jerked up the gun, the driving feet of Larrimee went home. Just at the pit of the stomach they sank into the body of the masked man and doubled him up. The revolver exploded harmlessly, and the next moment Larrimee wrenched it away and shoved it under the chin of the gasping man.

V

"AN EXCHANGE OF COMPLIMENTS"

The arms of the intruder were clasped tightly around his own stomach, the seat of pain. His eyes rolled, and his mouth was wide, as he gasped for wind. Larrimee caught up his own gun, that had fallen on the bed, and stood away to the center of the room, with both weapons directed at the masked man. At the same time hurrying footsteps passed down the hall, and a heavy hand knocked at the door: "What's all this noise about?" demanded an angry voice.

"Getting ready for an early start?" said Larrimee cheerily. "Cleaning my gun, and the damn' thing went off. Sorry!"

There was a growl from the hall, and a voice muttered something about — "No peace, no sleep, no nothing around this hotel!" Then the proprietor retreated, and Larrimee centered his attention on the thug. The latter had recovered his breath sufficiently to say: "And think of me being took in by a dirty little trick like that . . . so old I wouldn't never have dreamed of it! This'll make a joke out of Bill Wren!"

"Maybe you'll have your chance later, Bill," said Larrimee. "Maybe we'll meet again."

An expression of childish joy passed over the face of Wren. "Man, man," he said, "when we do! Now what you got up your sleeve? What you want with me?"

"Nothing important," said Larrimee. "All I want to know is where Lefty and the girl are."

Wren blinked, then answered smoothly enough: "That ain't

216

much. They're on the north road at Henline."

"Where?"

"They's a hotel at Henline, and they've put up there."

"How is it that Lefty stays at the public places? Doesn't he know that's dangerous?"

"You know why he stays there . . . because he's pretty sure that old Wheeler, the rat, is looking north for the girl, and has only sent you scouting out this way on a chance. Lefty feels safe enough, once he's dropped you."

"Once he's done that, I suppose he is."

"You think he can't, eh?" asked Wren. "Well, son, the only encouraging thing about your prospects, right now, is your life insurance, if you got one."

"I haven't."

"Then I hope you ain't got a missus and kids."

"You're a cheery fellow," replied Larrimee. "But about Lefty, where is he?"

"Didn't I tell you plain as plain? He's in Henline, at the hotel there."

There was nothing to induce Wren to tell the truth; there was much to keep him from it. Larrimee determined to venture another step in the dark, since he had successfully negotiated so many of them up to this point.

"Listen, Bill," he said as evenly as he could, "that's a pretty large lie you've just told me. Understand this . . . I know just about where Lefty is cached, only I'm not sure to within a few miles of the place. But I know it isn't Henline, or anything near Henline."

"You do, eh?" asked Wren, and his sullenness was an admission of his lie.

"Now," said Larrimee, and he glowered upon the thug, "you suggested a way of getting information out of a fellow. If I put another little scar around your head, Wren, d'you think it

217

would make you tell the truth?"

The other changed color, and his eyes bulged a little. "You'd do that?"

"The thing you were about to try when I kicked you in the stomach? Why not?"

"I was only bluffing. You know that," said Bill Wren.

"But I'm not bluffing, Bill. I'm a fairly hard man, and I'm going to find out what I want to know, with your will or against it. Suppose I give you a minute to think it over."

The dawn was breaking rapidly. Larrimee now puffed out the lamp and saw the face of Wren change, as the bitter gray of the day filled the room.

"Well," he said, "what harm does it do, except to you? I'll tell you, bud. He's straight down the west road. He's at a farm, about ten miles west and right off the road. Only one inside of five miles either way, so's you can't miss it . . . if you get there."

"Thanks," said Larrimee. "If you'd stuck to Henline, Bill, you might have sent me in that direction, but I think this second one is more apt to be right."

"Bluffing, were you?" demanded Wren. "You're one of these smooth gents, I see."

"Except with my feet," replied Larrimee.

"Yup, like a jumping frog! But give it to me straight, kid. Who are you? What you done?"

Larrimee could see the hungry pride of the man, eager to hear that he had been beaten by a celebrated fighter.

"I'll tell you," said the Stillwater-Larrimee scion. "I'm fair with a shotgun, rotten with a rifle, and absolutely no good with a revolver. Haven't fired fifty shots in my life, and those were at stumps I never hit, or squirrels that weren't even scared into their holes. I've never had a gunfight in my life, or a knife fight. I've squared off a good many times with gloves, or even fists, but the most I've ever done in the way of fighting, Bill, has been

218

to break a few noses and knock out a few teeth. I've wrestled a bit, too, but never inflicted more than a few bruises. So you see, Bill, I'm a very ordinary sort of a fellow."

"Well," replied Bill Wren, "curse my eternal eyes! If I'd knowed the third part of that I'd never have wasted ten seconds on you! Why, you. . . ." He was unable to find a word strong enough to fit the impostor.

"You see," said Larrimee, "I haven't a shred of reputation, but I'm going to keep on. I've a feeling that I'll get through Lefty's men and meet the great Lefty himself. How do you think that would come out for me?"

"Huh! Get over being proud of yourself, kid. You pulled one on me, right enough, but I'm a simp. I'm the boob of the crowd. You'll never pull the wool over the eyes of the rest . . . not a hope! And, if you ever meet Lefty . . . well" — here he rubbed his broad hands together — "I'd sure like to be handy for that meeting . . . that's all."

"I suppose you would," returned Larrimee, "but I'm afraid I'll have to detain you here for a few vital hours. Sorry, Bill, but I'll have to ask you to lie face down on that bed and put your hands behind your back."

The latter glowered at him a moment, and then he obeyed without a word. Plainly he realized that the humiliation was inevitable. Only when the cords were wrapped tightly about his wrists did he pour forth a brief, but moving, stream of profanity and a heartfelt promise to run the impostor down and tear him to small bits. Larrimee went methodically ahead and bound his man, hand and foot, and gagged him thoroughly.

Then he dressed, threw the thug's revolver out the window and into the bushes beyond, and went downstairs. The proprietor was up, so he paid his bill and went out to the stable, where Belle greeted him with an eager whinny. That short night of rest had completely washed the effects of the hard ride from her. The line of her belly was straightened a little, to be sure, but otherwise there were no visible effects of the journey.

He groomed her thoroughly, being enough of a horseman to know that, in the long run, time spent on grooming is not wasted. Then he saddled her, took her to the watering trough for a short drink, and swung into the saddle. A moment later she was rocking down the road, her ears pricked, her head high. Truly she was a gallant little traveler, and the heart of the rider went out to her.

The sun was just coming up, sweeping the dawn colors from the sky, when he came in sight of the ranch, and here he slackened his pace to a trot. However the need of a cautious approach was done away with at once. By the roadside he met a middle-aged fellow at work, restringing a fence, with a wire pull, brackets, and hammer. Larrimee stopped beside him.

"Some friends of mine stopped by this way last night," he said. "Are they still at the house?"

The other eyed him for a moment. "Friends of yours, eh? Well, they ain't at the house. If you aim to catch up with 'em, you'll have to travel fast."

"How's that?"

"Look yonder. See that corral and them five hosses? Them are the ones they left behind, and they took the best six nags they could find in my outfit. Made a trade out of it. It was a good trade for me, but they seemed to want only a tolerable fair hoss, so long as it was all fresh, rather than a darned good one that was fagged. Say, where they heading for? Has they been a gold strike somewheres, maybe?" He chuckled. "If they is, I'll bet on the skinny gent to smell the metal a hundred yards under rock. He sure looks hungry enough!"

Plainly this was not an adherent. "When did they start on?"

"About an hour ago, and they started fast."

Larrimee thanked him and went on. His eye went mournfully down a long, straight stretch of road. By this time they might be ten or twelve miles away. Why they had started without Bill Wren was a puzzle, unless they had allotted a definite time in which he was to complete his work, and, as soon as that limit was exceeded, they had pushed on remorselessly and allowed Bill to shift for himself. That must be the explanation, and it gave Larrimee some idea of the coldness of the brain of Lefty. He was one of those who believed in forced marches, those who dropped out, unable to stand the pace, being permitted to lie where they fell.

There was a temptation to force gallant little Belle to a faster pace, but he wisely desisted. She knew her own strength better than he, and she had proved the day before that her generous nature would give all it possessed. Perhaps the freshly mounted group might distance her today, but Larrimee had his doubts, and they were strong ones. His own opinion leaned toward a good tired horse rather than a fresh poor one, and he felt that, no matter how well Lefty's people covered ground in the forenoon, they would begin to fall back in the heat of the afternoon.

So he let his thoughts rove back to the problem of the girl. Much had been cleared up, or a clearing suggested, by the talk of Bill Wren. Wheeler, a distant relative, perhaps merely the guardian of the girl, had attempted to force on her the hand of his son in marriage, and, to escape from this predicament, she had fled toward a man named Tucker, under the care of Lefty. Why Tucker himself had not joined the kidnapping party was not explained, and the relation of Lefty to the affair was indistinct. He might have been hired by Tucker to do the work; he might have been hired by the girl herself; or he might have undertaken it for sheer deviltry and hatred of Wheeler, who seemed to be an abomination to the whole gang. At any rate, there was one thing free from the shadow of a doubt — the girl of the glove was riding full speed to find Tucker and marry him.

How long it would take her to reach him was, of course, unknown, and he began to regret bitterly that he had not discovered from Wren the location of the fellow.

There were other things about his interview with Wren that made him set his teeth and frown. Of course, he was a rank idiot to have confessed his inability with a revolver. And Wren, who by this time must have made enough noise to attract attention and get himself released, would certainly have run to the inevitable telephone and sent word ahead as to the nature of the trailer. Lefty, infuriated and contemptuous, might then lay an ambush at any point on the road and wipe out the gadfly annoyance.

In the meantime Belle rocked stoutly along with her unfaltering gallop. At noon they reached another crossroads town, and here he halted for the midday meal, having seen as usual that Belle was well cared for.

VI

"UNHORSED"

He found the restaurant, which was under the same roof with the inevitable general merchandise store, very nearly deserted. The rush of diners was just over, and they were now idling under the shade of the verandah in front. Larrimee often wondered just what proportion of their time Westerners spend sitting still and rolling tobacco into meager cigarettes. But he was too hungry to waste much time on observations, and he went straight to a corner table and ordered a large meal. There was some hesitation over serving him, since the regular meal hour had passed. When two more men came in, burly, blond-headed fellows, all doubts were removed. Three were evidently worth some extra trouble.

Larrimee ate leisurely. Not that he was not eager to get onto the road again, but he knew that it would not do to hurry Belle over her midday rations. Fifteen extra minutes for her here might mean many an extra mile before the day had ended. The big fellows seated before him, however — and he noticed, particularly, that they were as alike as two peas in a pod, straight-backed, wide-shouldered, with steady, pale blue eyes — hurried through their meal and went out, followed by admiring glances from the waitress.

In due time Larrimee followed, took a refreshed Belle from the stable, and again struck the road. It was no longer one on which the mare could maintain an even gait, for now they were winding into the foothills, with the bold-sided mountains close above them. It was an up-and-down course. Sometimes Belle lurched into a strong gallop downhill; sometimes she loped over a level stretch, and more than once she was reduced to a laboring walk up a grade. Larrimee let her take her own time about it, riding with a loose rein. Now and again he encouraged her with his voice, or the patting of his hand. She seemed to be constantly watching for the latter sign.

It was on a fairly level stretch, thickly wooded on either side, with Belle swinging on in her habitual canter, that Larrimee heard a shout, and straight before him, spurring out of the brush, came the two big blond fellows whom he had seen in the eating room. Each carried a poised revolver.

"Stick up your hands, bud!" shouted the leader.

But Larrimee had gone over the side of his horse, like an Indian. With guns he might be an amateur, but there was little that he could not do on a horse, from his very childhood up. As he swung down, with a hand clutching the mane of Belle, his left leg gripping her behind the cantle of the saddle, he drew his revolver, swayed still lower, and looked from beneath the throat of his horse.

She had come to a dead stop, alarmed and tossing her head, while the others, cursing with their surprise, spread across the road to get a new aim at Larrimee.

All this had happened in a breathing space, then Larrimee fired at the nearest man and missed. Then he fired again without hope, but simply with a sense of pointing direction, with one chance in a thousand that he might strike the target. The one chance was his. He heard the fellow yell, saw him drop the revolver, and clutch his right shoulder with his left hand. Larrimee swung his gun on the second man.

He delayed his fire in time. The man had leveled his own gun, and the trigger snapped, but there was no report. With a yell of rage and fear, the fellow cast the weapon from him and tugged at his rifle in its case. But the rifle was long. It stuck in the case a vital instant, and in that instant Larrimee was upon him. He did not come, gun in hand, for he would not shoot at one who was even temporarily disarmed. Instead, he sent Belle forward with a shout, swung himself back into the saddle, and so charged down on the enemy. He caught him in the critical instant. The rifle was free in his hands, but he had not yet swung the muzzle around, when Larrimee struck.

With the weight of his surging body, with the force of Belle's gallop behind his fist and stiffened arm, he struck as he had never struck before. The blow landed flush on the fellow's jaw, and, throwing up his hands, with a queer bubbling sound in his throat, he went backward over the cantle of the saddle, as if he had been unhorsed with a spear in the days when knights jousted.

At the touch of the rein across her neck Belle turned, as only a cow pony knows how, and she turned barely in time. The man who had been struck by Larrimee's fist was no longer the chief danger. He lay on his face in the dust, quiet as a log, his arms and legs sprawling in positions that showed that he had been completely stunned. But the man who had been wounded in the shoulder was in the act of slipping out of his saddle. His purpose was patent. Half buried in the dust, but still with a spark of sunshine gleaming on it, was his fallen revolver. If he could reach that he might, if he were at all ambidextrous, shoot Larrimee from his horse. For the latter had dropped his revolver to go at the second man with his fists, and now he was completely unarmed.

He had no time to mourn his chivalry in discarding the gun and fighting an equal with equal means. Belle, at his yell, spurted away at full speed, and Larrimee, loosening his feet from the stirrups, swung far to one side and, using the impetus of Belle as the charge and his own body as the missile, flung himself at enemy number one, as the latter was in the very act of scooping the gun from the dirt.

The impact stunned him, but, luckily, he struck, football fashion, with his body turned and the shoulder presented, and this hard mass of bone and muscle struck the other fairly on the exposed ribs. There was a crunching of bones, and Larrimee rolled over and over. Then he staggered to his feet, gasping from the shock, to see the other man writhing on the ground and groaning in his agony.

The battle was ended, and there they lay, each of them too helpless to resist the attack of a child. And, as though there was someone to hear, Larrimee shouted like an Indian in his triumph. It was not vanity; it was simply joy in his luck, for luck he knew it to be. Every chance had favored him. Otherwise those expert gunfighters would have blown him to bits. Even in a square fist fight, considering their bulk, they would doubtless have pounded him to a pulp, and there they lay.

He took stock of the surroundings as, for a first measure of precaution, he picked up his own revolver and those of the other two combatants. Their horses were galloping with wildly tossing bridles, far down the road to the east, and that removed the rifles from the scene. As for the two revolvers, he hurled them with all his strength into the brush, then he turned to the stricken fighters.

His first impulse, naturally enough, was to mount Belle. The mare had halted and was trotting slowly back to him, as if to inquire if she could be of further assistance. He wanted to leave the two miscreants to take care of their own wounds, but his better nature prevailed over impulse. Besides, there were things he might learn from them.

First he turned the stunned man on his back. Perspiration and dust had clotted the fellow's face with dirt, but he breathed, though faintly, and would shortly be on his feet again, none the worse, save for a rapidly growing wale on the left side of his jaw. The other was in a more serious condition. Larrimee found him gasping for his breath and writhing in vain to get into a comfortable position. A crimson stain had issued from his shoulder and spilled over his clothes and the white dust around him. Altogether he was an unpleasant sight when Larrimee began his ministrations.

From the fellow's own shirt he made a rude bandage, knotting the strips together, and this he bound securely around the wounded shoulder. Then he made him turn on his left side and lie quietly, for only in this manner could he give some relief to the pain of the broken ribs on the other side.

All this had been done without a word spoken, and now Larrimee turned to find his other victim heaving himself to a sitting posture and gazing stupidly about him. The approach of Larrimee brought him to his senses, and he started to his feet, but the latter covered him instantly with his revolver.

"The game's up," said Larrimee calmly. "There's your partner laid out. Your gun is safely out of the way. Suppose you think it over and see that you haven't a chance to get back at me?"

"It was Skinny's gun," he said explosively. "It stuck. He was always a pig in taking care of his things. That's all that saved your bacon. You can lay to that. But. . . . Oh, my jaw!" He had been using only one side of his mouth for speech, and now he tenderly fondled the bruised place along his jaw.

"What hit me?"

"My fist," said Larrimee, unable to control a grin.

"Fist nothing! Must have been a gun butt . . . my jaw's broke."

"You wouldn't be talking if it were," Larrimee assured him. "But let's take a look at things, my friend. Your partner . . . ," he paused, remembering many things. They were as alike as

227

two peas, these fellows, and now he recalled what he had heard of the twins in Lefty's gang. "Your brother," he corrected himself, "is badly hurt. That wound in his shoulder is only a scratch through the muscle. It will heal in a couple of weeks, if any care is taken of it. Worse than that, however, he has some broken ribs. They're not a matter of life and death, but, if I were you, I'd go back to town and come out for him in a buckboard. Understand?"

The other regarded him in gloomy silence and gave no sign. In the pause they heard the faint groaning of the stricken man. Presently he of the bruised jaw spoke: "And you're the gent that can't do much as a fighter, eh?" he asked bitterly. "You're him, are you?"

"I had all the luck," said Larrimee with due modesty.

"Lefty, the skunk, told me that Wren had phoned a message in about you . . . said you'd be easy. I come out looking for a cinch, and here we are. Made fools of! Why didn't Lefty tell me the straight of it?" he demanded. "Did he think I'd be scared? But I wouldn't have rode out like a fool into the road . . . they wasn't any sense in that."

Plainly his pride was far more severely bruised than his jaw. Larrimee determined to work on it. "It was a dirty trick, partner," he said. "But is it the first one Lefty has played on you?"

"Him? Oh, everybody knows Lefty. He'd give up a gold mine, if he could get a chance to land somebody in trouble. Just nacherally mean, he is."

"Suppose," said Larrimee gently, "you were to give me a chance to play the trick over again with Lefty. Would you do it? Will you tell me where I can locate him?"

Words, obviously, came tumbling up to the parted lips of the other, but he choked them back and stared cautiously at Larrimee.

"Why not?" asked Larrimee. "I ask you, man to man, partner, has Lefty played square with you?"

The other flushed with anger, but he shook his head. "It's too late, anyway," he said. "Best thing for you to do is to go back and tell your boss, old Wheeler, that the game's up. By this time they're married."

"Married!" demanded Larrimee, his heart shrinking at the thought.

"Sure, or they will be, a long sight before you come up with 'em . . . but you don't figure on tackling Lefty and Skinny, you all by yourself?"

"I'd tackle the devil, if I had to," replied Larrimee. "Partner, is there certainly no chance?"

The other shook his head, seemingly divided between admiration and wonder. He bore strikingly little sullen anger against his conqueror, a true attribute of the fighting man. His rage was solely concentrated on Lefty, as a champion's would be on his manager who advised him to meet a reputed set-up and found the set-up a tartar.

"No chance in the world, bud," said the blond giant. "They'll have the sky pilot and everything. Along about sunset time he's due, and they'll be waiting for him."

"Fifteen miles off. Can I make that by sunset?" He grinned sympathetically and shook his head. "Fifteen miles!" he exclaimed, and turned and looked at Belle.

The gallant little mare had come behind him, and, as he turned, she pricked her ears cheerfully. She was wet with sweat, for the afternoon was burning hot, and her pace had been a steady one since the early morning, and yet there was life in her still. She did not free a leg to stand at ease, and the spirit looked out of her big, kind eyes.

"Fifteen miles!" repeated Larrimee, and the other caught the hope in his voice.

"Might kill your hoss . . . that's all the good you could do.

The doc will be there at sunset sharp . . . he's prompt, too. Never doubt that! Nope, son, you're beat. You've sure made a good stand, but you can see for yourself. The old Johnson place, where they're going to meet, is over on the side of that mountain yonder . . . Glory Mountain they call it . . . that one that's chopped in two on top and looks like a couple of ears. You see? Can't make that by sunset, partner."

He had grown almost friendly. Larrimee looked away through the blue distance, for the afternoon was hazy, and marked the mountain in question. He sighed again. "I'm going to try," he said through his teeth.

"But listen . . . ," began the other.

"No time," replied Larrimee, and cast himself into the saddle.

VII

"ON GLORY MOUNTAIN"

Belle fell at once into her accustomed lope, and, as they swept around the next turn, Larrimee turned and waved to that friendly enemy who stood in the center of the road, gaping after him. Then the rock wall of the valley cut him from view.

Larrimee looked to Belle. She was cantering so smoothly that his heart leaped with hope, only to sink again when he raised his eyes and saw Glory Mountain, smoky in the distance. There was no hope to outfoot the leading riders. That was the meaning of their change of mounts that morning. They intended to sprint the heart out of those horses in order to make sure of getting to Glory Mountain before sunset. At least, they would be on hand when the sky pilot arrived to keep his appointment. In case he were early and found no one there, they would arrive before he left. Even a poor horse could do much, if his strength were squandered for a single day's run.

To reach the base of that mountain before sunset was overtaxing even the gallant spirit of Belle. Yet she rocked stanchly along, with never a sign of faltering. He did not touch her, and yet she seemed to realize that now there was a greater need of speed. She trotted up steep slopes that she would ordinarily have taken at a laborious walk, and she galloped heavily up places where she would have trotted. On and on she went, while the sun slid down through the western sky with an alarming velocity. How many times in his mind he had cursed the slowness with which that hot sun sank and the cool evening

231

came! But now it seemed to him that it made visible progress downward, every instant.

Presently he was out of sight of Glory Mountain, laboring on a faintly worn trail, behind one of the subsidiary ranges of hills leading up to the peak. Here, Belle began to weaken perceptibly — she began to pound in her gallop — her head lowered, and her breath was a harsh gasp. A dozen times Larrimee was on the verge of bringing her to a walk and giving up the hopeless contest, but, instead, he waited for her to stop of her own accord. Little did he know the generous spirit of the mare. What could not have been spurred or whipped out of her she gave with utter freedom to this man who brought up to her memory the ghost of the boy with the bare, brown legs. She gave greatly, too, for the sake of the kind voice of her rider that was rarely still. It was a reward even in the midst of her labors.

Larrimee rounded a shoulder of a hill and saw before him the round red sun, poised like a ball of fire-hot copper on top of Glory Mountain. He was too late. And yet he was not much in arrear of the appointed hour. He looked up the rough side of the mountain, thickly covered with lodgepole pine, and in a clearing, not a mile away, he made out the house. It was a big place, as he could see even in that distance, and it was also in ruins, as he could tell by the manner in which one side of the roof sagged in.

"Now, Belle!" he called, as he slapped her wet neck encouragingly.

She answered with a toss of her head and then gave herself to the climbing of that slope. But it was bitter work, and her strength was failing. The moment she struck the upgrade her forefeet stumbled. It was a process of weary stumbling, pitching, scrambling, that climb up the side of Glory Mountain. The trail went completely blind, and they were feeling their way through a tangle of the pine trees, sometimes forced into detours, when the growth grew too thick for them to make their way through.

At length, alarmed by the sudden tremors that were passing through poor Belle, Larrimee threw himself from the saddle and looked her over. Her head was dropped, her ears lay back, foam covered her muzzle and the sides of her neck, where the reins had chafed. She was far gone, very far.

He gave her one low, cheery call, and in answer she merely pricked one ear. It told him, plainer than words could have done, that her strength was ended, that another hundred yards might be the death of her. But that must not stop him. Not that he had a hope; not that he knew how he could act, even if he forestalled the arrival of the minister to consummate the wedding. But, by this time, he had worked so long toward this end that he merely felt the blind necessity of driving forward.

He began to run through the pines swiftly, working the cramps of riding out of his legs in the first hundred yards, then making very good time through the thickets. At the end of five minutes of dodging trees and leaping over fallen logs, five minutes of wind-breaking work, he came to the edge of the clearing, in full view of the house. Clearing was in reality a false name for it. The ground, that had once been swept clean, was overgrown with a thick mass of shrubbery. The forest was washing back across the land and reclaiming it for its silences. Right up to the walls of the house the waves of green ran.

It was a far larger dwelling than he had imagined. How the sawed timber for it had been brought here was a mystery, but the place must have been standing a full twenty years. What was now an obscure, almost a blinded trail, might have been an open wagon road at that time. A mine nearby, or a lumber camp, might have explained why such a location was selected. But Larrimee gave only a moment to running his eye over the desolate outlines of the building; he marked the falling beams,

233

here and there, and the broken roof and the darkening window gaps from which the lights had been dashed out many a season since, by wind and weather. His chief attention was fixed on the group that sat on the front verandah — a broad-faced man with the build and the manner of a lion, a hawk-faced fellow beside him of prodigious length of limb, a slender, handsome youth, and the girl. There they were under his eye at length — Lefty, Skinny, Tucker — and she who had been made in his mind and his heart of hearts and now was molded into reality.

It was very rash work to stalk two men like Lefty and his lieutenant, but, rash or not, Larrimee was determined to get nearer. He began to work stealthily under the cover of the shrubs, using the most minute precautions to keep sheltered from a spying glance and from putting his foot on a dry twig. In spite of all his care, however, his knees presently fell on a stout little branch that snapped loudly under him. A deafening report it seemed to Larrimee. And right before him — he had not dreamed that he had worked himself so near — sounded several voices: "What's that?"

Then a moment of breathless silence followed, while Larrimee felt that the beating of his heart must be heard by the listeners. By a very slight maneuvering of his head he was able to peer through the branches of the shrub behind which he was sheltered at that moment, and he saw on the porch the girl shrinking back toward the door that opened into the dark interior of the house, Tucker, standing close beside her and apparently willing enough to accompany her inside, and Skinny and Lefty with drawn guns in their hands.

Presently Lefty himself smiled — strange, indeed, to see such an expression on that scarred and horrible face. "Put up your gat, Skinny," he advised. "They's nothing there. You never can tell what sort of noises you'll hear in a forest full of dead wood like this," insisted Lefty. "Any bit of wind stirring makes a noise like ten men walking. But who could be down yonder?"

"What about the crazy cayuse that had the mix with Wren? What about him? Maybe he's tripped up Walter and Charlie, and now . . . ?"

"Maybe he's done a pile of things," said Lefty, "but he sure ain't tripped Walter and Charlie. They're fighters, son. They take to a rumpus like a duck takes to water, and they don't stop fighting till they's nothing left on its feet but them. Ain't I seen 'em work? They'll smash this spy of Wheeler's to bits!"

There was a faint cry from the girl, as she turned to Lefty, and for the first time Larrimee could see her face. Even this fleeting look showed all that he had dreamed of her. He understood, moreover, why five men had been employed to guard her, and why many more, perhaps, were hunting her through the countryside. Every detail of that picture he took away with him — the simple clothes of olive drab, the broad collar with the blue tie knotted loosely at her breast, the curling of the golden hair beneath the stiff brim of the sombrero.

"Mister Morgan," she said eagerly to Lefty, "you promised me there would be no violence. You promised me. If there is a single man injured because of me, I'll never forgive myself . . . or you!"

Lefty rubbed the flattened place which had once been a nose and, turning his ugly mask of a face toward her, attempted to smile winningly. The result was a terrific grimace before which the girl winced.

"Look here, little lady," he said. "Ever seen a hoss broke?"

"Yes, of course."

"It ain't pretty, maybe you'd say."

"No, and I've always thought it unnecessary. I've never heard of a horse that couldn't be handled with kindness."

"Sure, sure," said Lefty smoothly. "Kindness is all right

235

when you got the time, but when you only got a week to bust fifty hosses . . . what you going to do? Got to be a little rough. Same way with this rattle-headed idiot that Wheeler turned loose on our trail, I figure. Hurt him? I wouldn't no more hurt him than I'd hurt a baby that didn't know better'n break its toys and things. But he's a nuisance, ain't he? He'll raise a pile of trouble, if he ever catches up with us, won't he? Well, it stands to reason I had to head him off, but I told the boys to be easy with him . . . not even to break the skin, but just to find out what he was after, and then rap him on the head and put him to sleep."

The girl gasped.

"What's the matter?" asked Lefty. "Hey, Tucker, you talk to her. She and me don't talk the same language!" He turned away disgustedly and looked toward the shrubbery.

"It's perfectly simple and perfectly necessary," said young Tucker, and Larrimee loathed the very sound of the voice. There was not an inch of that lithe, good-looking youth that he approved. There was not a turning of the dark eyes that did not remind him of something sneaking and feline. "You see, as Lefty says, sometimes a little violence saves a great deal of damage. He simply wanted his men to knock the idiot down and tie him and put him away until he came to his senses . . . and . . . and the marriage was ended. You see?"

"But if they couldn't?" asked the girl. "If he fought back, and he seems to be that sort of a man . . . ?"

"Nonsense!" said Tucker. "He gave Wren some trouble, but Wren was always thick in the head. Walter and Charlie are different . . . they'll simply step out and lift him off his horse and tie him up. That's all there is to it."

She seemed somehow appeased by this sound reasoning, and Larrimee could not help smiling when he remembered how he had left Walter and Charlie on the road.

"But why isn't the minister here?" asked Tucker in great irritation. "If old Dan Wheeler is on our trail and comes up with us. . . ."

"Wait a minute, will you?" demanded Lefty. "The doc will be here, right enough. Give him a minute or two after sunset, won't you?"

"But he's not even in sight."

"Sure he ain't. He comes over that hill, yonder, and you won't sight him till he trots his old nag over the brow. Let's go inside and find some boxes or something and sit down. I'm plumb fagged."

VIII

"IN AMBUSH"

Larrimee dared not move until the little group had filed through the door; but, once they were out of sight, he turned and speedily worked his way back to the edge of the pines. Once behind their shelter he turned, and, running as he had never run before, he skirted the clearing and so came at length to the shoulder of the mountain over which Lefty had promised that the minister would appear. He arrived there winded and gasping and barely in time. Straight up the slope beneath him came a minister, with his little cow pony trudging along at a walk, his hands folded calmly on the pommel, his face lifted to the color of the sunset sky — a quiet, gentle face framed by the sober color of the hat and the black collar of his coat. For a moment Larrimee's heart misgave him as to the part that he must play, but there was no help for it. If he tried gentler means a single outcry could reach those three men in the house. As for Tucker, he hardly counted, but, from what Larrimee had seen of Skinny and Lefty Morgan, he judged that either one would be more than a handful for him to meet — certainly they would more than overmatch him, if it came to a gun play.

Carefully he worked around the trees, until the end of the house disappeared from view. He would be safe from observation if he could only manage the thing without making noise. But that was by no means a simple matter. The minister was past the prime of life, but his frame was still broad and stalwart, and the clear tan of his face suggested muscles and nerves in good working order. In time of need he might make himself a very dangerous antagonist. Larrimee crouched, tensed, panther-like, edging to the very side of the dim trail. He was afraid that, even if the dreamy eyes of the man did not spy him, the horse might see and give warning with a leap to one side.

But the horse had apparently taken over some of the habits of the master. It came slowly, methodically along, stopping here and there to pluck up a bunch of dried grasses, reached the place where Larrimee waited, passed a pace, and then Larrimee issued from hiding.

One long, silent stride brought him up to the rump of the cow pony; a leap carried him high in the air and crashing into the minister, but his right arm, shooting about the neck of the luckless rider and crushing into it, prevented an outcry. An instant later the minister was torn from the saddle and tumbled heavily to the ground. The frightened pony jumped a length ahead, but then turned and wandered back, apparently feeling far more curiosity than real terror.

As for Larrimee, he found himself looking down into wide, dazed eyes. It turned him cold to think of the brutality of his treatment of this good man, but it was a stern necessity. He jerked out his gun and shoved it under the chin of the minister, at the same time summoning a prodigious scowl.

"Friend," he said sternly, "I mean business. If you let out one yell, you'll bring three men from the house. That's why you've got to be still. And, if you yell, you make sure that I'll finish you before I attend to them. Will you give me your word?"

There was a muffled acquiescence. Anything louder was prevented by the stifling grip of Larrimee's other arm, but the latter at once released his hold.

"Now, sir," he said more gently, "I have to do something which I don't want to do. But this is a rotten business, and, since you're mixed up in it, no matter how innocent, I have to fix you so that you'll not be a danger to me. I have enough on my hands as it is."

"My friend," said the minister with a calm that astonished Larrimee, "work your will on me. I am not afraid."

"You'll lie where you are and swear not to move or raise an alarm?"

"I have given you my word," said the other with dignity. "Is it sufficient?"

"It's enough," said Larrimee.

Two slashes of his knife, as he rose and turned to the pony, severed the reins at the bit. Then by the halter, which the horse wore under its bridle, he tethered it to a nearby tree, lest it should wander into sight of the house. After that he strapped the minister's hands and feet securely with the leather and paused with his handkerchief rolled up for a gag.

"Listen," he said. "You need not be uneasy. I shall return and free you . . . or, if I'm unable to return, I'll give warning of where you are. One thing more. You are free to work out of these knots if you can, but I'm going to ask for your promise not to shout out for help for a certain space. If you'll give it, very well . . . if not, I have something here with which to gag you. But gagging sometimes comes near to choking a man, and I don't want to make you suffer. Will you pledge me your word?"

"My son," said the other, "you speak like one who has been educated. You should know better than to mix in with affairs of violence in this manner. Reflect now before you have gone further. There is good in you, for otherwise you would not trust in my unsupported word. Consider again before you take another step."

"Sir," answered Larrimee, "my conscience was never so clear in my life as it is tonight. If I had time, I could prove it to

240

you . . . but I have no time. All I can say is that there is fate in what I am trying to do tonight."

"Ah, young man," said the other, "the world is filled with those who have followed what they consider the dictates of fate, when it was only the urge of their own wicked desires. Once. . . ."

"I am leaving you," broke in Larrimee, "but the time will come when you will know I have kept you from taking part in a horrible piece of work. Good bye for the present."

"Good bye," murmured the victim. "Whatever you are attempting, may the mercy of heaven accompany you."

Larrimee turned back over the crest of the hill and looked down on the rapidly darkening outline of the house. For, since he had last looked on it, the brilliance of the sunset had passed, and in its place the twilight was gathering rapidly across the mountains. It seemed larger than ever and was like a symbol of the difficulty of the task that lay before him. Much had been done, to be sure, but it was only a clearing of the ground for the more and more difficult task which lay before. All the others, compared with Morgan and Skinny, were nothing. Even suppose that he had the astounding good fortune to clear this formidable pair from his path, how could he hope, in spite of that, to do anything with the girl? Force was the strength of the others, and, with force and luck to aid him, he might overthrow them, but force was the last engine that he could use with her.

So great did the puzzle loom in his eyes that eventually he dismissed it from his mind. Only so could he keep up his hope. Again he approached the house, skirting as before, until he was in front and below it, then edging in rapidly through the shrubbery. When he was very close to it, there still remained the main step, and that was to get in touch with the people inside of it. They might be in any room. Because he heard their voices signified nothing. In their weariness after the long flight they might be resting.

Then, while he paused to consider, he was thrilled by the thought that the danger which had driven them so fast had been his speed on the trail, or rather the speed of gallant little Belle and the courage of her big heart.

He could not crouch here in the growing darkness forever. He must make some move. The one he selected certainly showed that he was never meant for cunning ambushes, surprises, and attacks. He simply rose from the bushes and stole up the front steps of the house. A child would have found some better strategy.

Once on the rotten boards of the verandah, too startled and confused to be grateful because the boards did not creak beneath his weight, he started for the front door. As he did so, he heard steps and a voice approaching down the hall. Someone was coming straight for that same door, and what could he do now? It was far too late to dart back into the bushes. Larrimee flattened himself against the wall of the house and offered up what was in substance a prayer.

IX

" 'BABES IN THE WOODS' "

Well might he pray, for there came now to the door of the house no other than the dreaded flat profile of Lefty Morgan himself! Had he been a trifle closer Larrimee would have followed a first desperate impulse and flung himself at the throat of the leader. But he was too far to be reached, and, when the spring failed of its object, there would be a revolver to encounter. The keen eyes of Larrimee, in that failing light, rested on the hand of Lefty as it was raised to his lips, with a glowing cigarette butt. All the rest of the man was broad and stocky, made for endurance and great muscular power. But the hand, by a freak of mother nature, was long-fingered and lean, a hand that spoke eloquently of agility and speed. It was the hand of an artist, and well Larrimee could guess in what the artistry of Lefty lay — it was with a revolver. That left hand of his remained sacred to those uses only. Even when he threw away his smoked cigarette and rolled another, it was the right hand that took out the paper, selected one, and opened the tobacco bag. The left was called into play only to shake a fluff of the brown and flaky tobacco into the waiting leaf. After that the dexterous right, all by itself, took up the task of rolling the paper, a feat that Larrimee had heard of, but never seen. A twist, a whirl, and the cigarette was made. The lighting, again, was done with the right hand; the left was unemployed, as though such menial work was beneath it. It seemed to the fascinated Larrimee, by the flare of the match, that the left hand was even slenderer than its companion, but that, perhaps, was the result of his own imaginings. At any rate the idea grew in him that Lefty's hand in action would be as swift as the flash of lightning and as cruel as the thunderbolt itself.

All of this, naturally, passed through his mind in the space of half a minute, while the leader had discarded his former cigarette and rolled and lighted another. How he escaped the observation of those keen eyes was a miracle, but Larrimee himself had often noted that people are very apt to see only the things they wish to see. Lefty Morgan expected to find no one on the verandah of the old house, and consequently he did find no one, but kept his eyes fixed toward that shoulder of the hill, over which the trail of the minister led.

"Doc ain't in sight yet," Lefty said at last, without turning his head. "The old idiot must have got to dreaming about something and took the wrong road. Wasn't for that hoss of his, he'd lose himself about every day in the week, but the old hoss has got more brains than the doc ever dreamed of having."

The voice of Skinny, which was an enormous and musical bass, absurdly out of proportion with his frame, came rolling from the interior of the house: "Maybe he's got hold of somebody to save . . . that'd hold him up . . . or, maybe, he's run across a rabbit with a busted leg. That'd hold him up. Almost anything plumb foolish would hold him up."

The leader turned from the door with a suddenness that was the equivalent of a curse. "If we stay here all night, maybe old Wheeler will have his men on top of us. The old rat can smell trouble a hundred miles off, pretty near." His step passed down the hall. "Tucker," he was saying, in the interior room, "why didn't you pick out a wide-awake sky pilot?"

"He knew my father, and he knows me," said Tucker. "I thought it'd be better to have someone I could trust, and who trusted me. A good many ministers wouldn't do a thing like this."

The voice of the girl came small with distance to the straining ear of Larrimee.

"Why not, Henry?"

"Well, it's a little irregular, you know. Isn't done every day, this meeting of a girl in a deserted house, where she has been brought by some wild fellows. . . ."

"What sort of fellows?" This was a roar from Skinny.

"You wouldn't call yourselves 'babes in the woods,' would you, Skinny?" asked Tucker. "At least I wouldn't. I mean you're not the sort of fellows one would ordinarily send about to escort ladies in distress, you know."

"Don't know anything of the kind," declared Skinny. "As safe with me and Lefty as she'd be with her mother . . . safer, because I'd be able to take care of her. I dunno what you're driving at, Tucker, but, whatever it is, I'm here to state that I don't like it!"

"If you don't know what he's driving at," broke in Lefty, "how d'you know whether or not you like it? Say, it's getting dark. Where's a light? Bring any candles, Skinny?"

"Yup, I got some in this oiled paper."

"Then why don't you light one, instead of shooting off your fool mouth so much?"

A growl answered him, then a match was scratched, and Larrimee, craning his neck around the jamb of the door, saw the second doorway to the left down the hall faintly illumined. This, then, was their present point of assembly. Perhaps he could slip around to the side of the verandah and take stock of those inside the room. He was given a sudden spur to this change of plan by the voice of Lefty speaking again: "Let's step outside and wait for the doc there. He'd ought to be coming along, and, besides, these folks might have something to talk over with each other, eh?"

He laughed heavily at his own poor remark, and then two

pairs of feet came marching down the hall. Larrimee was across the doorway with the speed and light foot of a cat and slid down the verandah. Then he turned the corner, and, just as he made the turn, the voices of the two came out of the dark hall and enlarged suddenly in the night. Had they seen him?

No, fortune seemed to have favored him again, for they went straight across the porch and down the front steps. But the direction of their walk was around that side of the house. There was only one thing to do, and Larrimee did it. He flattened himself against the floor of the verandah, his face turned to the wall, for everyone knows that the human face is like a magnet to attract attention, even in the dark.

It was now that shadowy hour on the borderline between twilight and the utter dark. The brighter stars were out, but the faint distant hosts had still to appear. Larrimee hugged the wall and trusted again to luck that they would not turn their heads toward him. But his fear was ill-founded. He discovered in a moment that the level of the porch was well above the eye level of even Skinny. The voices had turned the corner.

"I don't like . . . ," Skinny was saying.

"Shut up, you fool," said Lefty. "I don't care what you like. I got you out here to tell you to watch your step. Tucker will take a lot, but someday you'll say too much to him."

"And what of it? Do I care when the little skunk has too much? The sooner the quicker, say I. I been aching to get my hands onto his pretty face ever since I seen him."

"Sure you have," said the leader, "because you're a fool."

"Look here," said Skinny in wrath.

"Talk soft, will you? I ain't deaf."

"All right." The huge, mellow bass was reduced to a thick murmuring that Larrimee could barely make out. "But I want you to know that you can't ride me, Lefty."

"Who wants to ride you? Who's trying to ride you?"

246

"You are, and you mighty well know it, but I won't stand for it. I ain't Charlie and I ain't Walter and I ain't Bill. I got a name as well as you . . . I been looked up to as well as you. And that goes, Morgan, if you was ten Leftys instead of one. You're flesh and bone the same's me. Bullets'll punch holes in you the same's they will in me. All I say is, don't press me too far, Lefty, and, mostly, don't start calling me a fool around that girl."

There was a moment of tense pause, and Larrimee, waiting in tense expectancy, was half prepared to hear the sudden explosion of guns. But it seemed that the leader was something of a diplomat. He said presently: "It sure takes me back to hear talk like this out of you, Skinny. Who've I always used like my right-hand man? Who've I always asked advice from when I never asked it from nobody else? Who've I always treated fair and square and given an extra split more'n your share, every time they was anything to divvy up? I ask you, now, who is it?"

"I don't say you ain't been square," said Skinny, somewhat abashed, apparently, by this yielding. "Only what I mean is. . . ."

The other broke in more sternly. "But I tell you straight . . . so long as you're with me, you got to walk the chalk mark. I try to use you right, but, when it comes to orders . . . well, they're orders, and they come from me! That's final! You know well I never give an order except when it's for the good of the gang."

"How come it's for the good of the gang that you shut me up in front of that little rat, Tucker?"

"What's the matter with Tucker, anyways?"

"I don't like him. I never did. Gives me the chills to think of a girl like that marrying him. It sure does."

"Say, Skinny, do you aim to marry her yourself?"

"I'll tell you straight, cap, I'd do better by her than that soft-eyed son-of-a-bitch!"

"Listen, Skinny, while I talk sense to you. Have I told you

247

what we stand to make out of this?"

"Nope. You know you ain't."

"Well, your share, if the thing goes through, which it's sure to, unless you spoil everything with your crazy talk, is just exactly two thousand dollars. Ever make it as easy as that before, without busting open a bank or something? Here we are all legal and fine and ready to collect in a big wad, and we collect it from Tucker."

"Are you sure he'll pay?"

"Say, son, can you imagine putting off a debt that he owes to me? Nope, he'd sell the house over his head first . . . before it got burned down. Oh, he knows me better'n that!"

"Maybe he does, but still I say it's a shame to let her marry him. She's just scared of having to marry Wheeler's brat, whether she wants to or not . . . that's why she picked up with Tucker. Running out of the fire and throwing herself into the lake, is what I call it. Dead both ways, and her life spoiled. Say, that'd rest heavy on my brain, Lefty! It'd haunt me."

"Would it haunt you two thousand dollars' worth?" asked Lefty.

"Hmm," said Skinny, "I ain't brought it down to dollars and cents."

"Well, you think it over, and. . . ."

Their voices, which had been steadily leaving the house, now receded to an indistinguishable murmur.

As for Larrimee, he waited for a moment, digesting the singularly brutal philosophy of Lefty, and then he rose again and began once more his crouching progress along the side of the house. At length he came to the square of a big window that was faintly blocked out with light from within, but so feeble was it that it sent no real shaft into the night, farther than the other side of the verandah, where a pillar was dimly etched. Moving his head gradually to the corner of the window space, Larrimee could make out the huge naked lines of the room within. He saw the candle burning lopsided from the draft through the window and sending a small trail of sooty smoke jagging sidewise. He saw the staggering old wreck of a table that supported it. He saw the forms of the girl and Tucker, sitting in the remnants of what had once been fine chairs. They were talking earnestly.

X

"VELVET CLAWS"

Tucker had drawn his chair close to hers, until the two arms well nigh touched, and he was bending forward, speaking with many gestures, but very softly. The girl was leaning back, with her head turned toward the window. In this position she was directly facing Larrimee, and it was very difficult for him to keep his eye on them without being seen. But it did help him to study her face at close hand. For the candle burned a little to one side — a slight, but vital, difference of angle, that blurred her features with shadow. There was one white splash along the round of her throat, and the ear, as it disappeared into a mass of shadowy hair, was roughly sketched; a grayer highlight was on her cheek, just making it possible to guess at the big eyes, a deeper darkness in the dark, and her lips which were visible as she spoke. But the chief reward of his study was the burning and tangling of the light within her hair, brilliant, priceless gold, more beautiful than that which he had dug out of the earth and washed in purity. Where the light fell directly on the golden masses, it shaded off to tones of copper.

Larrimee reached his hand around and touched the gauntlet which was still in his back pocket; and it seemed to his excited fancy that, in touching the glove, he had touched a part of her. It seemed to him, moreover, strange and foolish though it might be to others, that she must have felt the touch, and it almost surprised him that she did not sit forward in the chair, look more intently at the window. But her regard, obviously, was fixed not on him, not even on the gloomily lighted square of the window and the utter dark outside, but rather on her own thoughts. Could it be that the words of Tucker so entranced her?

"I don't wonder that you doubt now," he was saying. "What is wonderful is that you could have come so far and done so much. But don't you see, dear, that in following that instinct you were following the truth? You women know things in that manner . . . not by reason, but by the leap and flash of instinct . . . it carries you across the sea, while we poor men go plodding on and on. The difference is that we are sure of ourselves. You go so far in so little a space that, when you are across the sea, you begin to be afraid. Everything is so new that you want to jump back again. But don't jump away from me like that, please. Follow the first instinct. Do try to follow that, because I know it's right."

She hesitated a moment. "I don't stand up very well against your talk," she said at last, and the unconvinced quiet of her voice was manna from heaven to the thirsty heart of Larrimee. "I'm afraid you're a little too clever for me, Henry."

"Tush," he said. "Not at all! Not at all! Just a trick or two with words. Dear girl, don't tell me that I'm going to talk myself out of your interest?"

The lips of Larrimee formed silently in a snarl at the question.

"If so, I sha'n't say another word."

The better, thought the tigerish listener.

"Don't misconstrue me," she answered, and it was plain that she was fumbling for something felt, but hardly yet brought to the light of complete consciousness. "I mean that sometimes, when you speak, I am not at ease. You don't mind if I talk everything out with you?"

"Of course not. Bless your dear, foolish heart, talk it all out, and then the suspicion will be gone."

"Of course. Well, there have been times during the ride, and even after we arrived here, Henry, when I have wished that you were a little more like Skinny and Lefty."

"Great Jove!" exclaimed Tucker, stiffening in his chair and blinking, as if he had received a blow. "Good heavens, can I believe my ears?"

"Let me explain . . . I mean that I have wished that you had their simplicity and their directness, Henry."

"My dear, my dear, do you know of whom you're talking?"

"Well?"

"Of men known far and wide as killers, as murderers, dear. For heaven's sake, don't say you expect to find their qualities in me."

"I didn't know so much about them. I only know they're the men to whom you entrusted me."

Tucker, overwhelmed with embarrassment, gasped and swallowed, one slender hand caressing his throat, his eyes very wide. "I don't know how it's happened," he said. "Somehow you seem to have doubted about me until in another moment, upon my soul, my dear, you'll have me appearing to be in the wrong."

"Is that utterly impossible?" she asked, turning her head ever so slightly, as the light from the candle rippled over her profile in a line of white.

Ah, thought Larrimee, delighted past speech. *So you have claws, too, under all that velvet. Ah, good, good!*

"Don't you see," went on Henry Tucker in great haste, "that, in the first place, I needed strong and bold men to take you away from that terrible Wheeler?"

"Of course."

"And, besides, I needed men I could absolutely trust. You

felt safe in their hands, didn't you?"

"I'd go around the world with them in an absolute trust. I'd trust them anywhere, Henry."

Larrimee shook his head. *After all,* he thought, looking at the lovely profile, *I've never yet known a beautiful girl who has a grain of sense. Trust Skinny and Lefty around the world? Bah!*

"I knew you would." Tucker was murmuring, greatly relieved. "And so, you see, you're quite wrong."

"About what?" she asked.

"Why, about. . . . My goodness, I've twisted and turned about so often in this talk that I really don't know how the conversation is headed."

"Except you're sure I'm wrong."

"Now, don't be hard on me. You have a little way of popping out a fact, now and then, that's very disconcerting. It throws me quite off my guard."

"I suppose that's the strain of the Wheeler inheritance in me," she answered. "It does ugly tricks like that now and then . . . pops out disconcerting facts, I mean. My uncle was always doing it, you know, and I suppose I caught the habit . . . a little."

"But . . . you're so very thoughtful tonight and. . . ."

"I'm sorry, Henry."

"And cold, you know."

"I suppose that's because I'm thinking. I never could do two things at once."

"Two things? What two?"

"Well, thinking and acting the part of a girl about to be married, for instance."

"Hmm," mused Henry. "Well, I suppose not, but with practice you'll improve. It's like tennis. Amazing how the ball acts when you start, but in a week or two you're quite at home on the courts. Practice is everything. My father used to say

253

that. . . . I beg your pardon? Did . . . ah . . . did you yawn, dear?"

It was, in fact, precisely what she had done, to the unspeakable wonder and joy of Larrimee.

"I sighed, Henry," said the girl.

Well, thought Larrimee, *you'll bear watching in spite of your angel face, you little fox.*

"What on earth is there to sigh about?" asked Henry Tucker, leaning back in his chair and joining the tips of his fingers, as one prepared to pass on a matter.

"Well, suppose you had a sister, Henry."

"But I haven't one, you know, and that's one nasty complication out of the way."

"I mean, just supposing."

"Very well, if you wish."

"And your sister were to marry?"

"She'd get part of the estate. I mean there'd be a settlement or some such thing. I don't know just what. But you need not worry because. . . ."

"For heaven's sake, Henry Tucker!"

"My dear," he said, changing color with astonishment.

"Nothing. I mean, suppose your sister were to be in a place like this, away from any of her family, with a man she hardly knew . . . well, how would you feel about it, and how do you expect she would feel about it?"

"Why, she'd feel that it was perfectly all right if there were to be a marriage. My dear, you don't doubt the honorable nature of my intentions and. . . ."

"Please don't be excited. I'm only thinking. I'm only supposing. You wouldn't feel sorry for her, would you?"

"Eh?"

"You wouldn't worry about her?"

"Good God, my dear, what are you driving at?"

But her answer seemed to jump several necessary links.

254

"Has anyone ever told you that you are awfully English, Henry?"

"Oh, yes. And do you think so?"

"In some ways, yes."

"Thanks so much, my dear."

"Don't mention it," said the lady of the glove, without enthusiasm.

Great Cæsar! thought the eavesdropper. *You are a cat. I'd trim your claws for you, you vixen, if I had to die for it.*

"But do you know, Henry," she went on, with a singularly musical change of voice that went straight to Larrimee's heart, "I am just a little sad."

"Sad? By Jove! But I believe most girls are, just before they're married. Silly, though, isn't it? Never could explain it."

"I don't expect that you can."

"But come, now, what can make you sad? You're not marrying a poverty-stricken beggar, you know. And our two fortunes together . . . well, we'll be on the map with a vengeance. People will have to look at us."

"I was thinking of Uncle Dan's boy."

"Are you regretting that cad . . . after you've run away from him and . . . ?"

"Not regretting him, only I wonder how much he has to do with this marriage? I mean, if it weren't for him. . . ."

"What do you mean?"

"I don't know, Henry," she said. "But I wish you were a little bit quicker at conundrums."

"Never was any good at riddles and such stuff," he replied. "But come, come. Get this melancholy out of your mind. Why, there's everything ahead of us. First we'll get out of this infernal Western country. . . ."

"Henry," she interrupted, "do you know that, since we've met, you haven't told me once that you love me?"

"But why tell you that? You know I do, or I wouldn't be here."

"I suppose so. And you haven't asked me if I love you . . . not once."

"As a matter of fact I'm afraid to. You have such a way of keeping a fellow at a distance. But then, you're here, too, you know."

"Yes," she whispered, "ah, yes."

You blockhead! Larrimee raged at Tucker.

"And, even if you aren't terribly fond of me to begin with . . . well, time is what counts. These wild love affairs . . . never can tell. End up in a divorce court in a year or two, maybe. Love's blind, you know. Man thinks the girl is an angel. She thinks he's a knight out of armor. Don't expect any faults at all. First one they find . . . puff . . . there goes the whole bubble, sailing away."

"Did your father tell you that, Henry!"

"Why, yes. How did you guess?"

"I don't know. I just did."

"Hmm," said Henry. "You have a surprising way about you."

"Henry."

"Yes?"

"Do you mind leaving me here alone for a time?"

"Eh? Why, of course not, if you won't be lonely."

I'll answer for that, thought Larrimee.

"I'll try not to be lonely. I have a lot of things to think about."

"Well, if you wish, really."

"I do."

"I'll go out and smoke a cigarette."

"Smoke two, Henry."

"Will you be thinking as long as all that?"

"Quite that long, I imagine."

"You are a puzzler, my dear. Sometimes, do you know that you worry me?"

"Why?"

"You think so much."

"Do I? Then I'll try to get over the habit."

"Oh, it doesn't matter. Good bye for a minute or two."

He leaned to kiss her cheek, but though she made not the slightest movement of resistance, he changed his mind at the last moment and kissed her hand instead. A moment later he was gone.

XI

"LARRIMEE AND THE LADY"

As Tucker passed out of the room, Larrimee rose, waited an instant, and leaned across the window.

"Hush," he whispered.

He had not taken into account her natural terror at that unannounced apparition of a stranger. But her languor was gone; she whisked out of her chair and was at the door with the speed of a dead leaf caught up and whirled by a gust of wind. There she paused to look back and make sure, with her startled eyes, that she had seen a man and not a ghost.

He dared not speak loud enough for his voice to carry to her. He had only one agonized gesture to implore her back. Her glance flicked to one side, her lips parted to cry out. His whole fate hung in the balance, then the lips closed. She looked at him with less fear and a shade more interest, one hand clutching the side of the door to give her a flying start, in case it were necessary to flee into the hall.

Larrimee stepped through the window. His action sent her swerving out into the hall. She lingered there dimmed by the darkness, and still she had not cried out, or entirely fled from him.

"Lady," said Larrimee, "will you listen to me for thirty seconds? Every minute you listen, I'll keep my hands above my head, if you're afraid."

She came back a single step, then gasped with fear and sur-

258

prise. "I know you! You're the man Bill Wren described . . . the one . . . the tall fellow . . . who. . . . But Charlie and Walter . . . you got by them? You . . . you aren't killed, then?"

Certainly there was never a more stumbling speech. With a thrill of gratefulness he noted that it was whispered.

"But you must go quickly," she said. "No, you don't have to keep your hands over your head. You . . . you look honest, even if Uncle Dan did send you after me. But go quickly . . . out the back way. There are people in front. It's too late, I tell you. Everything is prepared. And, if Morgan finds you here, something terrible. . . ."

"I know," said Larrimee.

"Then why don't you hurry?"

"Because it's so wonderfully pleasant to stand here and listen to you persuading."

She stared at him. "I don't know who you are, or what you are," she said at length. "You seem too good a man to be injured in a brawl that might start on account of me. I tell you earnestly that you cannot help Uncle Dan now. You are only one, and there are three here. We are only waiting for the minister to. . . ."

"You'll wait a long time," said Larrimee. "Do you know where he is now?"

"Of course not."

"Lying tied hand and foot on the other side of the hill."

She gasped and took a step back. Indeed, she had been wavering back and forth all the time, approaching to persuade him to flee before harm overtook him, retreating when she realized again her position and his strangeness.

"But you see," she said, frowning again, "you've exposed yourself now. I have only to tell Mister Morgan where to find him."

"I don't think you will," said Larrimee.

"Is that a threat?" she asked, growing a little pale.

"You know it isn't."

"Then I don't pretend to make out the riddle of you. But I tell you again that there are three men about here, and you are alone. For your own sake you. . . ."

"Three men?" asked Larrimee. "Three men? I only know of two."

She started to explain, and, then, in a flash of her eyes, he saw that she had caught his meaning, and, for some reason, it pleased him immensely to see her flush to the hair with intense shame.

"You've been outside that window, eavesdropping," she said fiercely. "Oh, that's a shameful thing!"

"I really couldn't help it," said Larrimee. "Not without stopping my ears."

"You could have moved on."

"There were two gunfighters standing a very few yards away, and, if I had moved, they'd have blown me to pieces. Besides, once I'd heard part of it, I couldn't stop listening. It was so funny. Don't you think so?"

"Funny? What do you mean?"

"I mean that he was funny . . . just a little. Or, perhaps, you illustrate his father's maxim that love is blind."

"Sir . . . ," she began.

"Excuse me," he said, "I know I've been rude, but I haven't time to be polite."

"Will you tell me, once for all, what you expect to gain by staying here? Or are you one of those terrible gunfighters who have no fear of odds? Have you come here to earn Uncle Dan's money with . . . with a battle?"

"Lady," said Larrimee, "I've come here to battle if I have to, but not with guns. Matter of fact, I can't hit the side of a barn."

Her eyes opened wider than ever. "Then why . . . ?"

"I've simply come to ask you not to marry Tucker."

"Are you mad?" demanded the girl.

"If that's madness, thinking that he's not worth the weight of your little finger, then, yes, I'm mad. But it's not madness. You've been coming to the same conclusion. You sent him away because you couldn't trust yourself, if he stayed with you. You'd have laughed in his face in another moment. Oh, I know how you're placed! That ass of a boy of Wheeler's has been forced on you . . . you've taken this Tucker as the lesser evil. You pledged yourself to him, if he could get you away from Wheeler. But. . . ."

"I might have known," interrupted the girl. "Uncle Dan wouldn't send a fighter to get around another fighter. He'd send a diplomat!"

"I shall swear to you," said Larrimee gravely, "that I have never seen this uncle of yours, and that I am not in his pay and never shall be."

"Then how in the world do you happen . . . but don't stop to explain anything. Do you know, sir, that you are in mortal danger every moment you spend in this house?"

"I suppose I am."

"And yet you stay?"

"You'll not wonder when I tell you why."

"Then . . . ?"

"I was walking down the road the other morning," he said, "and I saw your glove on the roadside. Mind you, I don't expect you to believe a word of the crazy story I'm about to tell you."

But she was studying him thoughtfully; he felt the movement of her eyes over every one of his features.

"I found your glove, I say, and, though I'd never seen you, of course, I began to picture the girl who had worn that glove. When I came to the town I asked the hotel proprietor if such and such a girl, with blue eyes and golden hair, of about such a height, had been through the town. And he said you had!"

She smiled and shook her head.

"I know it sounds like a fairy tale," said Larrimee, "but I swear that I'm telling you the exact truth. He told me about your rough-looking escort . . . that you seemed to be in a great hurry, perhaps fleeing from some pursuit. Well, I jump to quick conclusions. Inside of half an hour I had bought a horse and was on the trail to learn what I could about the mystery. Very queer, I know, but having your glove in my pocket seemed to give me a right to know. Please don't think me an utter lunatic just yet. I'm asking you to listen, not believe me."

"I'm trying to do both," said the girl, with a sudden lifting of her head and a queer smile.

"Bless you," murmured Larrimee. "You are a trump. First I tangled with a blacksmith, and from him and his odd ways I guessed that there was really something guilty in your flight. He tried to put me onto the wrong road, but I managed to guess the right one."

"I knew. He telephoned ahead, and at the next town Bill Wren. . . ."

"Exactly! From Bill Wren I gained a little more information and knew that you were running away from a marriage which this uncle of yours. . . ."

"He's not really an uncle, just my guardian."

"At any rate, when you're near him, his domineering will makes you do pretty much what he wants."

"And yet you say you don't know him."

"Please believe me. So on I went convinced from what Bill told me . . . he's not such a bad fellow . . . that you were about to jump out of the frying pan into the fire. Before long, a couple of fellows stopped me, and we had an argument, and then I went on."

262

"You said you are not a fighter."

"With guns. I used fists on them, mostly. Besides I had all the luck. Next I came to this place . . . then I listened in the shrubbery under the verandah and heard about the minister and the way he was coming. So I scouted back and stopped him and tied him, as I told you. Then I came back here, and you know the rest."

He was prepared for any one of a thousand comments, exclamations of disbelief — anything save what happened.

"Will you let me see that glove?" she asked very gently.

He placed it instantly in her hands, and she turned and examined it.

"But," she said, looking up at him with that same queer smile, which was more in her eyes than on her lips, "it isn't my glove at all!"

"What?" asked Larrimee. "Not your glove? Why, it must be! Why, the whole picture of you grew out of it!"

"You see," she said, "it's much too large."

"Too large! Why, I couldn't get three fingers into the palm of it."

"But then you have large fingers, you know. I'll prove it."

She slipped on the glove. Obviously it was far too roomy. Larrimee passed a hand across his forehead.

"It's some other girl, and you'll have to go back and pick up the trail where you found the glove."

At that his eyes cleared. "It may be the wrong glove," he said solemnly, "but, I give you my word, the girl is not wrong. Do you know that when I saw you, I actually recognized you. I could have picked you out of a crowd. I tell you there was fate in it! Don't you feel that there must have been? It took me off the road, it put me on the back of a horse, it galloped me after you, brought me here."

"And then?"

"You won't believe me?"

"I believe every word you've said. I . . . I believe you're a very brave and chivalric man . . . but what is the end to be?"

"Of course, there's only one end. You're to go away with me."

"Go away with you?"

He flushed to the eyes and stiffened. "My name is Larrimee," he said huskily. His mother would have recognized both the voice and the stiffness. "My mother was a Stillwater . . . not that I pride myself a great deal on ancestry. I don't want to seem a prig . . . I've never even mentioned it before, or hardly thought of it. Only . . . there's never been the shade of a shadow on one of those names . . . never! And I can only ask you to trust me."

"I do," said the girl, "as profoundly as I believe all that you've told me."

"Bless you for that," replied Larrimee. "Don't you see that this is a mess? Tucker . . . why, it would be ghastly for you to marry him. You've been bewildered, that's all. He helped you to escape from your uncle . . . you want to reward him. Well and good, but not with a marriage. That's too much! I can take you to my mother, if you want protection, and she'd be a fighter for you. The whole world couldn't take you away, once she had you."

"Mister Larrimee," she said, "you're wonderfully generous . . . just as generous as you're quixotically brave. It makes my heart jump and get big to know that there are men like you in the world. But, perhaps, my family is not quite so old as yours. Its antecedents are chiefly business antecedents, but we have never yet, never one of us, gone back on a bargain."

He could only stare at her; no answer came. "Lady," he said at last, feeling that he had, indeed, come to the end of his rope, "I can't speak against your honor, and I can't pretend to be able to judge, just now, because I love you. And" — he managed the faintest of smiles — "as Mister Tucker's father said, I presume love is a trifle blind when it comes to matters of fine distinctions. There is nothing more for me to say. I am going."

He had turned away, when she called after him: "Wait!"

He faced her again. Truly the title of "lady" that Bill Wren had given her and that had been on his own lips so often during his talk with her had never fitted the girl as well as it did at this moment. She faced him now with the flush that his last speech had brought not yet died out, with a peculiar misty shame and happiness in her eyes, and yet with a willingness, a brave willingness, for him to see the truth in her face, the whole truth.

"Yes?" asked Larrimee. "Yes?"

And then, as she hesitated, he made a sudden stride toward her, and, though she winced at his coming, she did not retreat, but looked all the time steadily in his eyes. It was a power from the outside that checked him. Voices were clamoring down the slope and approaching the house, three loud, eager voices.

"Ah," cried the girl, "they've found him! Now go! Quickly!"

XII

" 'WITHOUT KNOWING HER NAME' "

Larrimee took in his own the hands that she cast out to implore him to leave. "Not until you have finished what you started to say."

"But that is it . . . I was going to implore you to go at once. Mister. . . ."

"That's not true . . . there was something else. It was in your face, you see. Will you tell me?"

"I swear," she pleaded, "that I was only going to ask you to hurry away . . . for your own sake. . . ."

"And a little for yours?"

"Ah, yes, for mine, too. I shall never forget you. If I am ever in my life tempted to be cowardly or weak or mean or ungenerous, I shall remember you, Mister Larrimee. Yes, for my sake, too."

"Then," said Larrimee quietly, "nothing under heaven can make me leave until you go with me."

"But didn't you hear? They're on the porch outside, now. Quick! They're coming down the hall."

"Let them come."

She saw his hand go to his revolver, saw his jaw set. Then she caught his arms with a little moan. "Not that! Ah, not that! That old curtain in the corner . . . get behind that."

At least she was right in that he could fill no purpose by remaining in view. He stepped behind the curtain, and, the moment he was there, he cursed the move. There was not nearly space enough behind it, and it surely must bulge significantly. How if he were killed like Polonius?

He had no time to think twice — the voices were pouring into the room. Tucker, Skinny, Morgan, the minister — all were speaking in an excited group.

"What's up?" Morgan asked of the girl. "You look as if you'd seen a ghost."

"I heard you all coming, shouting . . . it nearly frightened me to death. Mister Morgan, what has happened?"

"Nothing . . . everything . . . that devil that your uncle sent on our trail . . . I'd like to get my gun on him . . . must have busted through Charlie and Walter! How he managed to handle the two of them is beyond me. Anyway, he did. Got up here, learned our plans, waylaid our friend, here, tied him up, and now he's slipped away to lead on the rest of Wheeler's bulldogs. How many of 'em, and where they're riding from, I don't know. All I do know is that we've got to get out of here as fast as we can. Are you ready?"

Tucker interrupted anxiously: "Can't we take the time now? I have the license, the minister is here, and it'll only occupy a moment for the marriage, and then, you see, we'll have nothing to fear."

"You'll have nothing to fear, but what about us? He'd have our throats cut in a minute. No, my beauty, you think fast enough to suit yourself, but your thinking doesn't suit me."

"Then save yourself, Lefty, but leave the rest of us."

"Before I get my pay? Son, I may not be a financial giant, as they call 'em, but I'm a growed man, anyway. You'll come with me, and you'll come *pronto*. Are you ready, everybody? Get the horses around in back of the house, Skinny. You help him, Tucker. Doc, bring the girl. Jump lively, now. I know Wheeler's gang. They'll come shooting, and they'll ask their questions afterward. Hurry up!"

There was a rush of footfalls; then two voices remained. "Are you ready?" asked the grave minister.

"I . . . I . . . ," began the girl.

"What is that figure behind the curtain?"

He, of all men, had been the one to see. With one gliding side-step Larrimee came into view, and his gun was in his hand, his back to the wall. "Call them, then, and take the consequences!" he said angrily.

The calm of the old man was amazing; instead of calling for help, he folded his arms; instead of looking at Larrimee, he looked at the girl. "You knew he was there?" he asked.

"Yes," said the girl quietly.

"He came here for you?"

She bowed her head.

"Do you wish to go with him?"

"I cannot," she murmured. "I have given my word to. . . ."

"You have given your word, but where have you given your heart?"

She could only stare, her hands caught to her breast, her eyes going wildly from Larrimee to the minister.

"If you don't wish him to hear," said the minister, "you can whisper in my ear."

Then the grave old man bent toward her. Suddenly she was clinging to him and sobbing: "Tell me what to do. I've given my word to that . . . other man . . . my sacred honor."

"My dear child," said the minister, "you cannot serve such a sacred thing as honor with a loveless marriage."

"Sir . . . ," began Larrimee, not giving credence to his ears.

"Indeed, my boy," said the other. "I think I should have been lost eternally, if I had called them in."

"And this after what I have done to you?" exclaimed

Larrimee. "Why, sir, you're a saint!"

"Stuff and nonsense," said the minister. "I'm the father of a family. Be off with you."

Larrimee was through the window with a leap, as the voice of Lefty came thundering back to bid the laggards hurry. He reached to help the girl through, but she was already beside him, and, as he leaped down from the verandah, they heard the voice of the minister calling: "She went out the front way. Isn't she with you? I suppose. . . ." His voice died out, as he ran though the house.

"The blessed liar," declared the girl, as she raced at the side of Larrimee.

When they came to the edge of the thicket of lodgepole pines, he drew her down behind a dense growth of trunks. They could not flee now, he explained, without making a fatal noise.

Then a voice roared in the distance: "I'll stay no longer for any man. Let her stay! You'll pay for what I've done. I brought the girl to you . . . that was the bargain. Your fault if you didn't have the minister here in time. Now you'll come with me, son, and you'll stay with me till you've paid."

After that there was a crashing of galloping horses and a shrill cry of woe above that sound. In the heart of Larrimee was a wonder as to what manner of man this Uncle Dan Wheeler might be, the dread of whom had made terrible Lefty Morgan run from a shadow.

It was the first pink of dawn, when they came out on the hill above the town and left the forest behind them. Larrimee looked up at the girl, as she sat the saddle on Belle, and he caught the first glimpse of her by daylight. But the family pride of the Stillwaters was thicker in his veins than he himself imagined. Instead of breaking forth in rhapsody, he merely

269

said: "There's one thing my mother will never recover from."

"And that?"

"That I ran away with my wife-to-be, without knowing her name."